THE PAN SERIES

The Pan: The Trials of Jonathan Darling
The Pan: Michael's Ascent
The Pan: Wendy's Daughter

A Word from the Authors:

Whenever one undertakes anything new and creative, there's a sense of uncertainty and maybe even a little fear. I think it's in these times that one needs those around them who are inclined to encourage and support to really step up.

For those around me that did, I offer all the gratitude I have, even while knowing it won't be enough to show how thankful I really am.

First of all, in this long process, thanks to Rebecca. So many things have changed from the start of this whole thing to this point. Job changes, medical scares... Winklets. Through it all, my darling bride has abided. And encouraged. She's simply the best wife out there. Everyone else can fight for second place.

Marjut, Mary P., Lara, Jackie and the entire UW-Parkside crew deserve extra kudos for their support.

Thank you, Em, for your creative and technical editing prowess.

And finally, thank you to my boy, FJM. You are excellent at knowing when to push me and knowing when it might not be the right time. Thank you for your patience. Let's do it again sometime... maybe twice more?

m.

I would like to give a word of thanks to some people who were integral to getting this project off the ground:

First, to Emily, you are a wonderful editor with great tact. I am very proud of you and can't thank you enough.

Melissa, it's a pleasure working creatively with you. I know I can speak plainly with you and never worry about any ego getting in the way. It's been very easy, and the music is great.

Jay, the site looks wonderful. It's better than I imagined. Anyone looking for a good web designer should take a look at www.thepanbooks.com and contact Jay. He's dependable and creative and courageous.

To everyone who read this book and gave us your feedback, creativity, and support, we thank you with all our hearts. Special thanks in this category go out to my mom Jackie, and our friends Alexa, Kevin, Gene, Jim and Paul.

I must also give special thanks to Leia for not only putting up with me, but also for supporting me while I explored this new hobby. I love you.

I would also like to dedicate this to the people who thought it was impossible. Let me be clear. I am not bragging, but rather I hope this serves as a form of inspiration. If we can do this, imagine what you can do.

Mikey, I think I can be persuaded to write one or two more books.

f.

The Pan:

The Trials of Jonathan Darling

By Fionnegan Justus Murphy

And

Michael Winkler

"...[Fairies] were rather a nuisance to [Peter], getting in his way and so on, and indeed sometimes he had to give them a hiding."
-J. M. Barrie, *Peter and Wendy*

It Begins the Same as Always

Tinkerbell squirmed in her itchy prison tied to Pan's hip. The rotten pouch had been a second home to her for ages and despite all of her attempts to tear or reason with it, it refused to oblige. She repositioned herself just as a bit of saltwater doused the pouch, promising the tormented Fairie a special kind of discomfort later.

A cool mist of water from a crashing wave caught the breeze and alighted on Peter Pan's face, waking him from his afternoon daydream. The wide and flat rock on which he sat poked its nose a few feet out of the water and around Peter circled a hungry and increasingly impatient melody of Mermaids. Their iridescent scales reflected rainbows from below the waves.

The young boy took in his surroundings and frowned. He had no adventure to look forward to, and the last one was so long ago that he took no more joy from it. Even the Lost Boys were so bored that they resorted to fighting one another in their camp not far away.

Today Nibs was the center of their attention, again. Bloodlust had left Nibs long ago and the other Boys loved few things more than belittling their comrade. Peter grimaced. Nibs was one of the first Lost Boys, with Peter since the beginning. That he allowed himself to be treated with such disrespect made Peter's hackles rise in disgust. His sharp baby teeth clenched at the pathetic display.

He opened the itchy, rotting pouch on his hip and pulled out the small glowing fairie. "Tink," he whined, "I'm bored! And so are the Lost Boys. This *resting* is just unbearable."

"I'm sorry to hear that, sir," her spite for him curled from her lips like smoke.

"You know what we need to spark up a new adventure?" he asked, ignoring her tone.

"But, Peter, you just defeated the Vikings less than a week ago. Don't you want to recuperate a bit?"

"We've rested for long enough, I'm already starting to forget that last adventure, if you can call it that. Go out and get me an enemy, someone who's a challenge this time. The last few have been too simple, too frightened and timid."

"The Vikings took out more Lost Boys than anyone! How can you say they were timid?"

"Their weakness was the heat."

"Well, what about the Ninjas? They were formidable!"

"I've already fought the Dryads, and they were tough. Compared to them the Ninjas were a piece of cake. Besides, they had no leader. There was no *nemesis* for me. It was a worth-wile experiment, but boring just the same. Bring me someone worthy of fighting me."

One of her all too common rebellious moods swelled in Tinkerbell. She was wet and irritated, and if Peter wanted her to do something he was going to have to force her. She had limits, and it was time, once again, to put her foot down, no matter how futile the gesture. She wanted him to know that he hadn't yet broken her.

"I'm not going to bring anyone else here, Pan. There have been enough. You've killed enough innocent people. No more."

Peter rolled his eyes. The Fairies were a necessity to him. They played so many important roles in Peter's plans, but they were such a nuisance. Every chance they got they would drag their feet, or twist his orders around until he had to be utterly explicit with his instructions. They would occasionally get so completely in his way that Peter thought they enjoyed the beatings he dolled out. There were times when, despite what they told him about their deaths, he thought maybe they enjoyed dying and being brought back. Either way, he was too impatient to spar with Tink today.

"Just do as I say, bug, or your father will pay the price. Understand?" he asked, squeezing her just enough for her to feel his sincerity.

Tink's eyes narrowed to slits. She imagined the dark hole in which her father was imprisoned. Her mind twisted with the anguish she imagined Peter unleashing upon him.

"I understand," she said through clenched teeth and flew off to get started.

A new ruckus in the Lost Boy camp caught Peter's attention once again. The Never Bird had become involved in the escalating fight with Nibs. The other Lost Boys pushed him back until he stumbled into a bush where the Never Bird was gathering twigs for her enormous nest. So involved with taunting Nibs were the other Lost Boys that they only laughed while he fought in a panic to fend off the gigantic, deadly bird.

The Never Bird's aggression to defend what she felt was hers was so absolute that her sharp beak quickly drew blood. The fight to the death would have continued had a loud crowing not struck the group like a hammer. Peter crashed into the camp with such passion that the Never Bird chose to flee rather than pick a fight with this new challenger.

...

Ship's Log;
Captain James S. Cooper of the HMS Valiant;
12, May 1763

We arrived in port early this morning to restock our supplys. One tonne of flour, two tonnes of pork, two and a half tonnes of beer, and two and a half tonnes of potatoes were brought aboard. One tonne of rope has been replaced. The ship is undergoing various maintenance: All expos'd timber is being sanded and varnish'd, a fresh flag has replaced our faded and tattered flag of old. New livestock are being brought aboard currently.

The men will be given leave for the night and all of the day tomorrow. I will remain on board to inspect the ship and make sure she is seaworthy.

Regarding the subject of Smee; he has been acting more peculiar about this trip than most. I am afraid that he might be getting worse. This may have to be one of the last trips he sails.

My promise to keep an eye on him may soon be more than I can handle. He will be better off with others more like himself

...

Smee wandered through the market by himself, or so he thought. Captain Cooper did not like Smee wandering off alone, but loathed the idea of holding Smee's hand his entire life. The Captain made sure a few of his men kept a watchful eye on Smee from a distance. They stayed far enough away to not hover, but close enough to step in if need be.

"Buy a crystal, young man. Keep demons away," called a merchant.

"No, can't spend it on trinkets. Jimmy said not to," Smee replied honestly.

"Sir, this woven design will bring you peaceful sleep."

"No thanks."

"Try this elixir, my boy. It will bring the ladies swooning, guaranteed!"

Smee turned beet red, giggled, and pushed his way through the crowds. A young woman in a worn, but not worn out dress followed after him. She carried a green canvas bag with a big brass buckle on the strap. When Smee stopped at a wood carver's counter she settled in beside him to watch a demonstration of dexterity.

"Excuse me, but is your name Smee?" she whispered to him, looking at him from the corner of her eye.

"Who's askin'," Smee replied, but when he got a look at her his face beamed and he flung himself at her with a big bear hug. "Mom!" he said, laughing.

"Shh, Samuel," she whispered. "I need to tell you secrets and people are watching. Let's go for a walk. Big things are in store for you, son." She turned, unable to stop herself, and grabbed him by the face to look at him. "Oh, you've grown up so strong."

Smee could see tears brimming in her eyes. One of Smee's weaknesses was seeing a person cry. His face began to scrunch up, eyebrows together, eyes squinting, lips tucking in and nose wrinkling, but before his tears could start to fall she composed herself, cleared her throat and said, "It's okay, son. Come on. We've got a lot to discuss."

As they walked the pair grew more comfortable talking and the shadows grew long. The years since their last meeting melted away. Though his mother had noticed what a strapping young man he had become, she had not age a day. Smee did not notice.

"Darling, something is about to happen to you that isn't fair. But I need you to always remember a couple of things that will help you get through it.

"One, I love you and I always will. So does your dear uncle. He won't always show it, and you'll need to do everything you can to stay patient with him. He won't listen and he'll even grow cross with you at times, but don't forget that fact. He loves you deep down inside and that won't ever change."

The two walked through the market for hours, the young woman sharing her hopes, fears, and secrets with her son. When she had said all she needed to say, and Samuel had agreed to everything he needed to do, she kissed his cheek, looked for a long moment into his eyes, and disappeared into the crowd.

…

Ship's Log;

Captain James S. Cooper of the HMS Valiant;

13, May 1763

     Today is our second day in port and the men will return at sundown this evening. I have inspected the ship and declar'd it seaworthy. I completed the inspections in the late afternoon, which gave me enough time to step off the ship and enjoy a bit of dinner. Smee join'd me for my meal and we discuss'd the happenings of his day. He spent every last bit of money he had on trinkets and fygurines. These toys are merely some swindler's way of taking money off of wayfarers and half-wits.

     I spoke to Smee about my concerns with his behavior. He seems to have develop'd an irrational fear of going back out to sea. He was all a chatter during the meal, but whenever I mentioned the upcoming trip he grew quiet and eventually tried to get me to promise not to go.

     He continuously asked that I not "followe". He's been confusing his words more and more. This is just a simple example, and it was easy to translate what his intentions were. He said "followe", when I'm certain that he meant, "go". I'm concern'd for him, tho', because sometimes it is not so easy to decipher what he means, and I am wary of what will happen if he says the wrong thing to the wrong person. We will be setting out to sea soon and men who dare not hurt him will surround him. Being in port, however, always makes me anxious for him.

After our meal we went back to the market and I persuaded the merchants to give Smee his money back in exchange for returning the rubbish he bought. It took a bit of persuading, but eventually the threat of being press'd into service aboard my ship turned their minds. I do not like to abuse my Captain status, but I dislike even more when Smee is maltreated

On our way back to the ship we encounter'd a young woman who ask'd me to walk her home, as it was late and darkness was falling. Smee cried out and try'd to hit the young woman. I had to restrain him and send him back to the ship alone. I still have to deal with him. I explain'd the situation to the young woman and she was very understanding. Her name was Tina Bell. I escorted her back to her home safely. I then returned to the ship.

...

Tina Bell bumped shoulders with Captain James Cooper.

"Oh dear. I'm terrifically sorry, I'm sure," Tina offered to the captain. "I see the water in you, sir. A good sailor to be certain."

She was stunningly beautiful, with a close-cut bodice, a coat and tailored pants. Her hair was cut close to her face, too, and framed it perfectly. There was nothing of England in her. She walked with the confidence of a man and if she'd ever held the stifling social customs of a British woman in her heart, she'd long since abandoned them. Her bearing was free and easy and her thick soled boots struck the cobblestone with not so much a clack as a skitter. She seemed to dance along the street in her way. Her eyes didn't cast downward when his met them, nor did her shoulder turn her aside. She looked at him squarely, with her chin up and firm. Her tiny hands were hidden from him behind her back, but he instantly imagined them to be calloused and strong from honest work.

He couldn't not look at her. It took everything in his power to remember that he was no ruffian, that he was a man of the Royal Navy, the most prestigious international arm of the most powerful and respected government on the globe.

"Ahem, young lady. I do hope you're alright. Please forgive my clumsiness."

"There's nothing to forgive, Captain. Of course the fault is mine. My word, how the English do make their sailors these days."

Her hand very lightly brushed the back of his upper left arm, the way a gentleman's would were he ushering a lady to the dance floor.

"Walk me home, Captain. It's far too late for someone as delicate as myself to risk it, and you're far too strapping for me to pass up the protection."

Smee told her to shut her mouth and leave them alone and then swatted at her. Cooper, who would not tolerate such blatant rudeness, sent Smee back to the ship directly.

A Royal Captain does not blush, and so he didn't, but he wanted to. She was direct and lacked all of what an Englishwoman consider social graces. She had the demeanor of rough-hewn royalty, maybe forged in some sort of local martial culture. In any case, she knew what she wanted and how to tell someone to give it to her.

However, she wasn't coarse or base. Her grace and presence gave lie to the suggestion that she was in any way common, and the idea that she might have been a working girl never approached the outskirts of James' consciousness.

"Tell me about your world, Captain Cooper. I would like to hear about your relationship with the sea."

What an odd

way to put that.

"What is there to say, Miss Bell? I was made for it. My family is complete Royal Navy, to be sure. There was never a chance that I'd do other. Even if I'd ever wanted, which I never did."

"You're certainly made of the ocean, I can tell. I don't want to know what brought you to the waves, my good man," her laugh danced in the wind as so many crystal chimes. It played with his ears and flirted with escape, only to concede the point and settle in his head; where he made it feel as comfortable as he could, lest it grow restless and seek the breeze again. His neck grew warm.

You're an Englishman, sir.

Do not forget yourself.

Her voice brought him back to the moment as she continued her thought. "I want to hear what keeps you there."

In an effort to keep such a casual woman comfortable Cooper tried to let go of some of his formalities. "Might I presume to call you Tina, my girl?"

"Presume as you'd like, sir."

"Well, Tina, it's the sky. I'm not a poetic man, certainly not as gifted with words as yourself, but I love dependability of the sky at night on the sea. When I do come to port, be it here or in London or

Plymouth or Boston, I lose the sky. There's just too much happening down here. The men in their shops closing down for the night and cleaning; all of the night lamps lining the streets; it all just leaves no room for the stars and the moon. I'm a man of order. I love to be able to look at my sky and see the map it gives me."

"Order," she harrumphed. "I suppose order is fine, but I think there's something to be said for a little disorder. A little chaos is refreshing to the soul, some larceny of time, if not treasure. A little piracy."

Tina tensed, ever so slightly. This was always the risky part when she was searching for Pan's nemeses. Pan always wanted an enemy that could be completely changed. That was part of his game. If a Royal Sailor was going to be turned into a pirate, he had to despise pirates thoroughly, but also have the seed of the idea planted in his head.

"Piracy, young lady? I admit, I'm surprised at you. There's nothing romantic about a pirate. They're good for one thing, and that's feeding the crows."

"As you will, my Captain dear."

Cooper's arms flexed involuntarily under his uniform sleeve. Unconscious thoughts of what he'd like to do with and to this ravishing little thing danced in his head. Had he rooted them out he'd have been horrified, and he'd have taken little solace in the fact that they'd been placed there without his permission.

Tink had limited abilities in the real world. She couldn't put thoughts into a man's head, not exactly, but she could suggest them. One thing all men had in common, upstanding Royal Navy men and rapscallion buccaneers alike was that they were men. And all men, down to the last man, she'd ever met in this form of hers wanted her. She could only hope it would pay off.

"I don't know about maps and seaports and street lamps. When I look at sky, I see…"

"What do you see, dear?"

"I see freedom," she answered honestly. "I see potential, and the home of the birds and of the creatures who use it. I see flight and fancy. Release."

She'd grown wistful and more than a little morose. It gave Cooper at once an urge to protect her, as well as a fleeting sense of shame at his earlier urges, but only a fleeting sense. She was still beautiful beyond measure. He knew he could have her if he wanted. He wanted, very much.

"Why, Miss Bell, you seem sad. The sky is our strength, I think, yours and mine. I can't tell you why. I don't know. But we own it each in our way, as it owns us."

As they continued their walk, the talk continued on and flitted from his home in England to her home. She didn't say where she'd come from, or what had brought her to this place, but she didn't seem to want to be there, at least not entirely.

That night they didn't walk very far, but they did walk for a long time around the same street over and over again. James never recognized the time or the distance covered. They arrived at her "place" and he doffed his hat, said goodnight and found his way back to the ship, his id awash in conflict; his ego swelled by attention.

…

Ship's Log;
Captain James S. Cooper of the HMS Valiant;
14 May 1763

An event occurred during the night. We had set sail at sunrise. The winds were constant and sturdy out of the southwest at ten. We began making our patrol as normal.

It was during the night that unusual events began. A single star look'd out of place, as if it were much closer to earth than the others, although it was not any bigger than the rest. Then, as we got close it fell from the sky and hover'd, glowing over our mizzenmast. It could not have been much larger than an orange and it glow'd with a faint green tint. The whole of the crew stood and gazed at it. We were all transfyx'd for moments on end. It was not St. Elmo's Fire. There was no thunderstorm nearby, it moved silently instead of being fixed on one point, and it did not glow blue. I am not a religious man, but I can't think of any other explanation for this tongue of fire gracing our ship. Then it flitted from bow to stern, dropping glinting powder on everything.

A deafening howl broke out on the deck, shattering the silence and Smee rais'd a musket and shot a charge of grapeshot at our celestial visitor. His aim is terrible, lucky for us, and I had him taken below deck immediately. We could hear him wailing like an animal from inside the cabin.

When we return home I have decided that he will be admitted somewhere to be look'd after. I cannot risk the security of the men or the ship any longer. I fear I should not have had him on for this long.

After a short time of sprinkling, the small star darted off in front of us faster than I thought possible. Then, as if it were waiting for us, it stopp'd moving all together. I order'd a three-quarter speed ahead and we follow'd.

The night drifted by as a fog drifted in. By this point Smee was not the only member of my crew that was beginning to feel nervous about the experience. All visual was reduc'd to the faint green glow of our lead. I gather'd that time was important, as the light would accelerate and then wait for us to catch up. I was hesitant to go any faster. We were already going faster than the conditions warrnt'd, but I found myself giving all trust to this messenger of God. Soon I called for a full speed ahead.

We traveled quickly, but the anxiety of passing through waters in low visibility mix'd with the dreaded possibility that this might be a demon rather than angel, caus'd the night to move exceeding slow. But as the sun rose and the fog dissipated, an island on the horizon faded into view.

We sail'd 'round the island and found an ideal natural harbor. It's going to be a hot day today and I've order'd the men to stay aboard the ship and rest. I doubt anyone desires sleep, but I'm hoping that the fatigue of sailing hard all night will force their bodies to silence their minds. They need to recuperate before we put together an exploration party. I do not want my men on a strange island without all of their wits about them.

Smee is asleep, but he continues whimpering.

"He was a lovely boy, clad in skeleton leaves and the juices that ooze out of trees, but the most entrancing thing about him was that he had all his first teeth."

-J. M. Barrie, *Peter and Wendy*

$$\textcircled{2}$$

Captain Meets Pan

"Jimmy, I need to go to land with you because I'm supposed to, so I'm going along, okay?"

Captain Cooper was packing his tools and papers into a satchel. It contained his spyglass, a compass, a few matches, and a roll of paper with a pencil.

"Smee, I need you to stay on the boat until we can figure something out about this place. You stay on the ship, but after we see that it's safe you can go a'shore."

Smee had heard the order in Jimmy's voice and knew it was useless to argue. "Okay, Jimmy, I'll go on when it's safe."

"Good. We'll be back in time for supper. Just try to stay out of the sun until we get back." Tossing the bag over his shoulder he said, "I'll see you soon. Don't worry."

"Bye, Jimmy."

The Captain left his quarters and went onto the deck of the ship. The sun had just begun to rise and a few sailors were mingling around the rowboats lashed to the ship.

"Okay, men!" Captain Cooper called, "Load up three boats. Five men per skiff."

Each man carried a pistol with him, a blade, and their own water skin. Smee looked over the railing of the ship and waved for the entire descent. Then he quickly headed below deck and began to search out his best friends on the ship, but with over two hundred men aboard, this took some time.

They were not at their hammocks, which was the first place that Smee looked. Unfortunately his poor mind could not decide where to look next so he just wandered about calling their names.

"O'Neil? Smythe!" he called over and over. He checked the kitchen, but they weren't there, so wandered lower and lower into the ship until someone pointed Smee in the right direction. Finally, when he had returned almost all the way back to the upper deck, he found them cleaning out the cannons, which had gotten filthy overnight.

"Hi," he said simply.

"Hello, Boyo. How's the mornin' treatin' ye?" O'Neil asked, scrubbing the outside Long Tom, the ship's biggest cannon.

"Things is fair enough, but Jimmy won't let me go with him to shore, so I was wondrin' if you boys wanted to go do some fishin'."

The two were in time with Smee and saw through his trick.

"Smee, the Cap'n would bring out the cat if we did that. We can't sneak you ashore. We'd get ten lashes!" Smythe replied.

"Yeah, pro'lly," Smee said, "but you wouldn't if he didn't know it was you. I just need help low'rin' the boat. I can do the rest and I'll be back afore 'em."

"We can't just let you go off by yourself, Smee. No one is allowed to go exploring alone. We don't know a thing about that island, and can't go over there 'til we know what's what."

"But I'll be back afore Jimmy. And you won't be goin' on the island. You'll be fishin'. The waters can't be more scairt here'n anywhere else we've gone. We only sailed here in one night, so 'tweren't far'nuff fer monsters to pop up. No one will say nuffin'. You'll be okay."

O'Neil and Smythe looked at one another. O'Neil shrugged and Smythe said, "Well, I do hate cleanin' these guns."

To which O'Neil said, "'S truth there. I'd rather be out fishing. But just in the boat. We're not goin' on the island. Okay, Smee? Why don't you get the poles? We'll get some bait from the kitchen."

...

O'Neil had pulled Jameson's watchful eye away from his work in the kitchen and out into the mess hall. He was asking him about how they kept the drinking water from going stale as Smythe snuck into the kitchen behind them. Smythe had a few friends who worked in the kitchen. He offered to trade them some playing cards for a bit of cheese and a small ear of corn. He'd most likely win the cards back later on anyhow.

A few moments later, Smee, Smythe and O'Neil were rowing the long way around the island, attempting to find a little lagoon or harbor that would keep them hidden. They soon found themselves in a quiet spot where one giant rock poked out of the water about twenty yards from shore. Smee rowed their boat as close to land as he could and dropped a small anchor.

"I'm gonna go lookin' around while you fellas fish for a while. I'll be back," he told Smythe and O'Neil as if this were the plan all along.

"Oh no you don't," O'Neil said. "You're not going anywhere alone. It's one thing to sneak you off the ship for a bit of fun, but we're not gonna let you out our sight. And no one's settin' foot on that island. Got me?"

Smee felt an urge pulling him. He more than wanted to go to shore; he needed to. Being so close to the island made some faulty nerves in his brain snap to attention. He felt clarity just in front of him, the way one knows where something is in the dark. In the water below he saw Mermaids swimming lazily below their boat. While he was not surprised to see them there, he did suddenly feel sorry for them without knowing why.

...

Pan perched on a limb just out of sight of Captain Cooper and his party. He had hoped they would come ashore – the more the better. This next bit was going to be a challenge; it always was. But it was one that he had risen to before, and he'd do again this time. The first contact dictated a lot about the way his game would play out and it was a moment that he savored. He could feel the closeness of Smythe, O'Neil, and Smee, and didn't like them off on their own, but the Lost Boys would deal with them if they had to – or wanted to. Either way, the three mischievous sailors weren't likely to be a problem.

Peter closed his eyes and sent the Island its instructions.

Weaken them.

Slow them down.

Drain them of their energy.

Each step is more tiring than the last.

The Island smiled, softening its surface, stretching out the clay under each footfall. The Sun beamed and glared onto the Island, burning after each movement the sailors made. Tink smirked; the uncountable time she spent with Pan still hadn't numbed her to his immaturity and backhandedness.

Smythe and O'Neal shuddered slightly, feeling suddenly warmer in their skiff, sensing an approaching danger like a silent boat of pirates sliding up on their stern side in the night. Samuel Cooper steeled his nerves.

...

Sunlight had just begun to peek over the tree line, and already sweat beaded on the brows of Captain Cooper and his men. Not one of them could describe the feeling that swept through them as they stood on the beach and so none of them spoke up about it. The feeling was akin to seasickness, but oddly it didn't set in until they stood on shore. Nausea swept through them like a wave from the ground up. Its intensity subsided, but never went completely away throughout the day. Something else accompanied it as well, a sadness and fear. It was nothing they had ever experienced, and so they had no frame of reference.

This island ought to have had some kind of familiarity. On the surface it wasn't unlike other islands they stepped onto in the Caribbean. Palm trees, sand, rainforests; all of the traits they were used to and expecting to see were there. But the familiar setting did not serve as a mental anchor for the Captain and his men. Everything seemed to be covered in a glittering veil. It was so inexpressibly disconnected from anything they had seen or expected, and that terrified them.

It was their discipline as British Sailors that saved them from the insanity and permanent change that pulled at them. Their leader, the man they truly and deeply loved, the man who asked for patience and demanded obedience and earned respect demanded that discipline now. The change would have to wait. There was work to be done. King and Country asked James Cooper to do it, and so the men of the HMS Valiant had their own jobs to see to, as well.

...

"I'm just gonna be on the beach. I wanna touch the sand. Don't you? Can't we just sit on the beach fer'while? It's been so long, and if sump'n happens we can just push the boat back into the water. No explorin'," Smee pleaded.

"Oh come on, O'Neil," Smythe chastised, "We're already off the ship, why not take full advantage? You wanna go on shore, Smee? Okay, let's fish from land. What do you say, mate?"

"Alright, fine. But we're not goin' explorin'. Agreed?"

"Deal!" both Smee and Smythe said in unison.

Smee's feet touched the sand. And the sand touched him. An ill feeling barely made itself known to him before it was pushed aside by a second feeling. It was something he had never felt before. Like a prisoner stepping past the gates and out into the world, Smee was free.

Every part of his mind that was incomplete for his entire life had pulled together with his first step in the sand. His mind finally operated without the clunks, no more jerking thoughts without rhyme or reason, no more trouble holding one thought in his head.

For the first time in his life Smee felt whole, as if he had at long last come home after living in a foreign land. He shut his eyes and breathed his first breath as a complete man. The blood cursing through his muscles was steady, and for the first time he could control those muscles without his own brain betraying his intentions. When he opened his eyes the world was new. There was clarity. There was focus. He could feel the energy of the Island inside him.

And then there was another, more urgent feeling.

He felt danger and his every sense set to work to discreetly discover it. A breeze shook a cluster of trees in response to Smee's instincts, carrying both sound and smell. Hushed growls and barks drifted to his ears and acrid stink wafted into his nose.

"Shh," he said to Smythe and O'Neil, who were bickering over how to properly care for Smee. "There's something watching us." His voice was calm and he didn't stutter over his words. They flowed together without a gap of thought between them.

O'Neil and Smythe stopped moving. Smythe put his hand on the pistol in his belt. Smee noticed movement in the tree. He saw one figure with a bone horn slung around his neck; then more, encroaching through the bushes close to the beach perimeter. They were armed with nets and spears and their glare suggested that they would rather not talk things over. Smee knew this the way he knew that his hair was brown and his boots were wet. He felt a connection to them and understood their intentions.

"Hey boys," Smee called in a casual voice to his shipmates, "Look at this rock, its perfect for skipping!" He bent down to pick up a rock, and quick as a snapping whip, flung the rock hard at the horn-wearing figure in the tree followed closely by the knife kept in Smee's belt. Steel flashed, end over end, burying itself in young meat before Smythe or O'Neil heard their welcoming party.

Boys charged out of the bushes toward Smee and the other sailors. The boy with the horn and the one who was unfortunate enough to get in the way of Smee's knife fell before Smythe thought to draw his pistol. The boys were heavily armed and charging hard, but Smythe's humanity stayed his trigger finger.

"Stop, boys! Or I'll shoot!" he yelled.

But it was too late. A boy with the bone through his earlobe lunged through the air with a two pronged spear aimed for Smythe's neck. The end of the spear tickled Smythe's Adam's apple but went no further, thanks to Smee. He smashed his shoulder into the boy's ribs, knocking him out of the air, careening into the water where Mermaids swept over the drowning boy, pulling him under in roiling froth and gulping howls.

O'Neil froze with shock, watching the churning water stain dark. So preoccupied was he that when he turned back around to face the shore, Smee was the only body left standing among five small corpses. The stone statue, calmed by a deep breath, scanned the area once again. A peaceful silence returned to the beach.

"S...Smee...?" Smythe asked, his voice shaking.

"Be still, men. Get back in the boat and head out a few dozen yards. They won't chase you out on account of the Mermaids. I have more business here, but you two cannot come with me."

O'Neil helped Smythe get back in the boat and rowed out with neither a thought nor word. This was a different Smee than they knew back on the ship. He was confident, strong and coordinated. Smee had become an ideal soldier in the blink of an eye. Even his face held a more adult posture. Once the sailors were safe in the harbor, Smee tossed the remaining bodies in the water and let the Mermaids take care of the rest.

"I need to find The Pan," he thought. "Bring me to The Pan, please," he asked the Island and trotted off into the trees. Limbs bent out of his way, opening up a path before him that closed behind. Walk turned to trot, trot to jog and then run and Smee was pleased to find that the Island moved as fast as he did.

Soon the path closed and the canopy collapsed in tight above him, trapping Smee in a cage of branches and leaves. Growl, roar and crash reinforced Smee's trust in his surroundings; a trust manifested in patient stillness. From his vantage point he saw a bear rampage its way through the brush. Close behind, a small group of familiar monsters gave chase, wielding jagged weapons.

When the bear had gone and the din had dimmed, the forest resumed the accommodation of its guest, leading him to a shallow but wide stream and beyond. Before long another beach came into view and he heard talking. He slowed down and crawled on his belly to reach the edge of the tree line. Jimmy and his expedition were face to face with a large group of boys dressed similarly to the ones Smee had dispatched moments ago. Like Jimmy in front of his men, one boy was standing in front of the other boys. He had a golden short sword on his hip and was clearly their leader.

Smee willed the wind to blow in his direction to both mask his scent and carry words to him. It worked for a moment, allowing him to hear the introduction, but then the boy introduced as Peter Pan glanced in his direction and squinted. Peter then looked around, as if he were inspecting the wind and a second later there was none to speak of, robbing Smee of the conversation.

Eventually Jimmy took his crew away. Peter Pan's band stayed where they were, watching the Captain and his men leave. As soon as Jimmy was past the surf, Smee crawled back, deeper into the forest.

Pan stalked to the forest edge and peered in, but all he could see were the thick trees intertwining around themselves. He waved his hand and those woven trees separated, revealing further, deeper portions of the woods, but they did not reveal the grown man running far and fast away from him.

...

Smee stood on the edge of the shore. O'Neil had rowed back to pick him up, but Smee stared through him, deep inside his own mind. He was trying to decide between standing still and not moving. Then, reluctantly, he stepped into the boat and felt his synapses shrivel. His focus blurred and thoughts bounced through his head, scattering like marbles falling to the ground. His tongue and muscles seemed to pull in their own direction again and it took nearly all his force to keep them in line. The man he had become on the Island was shackled and thrown back into his oubliette. But Smee needed to get back to the ship or else Jimmy would worry about him and probably lash his friends. So he sat quietly on his bench as they returned, lamenting his loss and trying hard to remember how it felt to be whole. He would have to find another moment to slip away to deliver his message.

...

Ship's Log;

Captain James S. Cooper of the HMS Valiant;

15 May 1763

I drafted a search party to explore and map the island. It
succeeded to a point. We found that the fauna here are ferocious.
Bears, wolves, lions and tigers inhabit this small place, which is
most peculiar as they are from very different sections of the
world. I do not understand how they all came to be here together.
We found what must have been a small village of native men, but
we found no inhabitants. Constantly, wherever we went I had a
strange feeling like we were being watch'd from the trees, but
despite our best efforts no one came out to meet us.

We did not get to see the whole of the island due to the
brutal sun beating down with such intensity that the men were
becoming burn'd. We return'd to the ship, intending on going out
again when the heat subsides.

When we arriv'd at our skiffs we found one dozen children
of many different races inspecting them. They must have been the
children of the natives we discover'd earlier. They donn'd the
skins of the beasts from the island. Their parents must have been
near by. We miss'd them, I am certain, due to our stinging skin
and parch'd throates. When I introduced myself one of the
children stepp'd forward, declaring himself as Peter Pan, the ruler
of the island, which he calls Never Land. He was quite serious

and took umbrage when some of the men laugh'd at him, thinking he was playing at some kind of trifle.

Neither myself nor my two other officers laugh'd. We saw the golden short sword on his hip and notic'd that the other children were also arm'd. He was a good-looking boy of, perhaps, six or seven years old. He wore no skins. He was cover'd in leaves of all sizes and colors. Most of them had rotted away to the veins. Around his mouth and down his chin and neck there was a dark sappy residue, as if he had been drinking from the trees themselves.

His posture had not chang'd, but I knew he was willing, perhaps even eager to fight as hard as he could if it should come to that, and for a moment I saw unmatch'd brutality in his eyes. No day is a good day for hurting children, however. I quickly call'd the men to attention before the laughter went on too long.

I announced myself formally then as Captain Cooper of the HMS Valiant and requested a formal meeting. I hoped to uncover where we are and perhaps find our way back home. I also wanted to find out more about the island, where his parents were, how long they had been stranded here, and perchance offer them passage back to civilization.

He said to me "No, the ship is your territory. The island is me. You are my Pirates."

I tried to explain that we weren't pirates of any sort and that we could be trusted, but he only closed his eyes and was silent, taking many deep breaths before shouting in an alarmingly deep growl, "YOU ARE MY PIRATES!" None of the men laugh'd this time. He sounded like a lion, and his face twisted horribly.

Where did they get those weapons and how long had they been stranded here? They smell'd awful, like rotten leaves, and blood.

"While Peter lived, the tortured man [The Captain] felt that he was a lion in a cage into which a sparrow had come."
-J. M. Barrie, *Peter and Wendy*

Smee's Directions Home

Ship's Log;
Captain James S. Cooper of the HMS Valiant
18 May, 1763

  This place is taking its toll on everyone. I was forc'd to look back on this log to refresh my memory on how it was that we arrived here, where we were before here, and for how long we have been here. I knew that we were elsewhere, that there was a place not so brutal. The more I think about it, however, the more I feel as though I belong here. A part of me still believes that this is where I've always been.
  Paranoia is growing in me as well. I feel like I am under a microscope and every action I take is being watch'd. The heat is unbearable, and the confusion of who or where I am persists endlessly. Two-dozen boys attack'd us today. It is with great hesitance that I write these words down because I scarcely believe my own memories; another change I've recently developed. It must have been a trick of the heat, but they must have flown to our ship. It's the only explanation because there were no boats. We would have seen them coming, and they were not wet, so

swimming is out of the question. Peter Pan was with them and he fought like no other I have ever seen. He laugh'd as he cut through my crew, and he bark'd out orders like a general to the other boys running over the ship. I do not understand the reason for the attack. We made no offensive maneuver toward them and they were incredibly outnumber'd and outmatch'd in weight, weaponry, and skill. The entire confrontation lasted a mere minute or two. I order'd the men to disarm and take prisoners and not to kill unless it was necessary. I only just finish'd calling the order before Peter order'd the boys to retreat. A twinge of frustration curl'd in his voice. I could hear it. Each boy flung himself over the side of the ship, and when we peer'd over the edge we saw them gliding over the surface of the water, I think. It was then that I must confess feeling not myself. Peter Pan's yell echoed back to me again. He shouted once again that we will be his Pirates, and as he said it I felt an urge unlike anything I've felt before. I wanted to aim my cannons at the fleeing, flying boys and blast them out of the sky. I wanted to hunt them down and tear them apart. I longed for the free life of a Pirate.

Smee brought me back to myself. He call'd me Jimmy, his voice seemed so far away, and my mind was my own once again. This place is changing me and I have redoubl'd my efforts to find a way out.

No deaths occurred in the fray, but several of my men who were taken by surprise were wounded. Wallace, Henry, and Black will probably not return to full health if they survive the next few days. Henry was stabb'd through the upper chest. Wallace received a savage blow to the head and it is uncertain if he will *wake up. And Black was cut at the back of the knee. The surgeon Murdy is hoping that he will not have to amputate Black's leg. Perhaps just a splint will suffice. But he lost a lot of blood and is still asleep.*

We did take on two prisoners, which are currently being question'd. One of them wears a grey wolf skin over his shoulders and has a hand stitch'd pair of pants made of tanned hide. He has long slender bones tied in his hair that hang down the sides of his face.

The other is a shorter, rounder child; probably seven years old. He has no clothing above his waist, but has smear'd rust colored mud on his chest, back, and face. The designs of the mud make him look like a savage, but he is white skinned underneath. He wears a loincloth and has over it a skirt made of small bamboo sticks.

One of them must know of a way out of this place.

...

Smee entered Captain Cooper's cabin. He crossed over the wooden planks with purpose, but when he got behind James he merely glanced about the room, lost. He looked into the picture frames and twirled the golden rope that draped over the back of Cooper's chair. After unsuccessfully trying to focus on his work, James put down his quill.

"Is there something you want, Smee?" he asked without turning around.

Smee's eyes widened and he stuttered. He searched for the reason, any reason for disturbing Jimmy. Focus enveloped Smee as he tried to force his mind into constraints. Finally he let out an angry shout, "Why are we still here?"

"I've already told you, Smee. We're trapped here. We can't leave. Even when we sail off in a straight line we end up back here after the fog lifts."

More stammering and fidgeting, "But, um…did you try my idea?"

Sigh. "What idea, Smee?"

"The yesterday idea. The one I told you yesterday."

"You didn't tell me an idea yesterday, Smee. Are you sure you didn't just imagine telling me yesterday?"

"You say that every day. Write it down today."

James took off his glasses and rubbed the tension out of his temples and forehead. He swung his chair around and leaned back. Fingers splayed and touched in a peak. Jimmy closed his eyes and sighed, giving up, "Okay, Smee, tell me the 'Yesterday Idea' again and I'll write it down right here."

"Okay." Pride and accomplishment swelled from Smee.

…

Smee has an idea for leaving the island. Apparently going with the wind is the mistake. It pushes us into the fog and then brings us back around. We are not going in a straight line. We should, instead, follow the wind into the fog and then promptly turn around completely and push against it all night long with the oars. I promis'd him that we will do it tomorrow if the wind picks up. Right now there's no wind to speak of.

"...and [Mrs. Darling's] sweet mocking mouth had one kiss on it that Wendy could never get, though there it was, perfectly conspicuous in the right-hand corner."

"...but Mrs. Darling never upbraided Peter; there was something in the right-hand corner of her mouth that wanted her not to call Peter names."

-J. M. Barrie, *Peter and Wendy*

The Shadow Incident

A mother was telling her three children the bedtime story of Cinderella to get them to sleep without a fuss. It worked, like always. They were fast asleep, but she continued the story anyway because she enjoyed the way her mind spun the words together, like solving an intricate logic puzzle. It also gave her an excuse to sit and watch her darlings sleep, which always helped to make her drowsy. In fact, some of the best nights of sleep she'd ever gotten were spent in the large chair in her children's room.

She was at the point where the prince was having a rather difficult time locating the mysterious girl from the ball when something moved outside of the large window overlooking the street.

What was that?

Nothing. Just your imagination.
It was outside, after all, and there are
many things out there that could

casually pass by any window.

Nothing to be afraid of.

But what if it is something to be afraid of?

She froze, leaving her body, the room, and her darlings behind
as she retreated into her mind.

The dog's not barking,

so it must be your imagination.

No, something moved,
I know it.

No you don't.

Maybe it was just a bird.

Not all birds are friendly,
and they usually don't fly
around here at night.

A bat flew past, then.

Oh, that's much better.
Besides, it didn't move past the
window and you know it.
It moved from the center downward,
like a big spider.

It was already there.

You know what you saw.

No you don't.

Her eyes never moved from the window. She couldn't see outside. The only thing she could see was her own reflection sitting in the large chair looking back at her.

A slight shiver shook through her.

Had the movement

come from inside the room?

Is something or someone

inside with me and my

babies?

The room grew maddeningly quiet and for a moment she couldn't hear them breathing. She took a slow breath to calm herself and looked from bed to bed. There her angels slept, their blankets slowly rising and falling with their soft breath.

She roused herself and inched, one foot in front of the other, on the plush carpeting until she came within an arm's reach of the window. The street, three stories below, was unbearably still. Only their dog Nana moved below, moseying back toward the house after her late night constitutional.

Mrs. Darling reached up and flicked the latch, locking the heavy panes in place. Just as the latch snapped, Michael shifted in his bed. A ball of light about the size of her fist blinked outside the window like a large lightning bug or a camera flash. It blinded her for a second and vanished. She blinked to erase the residual negative

- 45 -

behind her eyelids. The image looked like a moth, a huge moth with a tired expression on its face. Next to the phantom moth was another design. Mrs. Darling blinked, desperately trying to bring the object into focus. Each blink made it smaller, yet clearer. When the image was too small to be certain, she thought she could identify the shape.

She was a small child in a haunted house, aware of the ghoul around the corner and unable to act. A shiver worked its way up through her spine to the top of her head. The phantom image was of a child, but not a child at all. Its face was hard and angular, like a bird's, and it showed her sharp, baby teeth.

She stepped back, barely holding in the sound of her gasp and drew the heavy drapes over the window. Backing up from the window Mrs. Darling began convincing herself that she didn't see what she saw, that it was her imagination. She was easily swayed because, after all, she was tired and her imagination was primed from telling the story. Besides, there was no way that after all this time he would have come to bring her back. And even if he had, the dog surely would have gone crazy. Clearly it was just a lightning bug and her imagination.

Then she saw the shadow.

Angela Darling turned and saw a shadow, which belonged to no one lying on the carpet. She did not dive into her imagination in order to defend what she saw, nor did she dive for a bottle. She did not go mad. She breathed slowly, as if to gather her thoughts, or sift through a memory. An urge to cry out at the universe swelled inside her.

It isn't fair to be reminded of that
... that...

Mrs. Darling would have called him a monster, a spoiled brat, the foul stink of all the worst parts of life. But she didn't. There was still a part of her on the right-hand corner of her mouth that remembered how fun and charming he was, and that quieted her anxiety.

But action was required; she couldn't just let the shadow stay on her children's floor. While her body braced with determination, a slight twitch at the right corner of her mocking mouth danced with the kiss that no one could catch, the relic kiss of Angela's own youth. It had been a time and place of mirth and dangerous excitement. She laughed a small devious laugh, almost a clearing of her throat, not wanting to wake her babes.

Bending down, she grasped the shadow by its collar, gave it a violent shake as if it were a piece of clothing fresh out of the dryer, then folded it neatly and walked down the three flights of stairs in her house. The shadow lay still in her arms as they moved through the grand kitchen toward another doorway, which framed more stairs leading to the basement. From there she went into the workshop and opened her husband's tool chest. She put the shadow inside and closed the lid. After turning the key that lived in the lock, she removed it, and slipped it into her pocket.

Finally.

...

Tinkerbell and Pan were spending another evening off Neverland. They weren't hunting, not tonight. Tonight they were simply observing. A kind of "bird watching." Although Tink hated the idea of helping Pan do anything, this was the most enjoyable part of her job as his slave. It allowed her a moment or two of freedom. She was free to fly as fast or slowly as necessary. She was free to daydream because who would know? Every part of her was allowed to wander.

Tonight she was jetting along particularly quickly. She wasn't interested in finding children this evening. Sometimes she was because she lived for their laughter, but tonight she was just happy to be on the air.

Let him find his own recruits.

While zipping along, Tink enjoyed trying to piece a whole person together in her mind using only pieces that caught her eye as she flew, creating a kind of collage-person. Tonight this person wore one shiny wing-tip shoe, something green with a buckle on it, a pair of jeans with a hole near the rear pocket which showed bare skin behind it, a baseball cap with a brown pony tail swinging out from the hole in the back, another something green with a buckle that might have been a sash, thick red framed spectacles, a kind of swirl designed engagement ring, worn black and white sneaker for the other foot, and something green with a buckle.

Tink equivocated what would have been a skid in the air. She was in the middle of an outdoor seating area of a restaurant, which could have been dangerous. Her senses returned to her and she darted to the rooftop before anyone could see what she was.

Is someone following me?

Chasing me.

What is that green strap with the buckle?

Something hot, like Pan,

but not Pan.

What else can fly and keep up with me?

Does it matter?

What's the worst that can happen?

Collecting her wits, Tink stepped toward the edge of the building to have a look around. She was given a start, but was not afraid, which was good. After all, what should she fear? At best this thing could grant her deepest wish and no one would be around to clap for her. At worst it would leave her alone, and that thought set her free.

She cruised off of the building, but stayed higher and went slower. A video store had just gone dark and a man exited to go home for the night got into his beat up two-door hatchback. Another young man walked down the street with his head up, gazing at the stars. The smell of fire slowly crept up on her. By the time that she realized that she smelled heat she couldn't place when it had started, and then, all at once, it billowed into her.

Tink stopped just as the green strap shot past her, trailing heat and wind behind it. At first she thought it was Pan because of how hot the air had gotten, but then she saw that it was a bird. Not Pan, but a different fiery bird. It was wearing a green bag with a tarnished brass buckle on the strap that was miraculously not burning. The heat and the wind were tremendous. Tink would have dashed after it if necessary, but the heat sucked her into its wake without any effort. It wasn't every day that one saw a Phoenix, Fairie or not.

The invisible blaze behind the bird was intense and Tink was forced to pull back a bit just to keep her eyes open. The earth was a blur: treetops, roads, lights, but no details and no people.

Finally the heat trail died. The phoenix must have burned itself up in its haste, and it left Tink facing a three-story building on the corner of Some St. and No Special Pl. There was a light coming from the highest of windows. Tink looked around for the Phoenix. She saw a young woman walking on the street below. Her head bobbed to a silent rhythm and on one upbeat she may have thrown a nod at Tink, directing her attention toward the window.

Disbelief knocked the wind out of her tiny body when she saw a woman through the window reading in a chair. Could it really be her? After twenty years to this woman, and what felt like centuries to Tink, could this really be Angela? Of all of the pathways out of Neverland, all of the where's and when's, the odds of this were next to impossible. Who was that girl on the street?

Without Pan's shadow on them as a beacon, they should be safe and impossible to track down. Impossibly, thought, here she was. It was Angela, one of two ever known to have left the Island. She returned home with her Dryad savior and was sitting in that oversized chair, reading a book.

But the mark of Neverland was still there. Tink could still see the tree in Angela, even if no one else could, because Fairies see things differently than people do. They see the stuff that makes up a person instead of the mask or skin that they wear. And with Angela, a few spindly twigs still reached out of her in places. Some even had a few buds on them, but the most telling of marks still clung to the corner of Angela's mouth. There sat an untouchable and overtly obvious kiss.

Sadness filled Tinkerbell and she turned to leave. Pan might not find them yet, and Tink would not give them away. In mid-turn something caught her eye. She almost missed it, and that would have been terrible. She saw beneath a blanket a pile of dirt in the shape of a boy. It moved from lying on one side to sprawling on his back in his bed.

Almost everyone and everything is made up of many bits of each element, and this is how Fairies see the world and the people in it: as the combination of elements. The blending of those elements helps Fairies see colors and shapes nearly the same way humans do. But sometimes, on rare occasions, a person is born with just one element in them. Peter, of course, was composed of Fire alone. Captain Cooper was made of the Sea. Elementals had the potential to be very strong beings with powerful wills and, if they could tap into it like Pan had, powerful magic.

Angela had an element son. It makes sense that he's Earth, what with her being part tree and her man being a Dryad, but it was still a miracle to behold. If something happened to Cooper, then she could get this earth elemental to the Island to take his place in the battle to overthrow Pan.

She scanned the rest of the room. An empty bed was directly in front of Angela, and at the opposite side of the room to the Earth Element was another impossibility. Beneath the sheets of this last bed was a spinning turmoil of wind. Tink saw it as a tornado in the shape of a girl endlessly curling and twisting about herself. Angela's daughter was a Wind Elemental.

Tink's heart nearly burst out of her tiny chest and everything went dark. Although the Wind and Fire combination would possibly be problematic, encountering two elementals in one night, in one year, in one decade was unbelievable. She fell a few inches and was caught by Pan, who had snuck up behind her to observe. He flicked her awake, harder than necessary but not as hard as he could have. Nights away from the Island always rejuvenated him.

"Find something interesting?" he asked her, not at all concerned with her well-being.

"That's your call, not mine," she said with more strength than she'd hoped to use, trying to hide her amazement.

"Well, let's have a look."

They stood on a shelf of air and watched a mother read a story to her children. Pan, of course, saw them as a mother and three children and not a tree sprouting mother and her elemental children. Neither did he recognize Angela, which was good. Tinkerbell wanted the children, not the parents. They had been through enough and escaped the Island. Good for them. Let them enjoy their freedom.

The irony in that thought struck her.

Leave them alone,

they've been through enough;

let's just take their children.

Tinkerbell laughed a little, which made her glow just a touch. She stopped immediately and fell into Pan's hand again while she focused on dowsing out her glow.

Angela must have caught a glimpse of Tink because she stopped reading, stopped moving all together.

"Tink, toss off my shadow so we can find our way back here," Pan ordered urgently, "She's suspicious and we don't want their guard up."

The Fairie hesitated. They had really been through enough. They didn't deserve to have it all come back this much later. They had moved on, and from the look of it, quite nicely.

"Tink! Hurry up. She's coming closer. Toss off my shadow, now!"

But she was caught in indecision. Disobeying him was a terrible price, but where did she draw the line? Could she draw a line? How much of her still belonged to her? Nothing, it seemed. Had she become nothing more than an executioner who was moral free? Just doing the judge's bidding? Just doing her job and shoo off to anyone else it may harm?

The latch snapped shut on the window and just then Tinkerbell saw a child appeared, or the outline of a child appeared, rather, shift in the middle bed before vanishing again.

What did that mean?

Another child?

A child with, what, no elements?

Two elemental children

and whatever that third one was?

A blank slate?

The shock of its movement blinked Tinkerbell's light for a moment, which was all Pan needed in order to shuck off his shadow, which slipped between the window sash and laid on the floor. Peter Pan snatched Tinkerbell out of the air before she could do any more harm and slung her into the pouch on his hip while he rocketed them both toward home.

"She was the cannibal of the seas, and scarce needed that watchful eye, for she floated immune in the horror of her name."
-J. M. Barrie, *Peter and Wendy*

$$\left(\,5\,\right)$$

Captain's Woes

Captain Cooper methodically stalked into his quarters. He kept his gaze at the floor. Slowly, he turned and grabbed the open door. He then spun quickly on his heel and slammed the door shut.

"Wretched children!!!"

It was the first time they the children defeated Cooper, and it threatened to push the good Captain off the ledge of control into a deep and bottomless pit of insanity. His memories were slipping like water through a sieve and the unrelenting heat burned away any patience from all but one on the ship. Hope of escape was quickly shriveling and another presence was beginning to push the strong and disciplined Captain Cooper out of the way.

His turn continued until once again his back was to the door, and his hair swung wildly to and fro before settling over his face. He let out a slow, grinding groan that stuck in the back of his throat, nearly a growl. Slowly, his hands raised to brushed hair from his view. Tension stuck in his jaw and his eyes wandered about the room. The muscles in his lips and face twitched and frustrated tears began to well. None fell.

The internal struggle shifted and for the moment Captain Cooper was back in control. He smoothed his coat and shirt and let out a smooth, calming sigh, squared his shoulders and approached the small and cluttered writing desk along the wall. One finger carelessly flipped open the cover of a book.

Hesitation.

He turned another page.

Dropping all of his weight onto his left hand on the desk, his right rapidly flipped through the book. His left hand crumpled a loose piece of paper on the desk.

Outside on the deck the crew shuffled around like children after they've been scolded. They scattered and tried to look busy when they heard the booming cry of frustration tear out from behind the door of the Captain's room.

...

Ship's Log;

Captain James S. Cooper of the HMS Valiant;

Date Unknown

Strange things are happening to us here. There is a change building up inside me. I find that my temper is running thin. The smallest impetus will set me off. There is no relief. I cannot recall how long we have been here. I do not remember where we came from, but I do know that we were not always here. I know it in my bones. I came to my log to refresh my memory, but all of the writing has vanish'd. I cannot explain it. I know that it is not a new journal because the ribbon is not in the right place and it looks worn closer to the front cover and crisp closer to the rear.

I know that. It is not new. This is not new. Someone has removed my entries. There are no phantom traces left. No clue to my past mind. No trace of our history. I hope against reason that this entry will be here tomorrow. The book is not the only thing that has chang'd. The portraits in frames on my walls are becoming faint. Perhaps they have always been so faint, but I do not like the look of them and I would not have kept them if they were. I cannot recall the names or relationships that go with the faces that remain. I remember the two children lock'd in the hold. They attack'd us. I assume out of hunger, but they are not telling me anything about where we are or why no one can remember any details about anything. They smell awful. I shall not be keeping these children on board my ship much longer. We are facing dangerous times and I will not be responsible for them as well. I will feed them and send them back to shore. I have already given the order and within the hour we will be dropping the main sail and leaving this place behind. I don't know where we will go, but it has to be better than this place. I have a constant headache from dehydration and squinting in the sunlight.

...

Knock Knock Knock Knock Knock Knock Knock.

"For God's Sake Smee! Just knock twice!"

...

...

Knock Knock.

Deep sigh. "Yes, Smee. Come in."

Smee came in, all sunshine and taffy.

"We're gonna leave."

"Yes, Smee, we're getting out of here just as soon as those children are off the ship."

"The wind's pretty strong. It's gonna be tough."

"Yeah...what's going to be tough? The strong wind will get us out of here faster."

"Yup. But then going back would be hard."

"That's the idea. Trust me, Smee, we're never coming back here."

And with that Smee grinned a wide grin and left Jimmy to do his important writings.

...

Captain Cooper's transition into Pan's newest nemesis and plaything was taking too long, and Pan's patience evaporated, steam from a boiling pot. They had already been at the Island for five days and the Captain had not yet come looking for him. It was time to push the envelope a little further. Peter wanted a pirate ship filled with pirates, but Cooper's will insisted on holding fast to that part of him that was still an upper-class gentleman. His will kept the beautiful Royal Ship of the Line from becoming the rotting pirate ship Pan desperately wanted it to be; and it had been five days!

Pan's Island was doing its job, as was the Sun and the Sea Fog. But his magic was just not sinking in. Tonight it would. Tonight everyone would participate. He waited until the Sun had set, knowing that the sailors would be out on the deck getting fresh air without its intense heat beating down on them. He called the Fairies to him and gave them their orders: twinkle in unison above the ship. He then waded into the water, which moved away from him ever so slightly, leaving a thin gap between his skin and the cool water. His entire self eventually submerged in the inky blackness. A shadow merging into a shadow, he vanished without so much as a bubble surfacing. When he finally walked back up to the shore the small wakes of crocodiles were seen swimming off out to sea behind him.

Cooper was a stone statue sitting in his chair. A hurricane spun itself endlessly behind his placid eyes. Anger. Frustration. Fear. Responsibility. Love. Reputation. Outside he was a pillar of strength and knowledge. Inside he was a criminal quartered in the town square. Any action he took would betray another side of him. The candle on his desk flickered and extinguished itself, leaving him in darkness.

On the deck, sailors silently mingled. Each one of them wished for a breeze to come by and blow away the day's misery. They stopped wishing for rain. Not one of them could recall the last time it rained.

Finally the wind picked up and ran its fingers through their hair. It caressed their necks and cheeks. It filled their lungs with its cool breath. Their eyelids blinked a little slower. Smee went downstairs.

The stars danced in unison above and the far off sound of the wind in the trees mixed seamlessly with the sound of the surf. Soon, so did their breathing. It was a slow, full breath that loosened the tension in their muscles. Some of the men leaned against the railing of the ship and melted into sleep. Others could not remove their eyes from the stars if they wanted to.

No one heard the faint wisp of wind over the surface of the water so far below. No one heard the short whispers hidden by the waves lapping against the side of the ship. It was the crowing that jolted them out of their meditation.

The deck was instantly filled with uncountable little boys. Each one armed with one kind of metal or another. In a flash of adrenaline and shock, the battle had begun.

Captain Cooper sprung from his chair and buckled his scabbard around his waist. He squared his shoulders and opened the door to his cabin, filling the doorway with his determination. His experienced eyes examined the fray as his ears found the pulse underlying the battle: the boots, the swords, the rigging, and the screams of men falling overboard into the waiting throng of crocodiles. It all made a pattern that he could read. There was something in the sound that was out of place, but he could not put his finger on what it was. Something did not belong.

They attacked a prone target,
but we will be victorious in the end.

Where is he?

Peter Pan was sitting on top of a barrel next to the railing playing his pipes, not paying the battle any attention at all. The sound of his instrument cut through the battle straight into Captain Cooper's nerves. Such arrogance and disrespect would be directly addressed.

Wait.

An officer follows certain protocol.
If he allows his body to take over
like a common soldier then
chaos will rule the fight.

A little chaos is refreshing to the soul,

That's what she told you on the dock.

Self-control will keep order
and ensure victory.

There's something to be said
for a little disorder.
A little piracy.

Cooper controlled his arm that wanted so badly to unsheathe his sword and bury it into that unprotected chest there, or that exposed armpit there.

A little piracy.

Control the squall.
Keep it in check.

The Captain marched up to his enemy a little more quickly than even he expected, and just before he could speak, noticed his mistake.

Piracy.

Pan had grabbed a rope and lassoed the Captain's arms quick as a flash. Cooper's hands instinctively grabbed the new leash leading back to the monster. He saw how this would play out in a fraction of a second. He would step closer to Peter and just like before Pan would fly. So he did. And he did. And with a flick of the Captain's wrist the rope slithered and coiled and caught the boy's foot.

Piracy.

He then heard his own voice call out "Take no prisoners!" and threw his body over the port side of the ship, still holding onto the tether tying the Captain to the Pan.

As their bodies passed, each rich, red timber faded, peeled, swelled and shrank. Boards cracked. Green moss sprung from the cracks in the newly rotten and faded wood. The wind changed direction and the Union Jack that proudly flew on the main mast billowed around on itself. As it did the red crossed lines became white bones. The royal blue field turned inky black, and when the flag completed its turn from west to east a skull faded out of the darkness and as it raised its head to look out onto the world it smiled.

Peter Pan smiled, too.

Splash!

The sea supported them both for a second. What rope was available was thrown and tangled around the two bodies by Captain Cooper's nimble hands. The waves threw them into the sidewall of the ship over and over again. The Captain allowed his body to take over. He would bite this and hit that, but as they sank his hands knew their most important job was to not let go of the rope.

Finally.

They rolled until there was no more up. The water pressed in on Peter Pan more forcefully than it ever dared before. It smothered him with its relentless, dark coolness and no matter how much he commanded it to back away it insisted on pushing closer. His bright, hot fire began paying the price and Peter felt, for the first time in a long time, disconnected from the world around him. He needed to be out in the air again.

This isn't the end. Up!

Up! Up!

But the Captain held firm to the tangling rope, and each attempt to rip free only expended more of Pan's energy. Soon, Peter was fighting with as much desperation as he felt, one of his few completely honest moments. A fist much harder than any boy's cracked the Captain's ribs. Nails much thicker and longer than any boy's opened his skin. Salt burned into his stomach. Everything grew darker as they fell further down.

Finally.

They hit something. It was too soon to be hitting the bottom, and it was no rock. Without warning the Captain knew nothing but pain. Drowning never existed. Peter never existed. The Island never existed. Pain was all there ever was and all there ever would be, and while one part of his brain screamed "Pain!" the rest of his brain confined that section, and set to work solving the problem.

Where is the pain?

Right arm. There it is.

His left hand did its job while the Captain faded into the pain, deftly feeling along his arm to the source. It felt along the hard and long snout and up to the eye. Enough pressure and it compresses like a hard-boiled egg; even more pressure and it breaks open.

The crock rolled in pain, tearing flesh and bone. Splashes broke the surface that suddenly came back into view. A pair of grown adult hands grabbed the Captain and pulled him up to the surface. They broke and before the Captain could gather a breath to shout, Pan was in the air and gone, flying off to the horizon. His laughter skipped off the water and bounced over the surface of the newly formed Jolly Roger.

Cooper drifted off into a place without nerves. The other sailors hoisted him back onboard and carried him to his room where they tied a leather strap around his bicep. They laid him down in his bed and let him sleep as an iron skillet was taken off its shelf and placed in the oven in the kitchen far below his room.

Four hands stoked and fueled the fire endlessly throughout the night. Drake, the master carpenter onboard, worked tirelessly to build the Captain's new namesake. His eyes dried and he continuously wiped oil and sweat from his face. The skillet glowed red and was shaped, glowed red and was shaped. Two men kept the fire raging while ringing pierced their ears with each hammer strike and the sound of saw teeth becoming dull grated on their nerves.

The Sun rose and the Sea was calm. It had taken its tariff and seemed pleased for the moment. The fire-stoking duo was sent to their hammocks and a fresh pair of bodies took over while Drake showed no sign of fatigue.

The Captain awoke in severe pain. What rum was left in storage was poured over tattered sinews, rent flesh and splintered bone. There were no signs of infection aside from the fever and incoherent speech. Like a loyal pet, Smee never left Jimmy's side. At times they would speak to one another, but about what no one could follow.

As the Sun set Drake had the Captain carried to the kitchen where the head of the hook hung out of the doorway of the glowing hot oven while the handle of it sat in the embers. A blade sliced away useless skin and muscle. A fresh saw evened out the radius and ulna. Finally, Drake put on a thick leather glove and removed the black hook that was once a skillet from the fire, revealing a forked end that glowed red. The captain's breathing grew quick and shallow as he watched the glowing terror approach him. His teeth clenched on a leather wrapped stick and sweat poured down his brow past frantic eyes.

Smee could not watch the rest. He turned his head away when Drake's leather gloved hand held the hook in place while the other recoiled a hammer, ready to drive the glowing points into the evened out bones. But something inside Smee forced him to keep his eyes open. If Jimmy would have to endure the procedure, then Smee would at least watch the shadows on the wall. He saw the warbling shadows play out the scene through his tears. The hammer swung, almost impossibly fast, and clanged against the curved edge of the hook.

Drake's apology as he wound up for the second strike was drowned out by the Captain. Pain rocketed out of his throat and filled the room, sending shivers through everyone in the room the same way the hammer sent spasms through the Captain's body as he fought against the men restraining him. Every head on the ship turned from bow to stern. Signs of the cross were made and prayers were said. Each strike of the hammer flung a louder scream from his shaking body. It took every bit of strength in four of his men to hold him down. Every curse in the Captain's vocabulary was slung at them, the screams darting over the water and through the woods. Fairies lowered their heads and stopped glowing. The Indians woke in wonder at what new god had finally come to the Island. Pan smiled and continued dancing while playing his pipes.

"Hook was not his true name."
- J. M. Barrie

MADNESS

There is a mutiny aboard my ship! I have been confin'd to my quarters and those DOGS have struck some kind of bargain with that damned Peter Pan! A curse has been thrust upon my head and I am haunted by magiks of all sorts.

There are 2 guards outside of my door preventing my escape. They whisper. They whisper continuously just loud enough for me to hear voices but no words.

...

"GO AWAY OR STOP YOUR MISERABLE DRIVEL!"
Captain Hook roared from inside his cabin. Quickly the two wards entered the room. Terror, rage and finally pain burst out to the world given life by the Captain's voice. Within moments, the two emerged with a pale bowl of red-stained water, which was pitched overboard, and a worn, drippy teapot that found its way below deck.

...

Two bears. They are not men but two mighty brown bears. Their heads nearly touch'd the rafters. I barely escap'd with my life. One held me down with his enormous paws, his razor claws dug into my chest, which is now soaked through with my own blood! The other tore at my wound and then poured a hideous potion down my throat. Poison, probably. I spit out most of it but I fear I may have swallowed more than a taste.

They are murdering me and the demon has taken all warmth from me. I see the sun, but I feel no heat, but then sometimes my skin boils and sweats and then I shiver again. He gives me the extremes of heat and cold. I want one so I get it in excess, then the other in excess. The sun in the frame comes and goes. Sometimes its people, sometimes monsters. I've only left one frame whole. The rest are kindling. I don't mind if they come, I just want to know from where they're coming. One way in. One door. One frame. They come and go. The fire comes and goes. Red and blue and green and black and stinking. It burns like fire. Black like coal. Black like iron sunken in dried blood. Iron. The sun comes and goes. I have no son. I have

...

"SMEE! WHAT HAVE YOU DONE TO SMEE!? YOU ROTTEN BEASTS! YOU SINFUL SWINE! TELL ME WHAT YOU'VE DONE OR TASTE YOUR JUSTICE!"

The smaller of the two wards shot as quickly as he could go below deck.

"All hands, all hands! Cap'n's raging sick! Find Smee! Bring the kettle!"

And with that, Jimmy fought in a self-created storm of tears, cold sweat and adrenaline against an unimaginable fury of beasts and monsters. His left hand was weaker than his right had been, but it was still fast and accurate; deadly, just the same. Finally, he drove the point of his still healing hook into the chest of a man-wolf. Lightning shot up from his bones into his lungs. His heart stopped for a moment or two and his chest tightened. Raspy gasps were all the air that would pass through his throat, and although his eyes were wide he saw only white.

He was restrained and tied down to his bed with twisted sheets. All attempts to fight them ceased, and the only sound he made was not of defiance or anger. It was the soft whimper of a broken heart, a lament to his beloved nephew.

*"...having been birds before they were human, [children] are naturally
a little wild during the first few weeks, and very itchy at the shoulders,
where their wings used to be."*
-J. M. Barrie, *Peter Pan in Kensington Gardens*

*"And whether you are a lady or only a little boy who wants a baby-
sister, always take pains to write your address clearly. You can't think
what a lot of babies Solomon [the Caw] has sent to the wrong house."*
-J. M. Barrie, *Peter Pan in Kensington Gardens*

(7)

<u>Pan Looks to the Future</u>

The clear sky was dotted with what were almost clouds, high
above the proudly flying flag that billowed softly in a balmy breeze.
The black flag overlooked the pile of rotten canvas, rope and flaking
soft wood: The Jolly Roger. Clinging to the bow of the ship was a
decaying corpse of what used to be a beautiful bare-chested woman
proudly pointing the way. She was nearly a skeleton now.

She had recently gained the company of other corpses strung
over the side of the railings: two slain goblins, the two slowest of Pan's
crew. One of them wore a grey wolf skin over his shoulders and had a
hand-stitched pair of tanned pants. Long slender bones were tied in his
hair that hung down the sides of his face, and his lower yellow-stained
teeth faintly cut up over his chapped upper lip. His small, muscular
grey and brown body banged against the hull on rough weathered days.
His jaundiced eyes forever looked down.

The other body was a shorter, rounder body. He had no clothing above his waist, but had rust-colored mud smeared on his chest, back and face. The designs of the mud made him look like a savage, but he was grey skinned underneath. He wore a loincloth over which hung a skirt made of small bamboo sticks.

One hundred meters away a pair of sharp eyes looked on with pride. Without moving his gaze, he removed a small ball of light from the itchy rotting pouch that hung at his side. "Tink," he said, clenching the ball in his fist, "We need replacements for those two slow slugs dangling over the ship. We should get one female, too. I may need a mother one day. Just in case."

Tinkerbell squirmed. Not to escape. Where would she go? What would she do? She squirmed for comfort and for air. Her teeth clenched in renewed hatred for her position and her captor. Tinkerbell and her Faerie clan would not be slaves to this masochist any longer than they needed to.

If one Elemental nearly destroyed Pan
and left him shaken, then he will surely
fold to the power of three.

No,
that family has been through enough.
Find another way.

There is no other way.
And why waste the luck at having
found all three at once?
It's fate guiding you, Tink.
Follow it.

"There are those brothers in America around 1988 that we saw," she winced. "The Komistras. They would fit in."

"Now, Tink," Pan sang, "I know what you've done with retrieving my Pirates. Their captain is very strong." Muscles rolled in his forearm making Tink clench her jaw and her breathing stopped. "You wouldn't be trying to play at some sort of coup, would you? He's an Element, isn't he? The water disobeyed me, and he wouldn't have taken so long to change if he weren't, so don't bother lying." He turned his filthy young face toward her and smiled, showing his sharp baby teeth, and raising an eyebrow.

"He wouldn't be a good nemesis if he weren't so strong," Tink wheezed, "You said to find a worthy opponent. What better than a strong Water Element for a strong Fire Element?"

Peter could not remember the last time an enemy had exhilarated him so completely. This adventure would be so wonderful and epic, yet experience pulled him away from his excitement to lay the groundwork before he got ahead of himself. Finally having a true nemesis meant that there was a chance, however small that chance was, that the great Peter Pan might lose. A safety net needed to be placed in case the worst happened, and in order to do that, Peter needed someone he could trust to call to his side if he found himself in danger. Whoever it was needed to be powerful like Peter, and just as clever. He or she should protect him as if they were family.

"Just the same," resuming his view of the ship and dropping the ball of light back into her home, "I think we'll take the Darling children. The two boys will do fine, and the girl would make a good mother one day." He tied the pouch shut with one hand, the other resting on his jutted out hip.

Inside the dark musty pouch, Tinkerbell hugged her sides and clenched her eyes shut to hold back any tears that might come, but upon hearing his final words about bringing the Darling children, her face softened and melted into a peaceful smile.

Finally.

If Peter was going to have a mother set aside for a rainy day, then he would also need a child in reserve. Some bird somewhere would have to volunteer to carry half of his power and be his support if he ever needed it. It would have to be an aggressive, ruthless, and smart bird; one with a weakness he could use as leverage.

A clever smile unfolded on Pan's face as he constructed his plan. He had thought of just the right candidate for the job, but she would not budge without a bit of convincing. Peter knew just the right bargain to offer, so he went out hunting for the Never Bird, the protective mother-to-be that lived on the Island.

The Never Bird's gigantic nest rested on a limb that hung over the Mermaid's Lagoon. No matter where she was off gathering sticks and mud for its creation, the Never Bird would return to her eggs before long, so Peter went to her nest to wait.

The eggs were the size of rugby balls and just as brown. Peter stepped up the tree and out onto the limb to inspect the five large shells. He could hear the dividing and doubling happening within the shells and couldn't resist touching them. With their mother gone and the eggs resting in the shade, they had become slightly chilled to the touch and Peter felt their discomfort, so he obliged with a little heat from himself. The chicks-to-be within shifted with their new comfort and went right back to dividing and doubling.

A terrible screech rent the air about him as the giant Never Bird crashed onto the limb across the nest from Peter. She squawked and cried and threatened his hand with her terribly sharp beak, but wouldn't dare strike him while his it rested on her delicate eggs. The cacophony she caused shook sparrows out of the trees around them and brought a few Mermaids to the surface to watch the commotion.

Finally, after hearing enough of her incoherent squabbling, Peter let out an echoing crow that shook her to her core and settled her tongue.

"There. Now we can talk like civilized creatures," he squawked to her in her own language.

"We have nothing to discuss, boy. Remove your hand or you'll lose it before this is through. If you harm my babies I will destroy you. You can forget about your precious Pirates or your flock of Lost Boys. I will eat your heart out of your chest in front of them all so they can see how weak you really are."

Pan did not remove his hand from the shell of her egg.

"Well, that is no way to start a business relationship with someone. I have come here to make you an offer."

"There is never any fair trade with you, we'll have no agreement."

"I want to make sure that for the thirteen months it takes for your chicks to hatch, and the entirety of their lives thereafter, neither my Lost Boys nor any of the creatures on the Island will harm either of them nor you; that's all. You know how much my Boys love hunting. It would be a shame for them to get it in their head to try to taste you or your babes."

"And what do *you* want?" she asked, looking at him with one eye on her turned head.

"All you have to do is agree to go see Solomon *if* I tell you to. That's all," he sang with a grin, "You get protection from my Lost Boys and me forever and there is a chance that you won't even need to do anything."

"To what end?"

"Should this new enemy gain the upper hand, I may want to bring someone else in to help me. Someone aggressive. Someone who defends her family with her life."

"So I am to become your family, then? Solomon will send me to someone and I will become the chick of you and whoever the mother will be?"

"It may not even come to that. There's a solid chance that I will not even call upon you to leave. I might just destroy this nemesis with ease. What do you say? Do we have a deal?"

"What if something happens to you before you send me away? Will your protection remain, even in your death?"

"If I die the Lost Boys will be on their own. I will have no control over them. You won't be protected anymore, no."

"So it's in my best interest to keep you alive, is it, you clever boy?"

"You could look at it that way if you want," he chirped and whistled with a smirk in his eyes.

"We have a deal, then, King of Boys. Now leave at once."

"There never was a simpler happier family until the coming of Peter Pan."

-J. M. Barrie, *Peter and Wendy*

Pan Picks Up the Darlings

The King of Boys returned to his scare of goblins that were milling about, still riding the high of the recent battle. Pan passed the time until sundown when he would be able to venture away from this prison. He enjoyed pretending that the Island was his to control, but in the end there were some rules that even he could not escape. As long as the Sun shone, he was forced to stay within Neverland's borders.

He would be torn away from wherever and whenever he was, and be flung back to the second star on the right and straight on 'till morning the instant the Sun began to peek through the surrounding fog. And although he would never admit this to any soul, it hurt him. It stung his eyes, his throat burned, and his skin felt covered with pinpricks. The few times it happened it left him shaky for what could have been days, and the very first time it happened to him he was torn apart, quite literally, into dust, leaving him useless and disoriented for weeks until he could pull himself back together and remember who he was.

So he passed the time detailing the finer points of his plan. Anyone paying attention, and there were always some who remained unseen and interested, noticed that he was simply going through the motions of his Neverland routine. His mind was clearly elsewhere and that usually meant that he would soon go off to catch up with it. And like a student in the final minutes of a class at the end of a long tiresome week, the Island began preparing for the break. Flowers that had been open for what could have been weeks began to pull in their petals. Palm trees that stood as tall as they could for possibly a month relaxed and allowed the weight of their fruit to dip toward the ground. The tide, which the overlord's focus had kept down for what may have been a day too long, snuck up on the shore slowly, avoiding detection.

And finally, when the Sun had had enough and the Night had covered that prison in her dark shadow, Pan ascended past the canopy and looked toward the horizon. A few skinny pillars of light shone like beacons to him, each a shadow calling him back to a place or family that was important to him. He noted the one that meant Darling and salivated with the adventure to come, but first Pan picked out the one symbolizing Kensington Gardens, London.

Peter knew of a bird, Solomon, in Kensington Gardens who had access to certain magic that Peter, having never been an adult, never understood. Peter considered he and Solomon friends and he hurried off toward the pillar of light leading to Kensington Gardens and Solomon to complete the first part of his plan.

...

It was 8:30 at night and Michael had been scooped up by his mother and spun around the room. Michael squealed in that way in which only children are capable. His dizzying tour of the large bedroom ended with a bouncy plop onto his bed. This riled up his siblings and soon everyone in the room was jumping and laughing and ducking from pillows that were flying through the air.

This moment of delight was broken when David barged into the room. Had he been present during the moment of spontaneity things may have ended differently. He would have taken part and enjoyed a moment to play with his kids. Had he seen it all come together he surely would have forgotten his bowtie in exchange for a quick tickling romp that certainly would have ended with he and the children all tickling Angela until she was breathless. Then he would have made another futile attempt to get the kiss at the corner of her lips.

However, while fun was being had in the upstairs bedroom, Mr. Darling had been in his master bathroom struggling with his bowtie, which brought his elegant suit together. The clock was ticking, and Angela was better at it that he was, so he went to the children's bedroom to have Mrs. Darling tie it for him. His stoic demeanor made him seem angry in the light of the mood within. He checked his watch and told his wife that she was not yet dressed and that they needed to be out the door in thirty minutes.

The laughter died out. Mrs. Darling's untouchable kiss faded away and the children, who also knew when to be transparent, went about their bedtime ritual: brushing their teeth, saying their prayers, and getting under their covers.

And while she moved close to him and focused her attention on his bowtie, Angela said in a quiet but still strong tone, "Do you remember when time wasn't more important than having fun?" She smoothed out the ends of the tie. Then she looked up into his eyes, rose onto her tiptoes and kissed his cheek. She whispered into his ear,

"I need to talk to you in the other room. I don't want to leave the children tonight."

David's eyebrows clenched together in a questioning look. Angela turned to her children who were under their sheets, waiting patiently to be tucked in. Both parents made their rounds, one clockwise around the room, the other counter-clockwise. Michael, who was in the middle, got two kisses at once.

"Mommy, it's hot in here. Can we open the window, just for tonight?"

"No, Michael, you know the rules. But we can turn the fan on higher. Would that help?"

"But mom..."

This time it was Mr. Darling who responded.

"Michael we haven't got time for this. The window stays closed and the fan gets turned up. That's it, now go to bed."

The parents left, turning off the light and shutting the door. When they were downstairs, away from the children's bedroom Angela spoke.

"David, I found a shadow in their bedroom. I'm afraid that he's going to come back to visit us, and if he does I don't want the children to be alone."

"What? When did you find the shadow?" asked Mr. Darling, curious that this was the first he was hearing about any of it and they had to leave in twenty minutes and his wife was not even in her dress yet.

"A few weeks ago. It got hot and sticky all of a sudden just a few minutes ago and I don't feel like going out anyway and I'm afraid that he's coming. Let's stay home."

"What did you do with it?"

"I locked it in tool chest in the basement."

"You kept it in the house! Why on Earth would you keep it?"

"I remember the first time. He was weak and sobbing and useless without it. I didn't want him to get it back this time. I wanted to pay him back for the last time. We owe him. Plus I've put up some things that should keep him out. They're just trinkets, but I read a book about keeping demons out of your house," Mr. Darling gave her the kind of look that suggested that the problem was solved. "But I don't know how much I trust that. It could just be some crazy person's ranting, you know?"

David the father was certainly concerned by the news. He wanted to keep his children safe, definitely. But he also wouldn't live his life afraid, paranoid. He would not throw away his reputation at the firm by ducking out at the last second. In the long run, keeping his reputation was the key to his family staying safe. It was, after all, what afforded them their three-story house with a bedroom on the third floor large enough to hold the three kids. The children would be safer together and there was no balcony or way of climbing to the window, so intruders were not a threat. They also had Nana, their large dog. Plus the babysitter would be around. She'd not let anything happen to them.

"Angela, listen," he told her, "Melissa is here and she'll watch the kids. Plus, there's Nana. The kids will be safe for a few hours. If Pan was weak without his shadow last time then he's probably weak right now. I'm sure Nana would kick his butt in a second."

That last line elicited the desired laugh from Angela and her kiss peeked out for a moment again.

"And it's probably hot and sticky in there due to all of the rough-housing going on. Right? In fact, it's probably much cooler outside than it is in here. We've not gone out in a while. You'll have fun, and when we get back we'll see what we can do about the shadow. But for now let's just try to have a good night. Okay?

"Everything will be all right for a few hours. And if you get a bad feeling while we're out we can shoot right home. I'll leave the number to the hall with Melissa. She'll call if anything happens."

...

The second star on the right flashed bright for a moment, like the flash on a cosmic camera. Pan blinked into existence and without hesitation shot through the night straight as an arrow fired at London.

Peter skimmed through the air over the great Atlantic Ocean. It was night because the park would be closed and he could move around without the threat of being spotted. Being spotted guaranteed some kind of adventure, and Peter didn't want to waste the Neverland night. He had plans to put into motion and every second counted.

He shot past the Figs, barely paying them any attention at all, and passed right into the Broad Walk. He zipped past Cecco Hewlett's Tree where a penny was once lost, and past the little wooden house in which Marmaduke Perry hid. He passed by the Round Pond and over to the Serpentine, a river that buries a drowned forest and supports a small island, which is the home of Solomon the Caw and many other birds that await Solomon's orders to become human children.

Peter alighted on the island, where a small gathering of birds greeted him.

"You're the boy who flies!" they chirped.

"The poor little half-and-half."

"The Betwixt-and-Between, poor Peter Pan."

"I am here to see Solomon," Peter interrupted, "It's urgent."

"Poor, poor half-and-half, belongs to no one."

"Peter is a sad story. Window closed and barred. Peter was replaced."

"I am not a poor little anything, finches! I am Peter Pan, the King of Boys, and I am here to speak with Solomon. Announce me!"

The finches were all aflutter after being so scolded and tried to quickly repair their rudeness by flitting around the island, searching for Solomon.

"Still flying, I see," came a strong old voice from behind Peter. This was not his Island, and Pan had forgotten what it was like to be startled. It excited him. He spun around to see Solomon perched on the limb of a tree behind him.

"Hello, Solomon," Peter said, "I need your help."

"Anything, my boy," the old Caw replied.

"I want a mother, just in case I want some help on Neverland. There's a new enemy there and he is better than any I've faced before. Teach me how to put part of myself into a mother so I can make more of me."

Solomon picked a bug out of his wing with his long black beak. "There's more to it than just that," he said. "You are special. You have so much of the Island in you now. You are part of it and it is part of you. The mother will have to take in as much of the Island as she can, as well as half of what you are to put in the chick."

"I can bring her to Neverland. That part is easy. How do I do the other thing?"

Solomon took Peter away from the gathering group of finches surrounding them. His magic was sacred and the finches knew not to follow.

Peter's origins were known only to a few throughout time. Solomon was one of those few. He knew Pan from the beginning. Part human, part bird, Peter Pan never fit in with any group. And after he left Kensington Gardens, he searched far and wide for a family to take him in. Solomon knew about the family that adopted him, and of Peter's foster-brothers. He knew what they taught him and how they raised him and he also knew that Peter Pan was no longer only part Human and part Bird, but he had become something far worse, and as long as Peter thought they were friends, Solomon would continue to do anything Peter asked, for he feared the consequences.

When Solomon had finished brewing a potion mixed with, among other things, Pan's hair, a feather, and one of Peter's baby teeth which was plucked from the back of his mouth, the resulting black liquid was dripped, two drops, into a hollow acorn and capped. Peter tied the acorn to a string from one of the finch's nests and wore it around his neck.

Then, with a glimpse of the boy he once was, Peter hastily shot off toward the Darling's where and when with his prize and without a word of appreciation.

Pan could read that the time here was 8:30 at night, according to the clock on the digital display at the bank on the corner. The Darling's window was closed, and special trinkets had been placed around the sill: a little figurine here, a crystal spike, and a woven tapestry hanging from the latch. They were worthless trinkets that children found fascinating and could be found in any flea market but acted as an invisible fence to one such as The Pan. He could still peek through, but entering was out of the question.

If the Darlings only knew what the rest of this night held for their future they may have acted differently. One side of Pan's lips curled upward, into a knowing and arrogant smirk. There would not have been any horseplay tonight if they knew.

He floated slowly across the outside wall until he was directly behind the middle bed on the opposite side of the paint, drywall, insulation, and siding. His hands uncurled and he rested them softly on the aluminum siding. His eyes were closed and he breathed slow, deliberate breaths through his nose. Then, just as Mr. Darling entered into the room, interrupting the pillow fight romping on the other side of the wall, Pan's arm muscles rippled and he got closer, positioning himself in a vertical pushup against the house. The tip of his nose tickled the wall and then, lowering his chin, he pressed his forehead against the cool aluminum.

He let out a breath and opened his eyes that had turned into glowing coals. Diluting ripples of heat poured out of his mouth, crashed into the wall and spilled up his face. Dark stains crept out from under his hands, spider webbing out on the aluminum siding. He breathed again, and again, until brown crept out from under his hands and forehead alike, staining the blue-gray siding.

"Mommy, it's hot in here. Can we open the window, just for tonight?" Pan heard from inside.

Yes. That's a good boy.

He let out another long and slow breath.

"No, Michael. You know the rules…"

Rules were made to be broken, boy.

Pan pushed harder and his eyes glowed brighter.

…

High above the leaving black town car, still safe in his bed,
Michael began to plea to his older sister.

"Wendy, it's so hot in here. Can't we please open the
window?"

"I know it's hot, Michael," Wendy said in a pleasant big
sisterly voice, "but you know the rules. Mom and dad said no."

Outside their bedroom, standing on a high ledge of air, the
King of Boys called upon his new subjects.

But it's unbearably hot.

"It is unbearably hot in here, Wendy," John said. "I think that
we can do with opening the window just a crack."

"But John…" Wendy retorted and was cut off.

"Mom and dad are gone and it's a stupid rule anyway.
Nothing bad's going to happen to us if we open the window. I know
lots of kids at school who sleep with the window open and you know
what happens to them?"

Yes, some of them.

Pan smiled to himself.

Assert yourself.

"Nothing. Nothing at all. I say that we can open the window
tonight. I'll tell mom and dad that I did it if they get mad."

Before Wendy had even put her feet on the floor to head off her brother, Jonathan was at the window, flinging it wide open. A breeze instantly filled the room. It was the wind that stopped Wendy. It felt so soothing in the sticky heat that she grew calm with relief.

"Alright," she said, letting the cool breeze fill her up, "But just for tonight. This isn't going to become a regular thing."

"We'll see," muttered John as he returned to his bed.

You'll have more than just
fresh air from now on, boy.

Pan slipped up onto the roof to impatiently wait for Sleep to enter the room and shuffle the children off to Dreamland before he appeared. Wendy must be tested by herself, first. Not just anyone can be the mother.

When the time finally came for him to enter the room he opened his rotting pouch on his hip and pulled Tinkerbell out.

"You know what to do. Keep an eye out. I'll keep the boys asleep. You mind after the dog and old woman."

"Of course," Tinkerbell humbly replied.

Pan slipped softly into the room and whispered into John's ear and then Michael's ear.

"Psst. Shadow. Out here with you, now."

In the dark room no one would have seen the paper thin shadow slink its way into the room from under the door, having easily slipped out of the tool chest and slither up the stairs. It spilled out onto the floor and inked its way over the carpet to the wall, where it slinked up into a standing position.

"We'll play 'Not Coming Home' and see what she does."

Then The Pan turned his face to look at Wendy. When the moonlight spilling in through the opened window hit him he changed. His features softened and the burning coals that were his eyes cooled into black pupils circled in a brownish red, the color of cherry wood. Then he sat on the floor and began to cry.

Wendy stirred and sat up, unsure if she was asleep or awake. A boy was sitting on her carpet and he was sniffling. Maybe even crying.

"Boy,"

She already knows my name,
even if she doesn't realize.

"Why are you crying?"

"I'm crying because my shadow won't come home with me. It won't stick back on. Besides, I wasn't crying."

"Oh my gosh! Your shadow fell off? How did that happen?"

"It wanted to look around and now it won't go back on." The great actor, Peter Pan, laid on the dramatics. His body collapsed on the floor and he moaned. "Now I can never get home."

"That's terrible. My name's Wendy Moira Angela Darling. What's your name, boy?

You've called me by one
of my names twice already.

"Peter Pan"

"That's all?"

I could tell you all of my names,
but you can't pronounce most of them.

"What more do I need? Besides my stupid shadow."

"Maybe I can help."

"You can't help,"

How strong are you?

"You're just a girl."

"What? I can too help. Let me show you," she shot a chilling look at him while she dug in her own nightstand for a spool of thread and a needle. "Capture it and put your foot on its foot," and then she muttered, "Just a girl. I'll show you what "just a girl" can do."

Outstanding.

Resourceful, creative, and tough.

Pan finally was able to capture his elusive shadow and did as he was told. Wendy knelt down next to the strange and mysterious boy and sewed the shadow back onto his feet. He smelled like fallen leaves and sea air.

The strange boy sprung up to his feet and tested her skill.

"Oh, how wonderful I am! Look at me, I've caught you, you tricky shadow. Now you're coming home with me!"

"How wonderful YOU are? Like you had no help at all. And stop shouting, you'll wake my brothers and make Melissa come up here." Wendy folded her arms and shrugged.

Incredible.

A mother's instinct and quick wit to boot.

She could make a great mother

one day. Just in case.

"Maybe you helped. A little. You should come with me."

"With you? I don't even know you or where we would go. Where do you live?" He also smelled like a campfire and his eyes...there was something in them that made it hard to look away.

"Neverland."

"Where's that?"

"Second star on the right and straight on 'till morning."

"What kind of address is that? How do you get there?"

Good so far.

How do you handle this?

"I fly, of course."

"Peter, come on. Where do you really live?"

Hmm. She's no fool.

"I'm not lying. Do you want to see? It's not hard."

She sat on the corner of her bed and raised her eyebrows in a disbelieving arch.

"Go ahead. Fly. Right here. I dare you."

Pan paced about the room. Then he noticed the doorknob. He rocked from his toes to the flats of his feet and back again. Then he jumped. But his jump was slow. And when he was coming down he placed his toe on the doorknob and balanced there. He gave Wendy a smirk. Then he pushed off and soared throughout the room. He back paddled through the air, flew like Superman, he even flapped his arms like it was actually providing some sort of lift. Then he came to rest with his face directly in front of Wendy's. She was sitting on her bed. He was laying on nothing, suspended nose to nose with the awestruck girl.

"You wanna try it?"

"I'd like to give you a kiss."

"Okay,"

Wonderful

Peter Pan held out his hand, palm up.

This was not what Wendy was expecting, so she opened her drawer again and fumbled around. She found her thimble from her sewing kit. She pulled it out and placed it on his finger.

"And now I shall give you a kiss."

The innocent girl closed her eyes and stuck out her lips. He removed the "kiss" from his hand and uncapped the acorn hanging around his neck. He poured the two drops of the magic that held half of his essence into the thimble and placed it on her fingertip. One half of everything he was got compressed and sealed onto her finger where the magic would wait until his command, forever if necessary.

The thimble seemed snugger than Wendy remembered it being, but she didn't pay any attention to that. Her hands must have grown since her last sewing project or swelled in the heat, that's all.

That was easy.

Now let's get you back to Neverland

before the Sun rises.

"Do you want to try flying now?"

"How does it work?" She sat up straighter and clapped her hands. The thimble didn't so much as tremble.

"All you need is some Fairie dust," Peter Pan said and whistled for Tinkerbell, who slipped into the room. "Tink, this is Wendy."

"You have a Fairie! She's amazing!"

"Wendy, this is Tinkerbell. She's the princess of the Fairies, and she's my ... helper, aren't you Tink? She fixes the pots and kettles," he smirked.

Tinkerbell's anger surged and she glowed brighter, but just for a split second.

"Go ahead, Tink, why don't you sprinkle the Wendy Lady with some dust so we can take her home with us?"

"I can't go home with you, Peter. I couldn't just leave my brothers here. That would be awful."

"Your brothers? They're hardly worth it, Wendy. Just look at them. They're too lazy. They'd never work out on Neverland."

Pan went over to Jonathan's bed and rolled him straight out onto the floor. He landed hard on the carpeting, but he never awoke from his dream, just as instructed.

"It doesn't matter. I can't just leave without them. They would be so disappointed."

There's no time for this.

Peter had been too caught up in his plan for a mother that he forgot all about replenishing the ranks of his Lost Boys

"Okay, they can come, too. C'mon, wake up, *boys*," Pan reluctantly said.

"Wake up, John. Wake up, Michael! This boy's going to teach us to fly and we're going to a magical place!"

John woke up and was incredibly disoriented. He remembered going to sleep on his bed, but now he was on the floor tangled up in his bedding. Michael seemed to bolt awake, as if he were waiting in starter's blocks.

"What? We're going to fly?! Wendy, did you say we're going to fly?" he almost shouted.

"Who is that boy?" Jonathan asked, getting up to defend his siblings.

You will soon call me Lord, boy.

"I am Peter Pan and I'm going to teach you to fly and we're going to go to my home, Neverland. Hurry up, Tinkerbell. Sprinkle them all and we'll be on our way."

Tinkerbell peppered the entire room with the Fairie dust. Michael was overcome with his own enthusiasm. He was jumping on his bed, laughing, because the dust tickled him to the core.

"What magical place? We can't just leave, Wendy. What are you talking about? Peter Pan, we can't go with you. I'm sorry." Jonathan was the voice of reason.

That is the wrong answer.

You WILL come with me,

and you will come with me NOW!

"There are all sorts of fun things to do there. There are Mermaids, and Indians, Pirates, and the other Lost Boys, of course. I'm the ruler there. There are more Fairies and you get to play all day long and have fun-fun-fun."

"I don't know. It does sound like fun."

That's it.

"The pirates, are they *real* pirates?" Jonathan asked, enticed. But reason quickly returned, "Wait...no. We really shouldn't go. It wouldn't be right."

NO! You are coming!

Who are you?

You don't disobey ME, boy.

"Why don't you all try flying and then make up your mind?"

"How do we do it? I'm trying now and it's not working," Wendy said, from the forgotten corner of the room and Pan's mind.

Michael, on the other hand had figured it out already. All of his laughter lifted him off of the ground in no time. He had been aloft the whole time Peter and Jonathan had been arguing.

"Ah, do like your brother, Wendy. Just think of a happy thought. Any happy thought you can think of and you'll become weightless. Sad thoughts make you heavy, but happy thoughts will lift you up and bring you home with me."

Wendy thought of earlier when she first saw Peter Pan. She thought of her mother reading to them. She thought of the pillow fight and the tickling that had happened…how long ago?

Soon her feet began to lift and she joined her baby brother up by the ceiling.

"C'mon John, you've got to try this! Remember when you intercepted the football at recess?" Wendy called down, trying to help.

John was never very good at sports. He was never picked last, but it was usually right near the end. Last week he finally made the play of the game. It was just before the bell rang, but he intercepted the ball. His team still lost, but he felt unstoppable. He was in the right place at the right time and his body took over. His mind had shut down and that feeling was incredible. It was the only time that he didn't think about what he was doing before he did it. It just happened. He stepped right in front of the receiver just as the football was thrown. Then he crouched down and pushed off of the ground. His hands instinctively went over his head and in that moment, eighteen inches off of the ground, cradling the football, he realized that he didn't decide to do any of it.

And in his bedroom at night, with Peter Pan and his siblings hovering over him, he looked down at his feet and once again felt that feeling. He was hovering. And what was more was that he felt like he knew how to move up here in the air.

He focused his attention and began to move toward the rest of them.

Pan could feel the atmosphere on Neverland begin to warm up.

"Okay, should we go?"

YES!

Let's go.

"Yes!" Michael cried.

"Let's go," Jonathan said.

"Alright," Wendy followed.

So, leading the way, Peter Pan shot home through the muggy night sky.

"Toodles excitedly fitted the arrow to his bow…and then he fired, and Wendy fluttered to the ground with an arrow in her breast."
"If Wendy's heart had been beating they would all have heard it."
- J. M. Barrie, *Peter and Wendy*

The Island

The mid-day Sun glittered through the canopy onto the trunks, bushes and dirt below. The humid air moseyed about the forest. It carried a bit of salty sea air with it and blended with the decaying leaves and moist dirt of the woods.

The breeze dribbled to a halt. Nothing moved and all was quiet. The sound of the waves on the shore was deflected back by the large, leafy monoliths standing guard at the edge of the sand. Birds had moved on from this area a while ago. In fact, all fauna had left this area.

Silence.

Stillness.

A single wolf broke through a line of bushes that may have had yellow flowers on them. In a full canter it glided and bounced through the woods, forging its own path. Its ears were back and its head looked forward, but was kept low. Something moved in the bushes just ahead and it broke off at a hard angle toward the mountain in the distance.

Where is the rest of the pack?

Path to the left. Blocked. Break off toward the rocks. Bounding frantically through a shallow creek. A paw slipped on a stone and a small yelp escaped the wolf as he splashed into the hard clay shore. A second later he was back to his feet and running, with just a shadow of a limp.

Are the trees moving, too?

That wasn't a tree.

Sticks were flying past and burying into the trunks on either side of him, guiding his route. An opening ahead. The woods end there, and then he could run freely, quickly.

He leapt out to freedom and got three good lunges before he skidded to a halt. A large rock formation stood like a sentinel in front of him, forcing him to move around it, but it was too late for that. Their stink was close now. His hackles raised and the ruff of his neck stood as he spun around, his back to the rocks. He gained a good two inches of size in every direction. The bushes were thickest just at the edge of the clearing. He could see some shadows shifting like those spirits he saw from time to time. This time, there were several of them, more than he had ever seen before. And instead of telling him where a warm den might be, or a fresh litter of bunnies, these were intending to hurt and end him.

One of those sticks that guided him before sprang out of the leaves and hit him in the rear shank. He yelped, but promptly growled, snapped and gnashed his teeth.

Another arrow into the other shank. Then another and another and another, all into his legs. Lying flat on the ground, he continued to howl and snap. Snarling to the end. Finally they stepped out of their cover. A whole scare of goblins. A slightly more round one from the rest of them came running up from the direction of the water, not from the trees. He threw down his sticks and shoved into one of his own kind. They pushed back and forth and the whole scare turned their sticks and pointed them at the slightly more round one. Just then a shadow passed quickly overhead.

They all looked up to see the Pan being chased by more delicious looking human children. Pan had brought them back replacements or a meal; either way it was up to them to catch one if they could, that one wouldn't have been worthy anyway. Pan never hunted for food because he never ate. Never.

The round one scuttled over to his sticks and fired one up into the air as fast as a frightened sparrow. It must have hit one of the shadows because there was a loud crash in the forest.

The wolf breathed more deeply, the adrenaline pouring out of his muscles. One of the other members of the scare turned and considered him. This goblin carried a longer, heavier branch. It shifted this in its hand and stalked closer to him. Then, ignoring his snaps and growls, it slowly but firmly put the sharp end into the wolf's ribs, just back from his front shoulder. Despite his twitches and lunges he couldn't shake it off. The goblin then collected all of the arrows from his legs and just before leaving him there, it pushed the spear down through him until it stuck into the earth.

...

John knew that at any second he would plummet from the skies and drop to the earth like a stone. It did not frighten him. He knew exactly how he would fall at any second in order to cause the least amount of damage to himself. Falling doesn't leave a person completely helpless. He could aim for the slope of that hill to soften the angle. He could land in that lake there. He could probably fall into those pine trees and be alright. Evergreens were a softer wood and he might survive that. In any case, he would have to go remember to not tense up. Drunk drivers survive accidents more often than the innocent sober driver because the sober driver tenses up and breaks, whereas the drunk flops about and bruises but doesn't break. Yes, going limp was the key, and he felt certain that he could override his own instincts to survive, no matter how hard they tore at his body. He knew his mind could overcome.

He may have even been right.

Michael had not yet learned that this was impossible. He had heard from his parents and his teacher that he couldn't fly, but he wasn't quite certain of that just yet. His parents weren't as convincing on the subject as they were about other things, and that always gave Michael hope. He believed that until this moment, he simply wasn't doing it right. Comic books and cartoons weren't impossible to Michael. Why couldn't those things happen? He knew that the world was bigger than he could imagine. So didn't it make sense that some parts of the world could exist beyond other people's imagination?

Yes.

And it did.

So Michael did not hesitate to swoop closely to the treetops and even weave through the branches, completely trusting his own control over this new talent. The water looked wonderful from far away, but watching it whip and ripple past just inches from his nose was far more exciting. Mermaids even reached up to say hello to him. One even grabbed a hold of his hand to shake it. Something about her reminded him of his mother. This Mermaid was young and cute and had jet-black hair with dark tan skin. His mother had brown hair and had very fair skin. But something about them was exactly the same. Then she flashed her teeth at Michael and he saw it then, plain as day. She had a kiss in the corner of her mouth, just like his mom, and she tried to pull him into the water, which Michael was completely comfortable with. It didn't matter that he couldn't breathe under water. She would take care of him.

Pan hovered behind Michael and stared fiercely at the Mermaid. His left fist rested on his hip. His right balled up on the handle of his sword. His head slowly shook from side to side. The Mermaid smiled lovingly at Michael and dove back down to the depths, letting him fly with Peter.

They were off flying again.

Wendy thought only of how lovely it all was.

Peter was wonderful.

She followed closely behind him, barely noticing the scenery beneath them. There was no reason to fear falling because he would protect her. Nothing bad could happen to her here because this was his island and it was a place of mirth and dangerous excitement.

As long as they were together she would be safe. She was sure of that. He led them around a large stone formation and over another collection of trees on the other side.

A sharp shooting pain didn't so much tear through her as it brought all of her focus to one point in an instant. She clutched her chest and felt the arrow in her heart and faded away.

He would save her though.

He would turn around and catch her.

He would fix...

Pan was by her side not one whole second after the ground touched her. John was the next one to reach her.

"Oh my God! Wendy! What happened to her? Who shot her? What kind of place is this? Wendy!" He checked her pulse. If the arrow hadn't killed her then it was the broken neck. Either way her heart stopped beating. CPR was out of the question. There was no bringing her back now. How would he explain this?

Peter sounded a loud and high whistle. He then tried to roll her onto her back.

"Don't you touch her!" John yelled, batting away Peter's hand, "You don't get to touch her ever again! You brought us here and didn't tell us that there would be arrows flying through the air. You didn't even try to shield us from them, or bring us higher-" he hesitated. His eyes grew wide at what this last thought meant.

"You brought us here to kill us. This was no accident. Look! It was a direct hit into her chest! This was no accident!"

Pan didn't pay John any attention at all. He looked past him and held up a hand casually, as if telling someone to stop. John whirled around and saw eight boys dressed like Indians come charging through the brush right toward them. They were carrying spears and bows and arrows and looked as though they wouldn't hesitate to use them. He spun on his knees and threw his arms wide to protect his fallen sister.

Michael was still nowhere to be seen, but no one noticed.

The boys got about three steps into the clearing before skidding to a halt. Pan yanked the arrow out of Wendy unceremoniously and looked at the fletching. The slightly more round boy, Toodles, slowly took a step backward and was swallowed up by the group of boys. He never looked up.

"Boys, I've brought a mother. This is Wendy. Say hello," The Pan said without a drop of concern in his voice.

John turned his head and looked with disbelief at the boy who was making these children say hello to a corpse. Peter had bent down and propped up Wendy by the shoulders, resting her on his bent knee. She looked like she was asleep, reclined in a chair. Her head lolled and dark blood crept quickly down her nightgown. That's when the chimes started.

Like a hundred crystal bells rung at the same time, or small raindrops in a dream, a sound came from all directions of the Island. It was getting louder, but not loud. Finally a dozen balls of light just like the one from their bedroom swarmed into the area and went for the marionette called Wendy.

John tried to swat them away, but Peter nodded his head at him and one second later eight pairs of hands were on him and carrying him a few feet away, but they did not put him down.

The old Fairies hungrily tinkled and rang over Wendy's body. They kissed it in places and tasted blood from others. One opened Wendy's mouth and had a peek inside. She discovered with great wonder that it kept going. She stood upon Wendy's tongue for a while and found that it was soft, but would not pull her into it like quicksand. Discovering that three of Wendy's teeth had been shot out of her gums and into her mouth, the Fairie meticulously put them back – good as new. As the Fairie did this, her thin, straight hair curled and thickened with a renewed youthfulness. She traveled further. Wendy's uvula was an exciting thing, but the Fairie's attention span was only slightly longer than that of a child in school on the first day when jackets are no longer necessary. And today was an exciting day. She continued her exploration further down.

A pair opened Wendy's eyelids and poked curiously at her eyeballs and then, after deciding that they were okay with the way these pools held their shape, they fixed their hair and cloths as if they were in a bathroom preparing for an evening out on the town.

Another two played a game of telephone through Wendy's ears. They cleaned out a bit of blood and tried again. It must have worked because their high brows shrank as a new widow's peak grew in and the lines around their questioning eyes grew taut. The pair moved on.

Wendy's fingers and toes began to twitch while Pan scanned the area for something. He picked up a small black pebble and held it tight in his hand while he closed his eyes and focused on a spell.

Wendy is no longer just another girl.

I've invested so much in her already.

I must have control over her.

Bind her to me, he thought, forcing the idea, the magic into the small stone he squeezed in his fist.

I will be her world.

I will do no wrong in her eyes

and I will possess all of her trust.

A cluster of Fairies gathered at the wound in Wendy's heart. They blinked like Christmas lights set to chase. Then, as if called, three of them flew up to her mouth. Pan tossed the smooth black pebble to one of them and they all dove inside Wendy. The group that remained on her chest sat down and began to fiddle with this and that. They inspected her buttons and pulled at her lace collar.

Moments later Wendy's head quickly flopped to the side. Peter kept his eyes locked on John's and he smiled, showing his baby teeth. John couldn't interpret what this meant. It may have been comforting. If Peter's not panicking, then he shouldn't panic? Was that it? Or was it intimidating instead? Either way, John could not look away.

An image flashed in his head like a single wrong frame in a film. Peter was bearing his teeth in – a sneer? A growl? – with a serrated beak and small horns and the boys holding him up looking like small filthy monsters. He blinked to pull focus but when he opened his eyes again everything seemed normal.

Wendy's head snap to the other side.

The twitching in her hands and feet had spread to her whole body. Not like a seizure, but like a person dreaming. Then one of the twitches shook her whole body into a sitting position and she began coughing. The Fairies that had been on her chest took flight and watched from above. Wendy knelt on all fours retching violently until she vomited a small puddle of blood and four Fairies with it. None of them had the small black stone, but they all looked younger, more vibrant, and covered in gore.

Peter then crouched down next to her and whispered into her ear while rubbing a hand on her opposite shoulder like someone consoling a friend. He slipped his acorn necklace around her neck.

"Are you okay, Wendy?" he whispered, "You would have died had the arrow not hit my acorn necklace."

"What?" Wendy asked quietly, trying to shake free from the cobwebs in her head.

"The necklace I gave you as a kiss in your bedroom. It saved your life."

Wendy looked down at the acorn necklace. "Oh. But I thought…" she reached for the thimble on her finger, but Peter caught her hand in his before it could get there.

"We kissed twice, Wendy. I kissed you while you were asleep. I couldn't help it. Didn't you hear me crowing?"

Wendy was overcome with happiness and with newfound energy she flung her arms around Peter.

"Oh, Peter!"

"Now for the first time we hear the voice of Hook. It was a black voice."

- J. M. Barrie.

Hook Emerges

A high wind pushed one large and somber cloud in front of the Sun. Moisture in the air teased the men standing on the deck and climbing in the rigging. A calm fell over all of them as they relaxed their brows and eyes in the refreshing shade. A soft creak shook the ship like a crash of thunder shakes windows in their sills. All eyes shot to the Captain's doorway, which opened with a low groan. No one breathed, anticipating what was coming; the flag was the only noise, applauding loudly in the wind.

One heel of a boot clopped on wood followed by another, and another until their Captain filled the doorway. He did not look up to see the anticipation on the faces of his men. His gaze was fixed on his new permanent jewelry; his deadly, black, arthritic finger, his iron hook. He contemplated its entry into his arm and dabbed at it with the bottom of his coat, staining the fabric a darker red than it already was.

"Dogs!" His shout pounded on all of them like a tidal wave, shaking them back to reality. "The wind is running away and the Sun is hiding for its life." He first raised his eyes to his transfixed crew, followed closely by the rest of his head, and in that instant their transformation into real pirates solidified. A muscle in his jaw twitched and those close to him stepped backward.

"They fear for their lives, and rightly so. I have looked into the face of death and have tamed it. And now I seek to sic my new pet upon my enemies!" His crew of pirates raised cutlasses and pistols into the air. They roared with approval. This would not be another day filled with waiting and hiding in the shade below in the stinking cabins. Today there would be action.

He raised his hand in the air and all but the flag stopped cheering. "I want to study this monster; to hunt him. He will not be harmed right away. He studied me. He knew what I would do and I will return the favor. He is dangerous and crafty, but I tell you – he can be killed like anyone. No one but me will touch him. It is my debt to repay. If anyone engages him they will find themselves the newest decoration on the bow of my ship.

"Boys!" he said, "Someone took my hand." This he announced as if it was fresh news, raising his hook for all to clearly see for the first time. "Go find him."

The order was spoken with all the quietness and venom of a jellyfish, and the eruption of yawps and howls that followed it leapt into the air and hitched a ride on the wind. The sound carried over the water and was slung into the trees at the end of the beach where Slightly was perched, waiting, and absently rubbing the horn he wore on a string around his neck. Above his eye a scab had formed, and a deep scar would eventually rise where Smee struck him with the rock and knocked him out of the tree the day he came ashore.

He scuttled down the shoulders and past the slender waist of the tree on which he sat and padded down a path that he had worn into the weeds and sprouting saplings.

Smee tugged on Hook's sleeve.

"Ah, Smee," he said, clasping Smee on the shoulder. "Good to see you."

"Are we leaving?"

"Some of the men are going ashore soon. We're going to learn as much about Peter Pan as we can."

"No, Jimmy. Are we going home soon? Are we going to do the yesterday idea today? We've got the wind for it."

"Smee, what are you blathering about? We are home. We live on this ship. Maybe one day we will be able to carve out a little section of that island as a port, but we live here Smee."

"But, Jimmy, what about leaving here? Getting out, remember? I told you how and you said okay and wrote it down and said okay and when the wind picked up and then you got hurt and now you're better and the wind has picked up and–"

"Smee! I don't know what you're talking about. We've always lived here. We never had that talk. That didn't happen. It was a dream. It's a good idea, I would like to leave the ship sometime too, but *this* is home."

Somewhere in the back of Captain Hook's mind, Cooper was shackled in the dark. He saw and heard everything Hook did, but was unable to break free. Fighting against his chains, Cooper tried to call out to Smee for help, but his cries went unnoticed.

"But Jimmy, you wrote it down and said okay and when the wind picked up and then you got hurt and that was after we got lost and we can go home and we just go off into the fog and…"

"Smee that's enough! This is our home." A ray of sunshine pierced through a cloud, momentarily shining down on Hook. "You know that no one can go into the mist. People have died in the mist. That other island was sunk when the mist came in."

Smee shook his head to clear out some cobwebs. Was there another Island? No. That wasn't true.

"No other island, it wasn't there. What are you saying?" Smee turned from Hook to address the pirates. "Keep the boats on the ship. *Keep the boats on the ship*! There was no island! It's wrong, go into the mist." The pirates hoisting the skiffs into the water turned to see what this new order was. "We have to go *home*! The winds are strong and we can go home!" Smee shouted again.

Hook's left hand was not quite as strong as his right had been, but it was just as fast and just as precise. It blurred up out of nowhere and stung Smee's cheek, making his eye burn like fire. Smee yelped and cupped his palm over the right side of his face.

"Don't you ever try to override my orders again. You may be kin, but mutiny is mutiny and I won't allow it," Hook's voice was a growl from deep within the ship on a still black night. "As you were, you worthless kelp! And as for this going home business, I don't ever want to hear you talk about it again to anyone, do you understand me?"

Smee stared at him with tears welling in his eyes.

"Do. You. Understand. Me," Captain Hook asked softer now than before, and all the scarier for it.

Smee hunched away whimpering, but managed a sound that resembled a yes.

"Of all delectable islands the Neverland is the snuggest and most compact, not large and sprawly, you know, with tedious distances between one adventure and another, but nicely crammed."
-J. M. Barrie, *Peter and Wendy*

Tink Shows Michael The World

Michael turned to see his brother and sister fall from the sky without him. Actually, Wendy seemed more to be plummeting than falling. For that matter, John seemed to be almost chasing her and the strange boy.

He was worried, but not yet to the level a six-year-old boy is capable. He wasn't wide-eyed, tight-stomached, clench-fisted worried. There was no imminent threat of uncontrollable tears.

Tinkerbell noticed a small gray cloud of worry flash over Michael's chubby little face. Fairies existed because of the joy of a child. They were that child's joy come to life. Seeing the worry on Michael pulled at Tink. She determined quickly that Michael ought to be spared the sight of Wendy's body lying lifeless in the short grass of the clearing. This could also be a good opportunity to find out what Michael was, and what that could mean.

"They're fine, Michael. Come with me. I have something to show you," she said.

With a lazy twirl up an invisible helix, the six-year-old boy and the thousands-of-year-old Fairie climbed the blue sky. Tinkerbell opened her arms wide like a bird, arching her head back and closing her eyes. Her arms widened, Michael was just an inch or two away from her, and she could sense the panic begin to rise again within him. She opened her eyes, turned her face to him smiling, and gave him a playful wink. The peace this small gesture brought Michael was sorely needed. He let himself trust this strange being, and copied her movements as best he could. He threw his face back into the sun, closing his eyes as well. His arms spread out in as close an approximation of her as he could manage. His feet weren't pointed as perfectly downward as hers were, but rather hung from the bottom of his legs like he was on a swing set miles in the sky.

I will never leave here, thought Michael. Any fleeting doubts or concerns for his parents and their reaction to his disappearance climbed up from his brain, perched on his earlobe and launched into the void, fluttering away from him in the rarefied air as dandelion fluff on a summer's breeze.

The excitement on the ground was soon lost to distance. As they scraped the bottom of the cool, wispy clouds with their heads, Tinkerbell finally stopped their ascent. She let them just spin in slow circles now, allowing Michael to take in his new surroundings.

First peering over the fuzzy fleece and plastic eyes of his bunny clad feet; Michael could see figures scurrying beneath him like tiny ants. Over there a little bit was a beach. The water sure looked fun, probably great for swimming. In it he saw the Mermaids who had tried to shake his hand not so long ago. They were swimming in packs now, some here, some there. Just off the beach was a ship. Even though the rest of the place looked crisp and clear to his eyes, this ship looked hazy, like looking at the distance through heat rising off the hot ground. The beach and the water looked warm; the ship looked hot.

Nothing moved on it but the flag. The men seemed to be standing still, watching someone speak, probably their Captain.

Where they seemed to be headed when Wendy fell was the far edge of the island. It was sort of below Michael and his little friend, but not quite directly so. They had evidently drifted on the warm breezes up here in the ether. It was a beautiful island, a perfect place. It only reinforced Michael's desire to stay forever. He'd never seen an island from above before, and he knew that there must be a lot of them all over the place. Just a million around Florida alone, John had said so. But Michael knew that he wouldn't have to see all of them to know that this was the most perfect one of all.

There was a mountain. It was more of a big rocky hill, actually. Michael knew that mountains were much higher than that, like a thousand miles, John had said. There were caves on the other end of the island, right down by the water, and some on the land itself. He strained to make out details, but couldn't.

Tinkerbell saw him squinting to see more clearly. Smiling, she crawled up his arm and perched herself on his shoulder. The experiments were about to begin. She noticed that his form grew more tangible as people around Michael got closer to him, as if he were changing his elemental makeup to match theirs. But what did that mean?

She leaned into him until she was resting her face on his, cheek to cheek, holding on to him with her hand on his ear. Her dragonfly wings tickled his neck, too. Michael didn't hate the feeling of her so close to him. She pointed to a specific place on the Island and when Michael looked there he could see all of the detail as though he were right next to it.

"Can you see that?" she asked.

What had been an indistinguishable tangle of green and brown resolved itself into a community of little people, just like Tinkerbell. They were as small as she, and their activities betrayed that. Some wove fine rugs and tapestries with multicolored spider webs. Some wrestled their tiny bodies one against the other or raced, both in the air and on the ground. And others just sat outside of their little homes, fashioned from all sorts of nature they had collected. Michael stared in awe.

"Yes, I can!" he said, amazed. "They're just like you!"

The scene retreated a little from his view. Slowly at first, it climbed back to its original perspective. Before long he was looking at the island exactly as it had appeared before. It was its normal size.

Tinkerbell pointed to a different spot on the Island. This time Michael knew what to expect and was able to adapt to it more quickly. He immediately saw a scene beyond anything he'd ever witnessed. There were many scenes that would fall into this category, of course, not a few of which he would experience in his stay in Neverland. Small boys crudely and poorly dressed like Indians chased each other, but not as playfully as the Fairies. There was an aggression here not seen in the other camp. To the north of this was a burned out tree trunk. Fire had not caused the gaping hole in the top of it. Michael had a vague and uncomfortable feeling that something much more sinister than mere fire was responsible for it.

"What burned that tree there?"

"What do you think it was, Michael?" Tinkerbell inquired, still testing his limits.

"Well, I don't think there was a fire. Was it a bad thing? Was it magic?"

"Sort of," she said.

Michael didn't notice just how assiduously Tinkerbell was steering his gaze from the scene with his siblings. As she steered his gaze, Tink made sure to keep tabs on Wendy's progress. She finally directed his attention to the part of the Island covered in snow. Michael didn't notice this section before as they flew over the Island. It didn't make up a huge section, but that he missed it completely was confusing. It seemed to waver in and out of focus as he glanced there. It looked cold, but somehow comforting.

"How did I miss that?" he asked, and Tinkerbell knew a little more about what Michael was, and what he might one day become.

Eventually, she let them float down from their perch of wind and toward the clearing where Wendy was now up and moving. John looked angry, a sight still unfamiliar to Michael, but soon not to seem out of place on his face at all. Pan glanced in her direction, and his face lit up with joy to see Michael in such good health. The tension between John and Pan seemed to break, at least temporarily.

"It is awfully difficult to catch a Mermaid. They are such cruel creatures, Wendy, that they try to pull boys and girls like you into the water and drown them."

-J. M. Barrie, *Peter Pan or The Boy Who Would Not Grow Up*

Mermaid Lagoon

"Where are we going now?" Michael asked. His thirsty mind wanted the next amazing moment to happen. He couldn't get enough.

"I could show you our tree, where we live; or..." Peter said. 'Or' hovered amongst them. It taunted them all, including the Lost Boys. They salivated just thinking of a more exciting alternative. The three new children picked up on Peter's inflection. Even John leaned in with anticipation. He had momentarily forgotten about the entire trauma he just witnessed. That one smile from Peter was all that it took to erase the horror he had just seen.

"We could go to Marooner's Rock and play with the Mermaids!" Peter finally finished.

The goblins hungrily agreed. A fine Mermaid dinner was always a treat, and the sport of it was dangerous enough to make it interesting. A canopy of blades was raised in the air and guttural growls of bloodlust were shouted.

Michael was overjoyed at the suggestion and hoorayed with the other kids. He jumped up and down and pulled on John's wrist.

"Mermaids, John! I saw one already. It shook my hand. Let's go play with them! Come on, John, can we? Please?"

John looked to Wendy for some sort of response. Wendy's hand was at her mouth and she cleared her throat. She looked at John and smiled.

"It sounds lovely to me," she offered. Absently brushing away a fly that had landed on the large bloodstain on her front, she looked down and admired the crimson flower that had bloomed on her chest. Panic was not even considered. Minutes earlier the top of her nightgown had matched the bottom in every way. It had been sky blue and had tiny white flowers embroidered on it, but as far back as Wendy could remember the giant blood-red flower had been there.

She remembered how she loved the feel of it. She had specific memories of touching the velvet fabric there with her fingertips while her mother read them stories. She loved the way it had a certain grain. It would resist the changing of direction, back and forth, back and forth, until she fell asleep.

Wendy was absently rubbing the bloodstain when a thought occurred to John.

When did that flower get there?

It wasn't there before.

Something inside him warned that he would be better off staying silent.

"Okay, let's go see some Mermaids, then," he said to his bouncing little brother.

"Yeay!" Michael cheered with the rest of the boys.

Peter turned and led the way to Marooner's Rock.

...

Three rowboats beached themselves on the Island and fifteen pirates disembarked to begin hunting their captain's nemesis. They crept as silently as they could, but land didn't move the same as a ship did. They were as quiet as pirates could be while tromping through a jungle. Twigs snapped. Leaves rustled. It was no surprise that the goblins; which are made for land travel and are terrible at managing water of any sort, heard the grown men coming almost as soon as they left the beach.

Peter brought the Lost Boys and the Darlings out into the open beach of Mermaid Lagoon, which was home to Marooner's Rock. He enjoyed taunting the Mermaids. He knew what they would do if they ever got the chance, but he was so strong, and his Lost Boys were all around. He could do whatever he wanted there and the Mermaids wouldn't do anything.

"Okay, so this is the game. It's sort of like," he searched for the word, "tag. What you want to do is swim out there to get their attention. Then you have to try to capture them. If you capture one and get it to shore by the other Lost Boys then you win. Are you ready?"

"But, Peter," John asked, "don't they try to capture us?"

"No, John. They'll not capture you as long as I'm here."

"And," John continued, recognizing this type of water, "what about alligators? Don't they…"

"John, we haven't got any alligators here. We have crocodiles. They're bigger and much more vicious."

Michael gasped.

"But don't worry. They don't get along with the Mermaids. They don't ever come over to Marooner's Rock; this is the Mermaids' lagoon. Trust me, we swim here all the time. It's fine."

"John," Michael whispered to his big brother, "I'm scared. I don't wanna catch a Mermaid. They seem nice."

"It's okay, Michael. We don't have to," John said and then turned his attention back to Peter. "We don't feel much like catching a Mermaid right now, Peter."

Pan sighed dramatically. "Okay, if that's what you want. I just thought you wanted to be a part of the group. It's part of the initiation. Everyone had to do it. I was even going to let you and your brother work together. But if you're too scared to do it then I suppose I can take you two home."

"But I don't wanna go home," Michael desperately said. "I'll catch one. It's okay," He caught sight of John's questioning face. "It's okay, John. Let's just catch one."

"Are you sure, Michael? We don't have to. He's just being bossy."

"No, let's just do it. Okay? I'm alright," Michael said as he slipped off his shirt and waded slowly into the water.

John glared at Peter who was sitting next to Wendy on a log nearby. Peter just smiled back at him. It was a grin that made John shiver. He took off his shirt and joined his brother out in the lagoon. He could see the sand through the water, it was so clear. Up ahead it got darker as a shelf dropped off. There were flashes of silver, gold, and pink slipping through that darker water.

"What do you do with the Mermaids after you catch them, Peter?" Wendy asked.

"You know, Mermaids are dangerous creatures, Wendy. When they can they try to drown boys and girls."

"That's horrible. What if they…"

"John and Michael are going to be fine. I won't let them get hurt so soon. Did you know that the Mermaids weren't always here? They started showing up a long time ago, but before that, nothing."

"Where did they come from?"

"I'm not sure, but there don't seem to be many of them. We've been catching them for a while now and although there aren't more of them they don't seem to ever lose numbers, either."

"What do you do with them when you catch them, Peter?" Wendy asked again.

"We have a celebration, the same when we catch a pirate. It's the only good thing to do after you kill an enemy, don't you agree?"

"Yes. I suppose it is," she said and turned her attention back to her brothers.

It appeared as though they had forgotten any fear that they had. They were both squealing and laughing. Water was splashing all over while the boys played with the Mermaids. One of them had even taken John down into the dark water with her. She showed him a tunnel that worked its way under the rocks and went further under the coral. When he needed air she placed her mouth on his and breathed for him. He held his breath for shorter and shorter periods of time the more comfortable he grew to the idea of kissing her. Each time he tried for the kiss on the side of her mouth, and each time he failed to get it. His head was spinning. He never wanted to leave. Before they came up, John thought he saw another young girl's face down in the dark water deep below them, but she turned and disappeared back down into the coral.

When they surfaced again Michael was laughing. One Mermaid was squirting seawater at him by squeezing her hands together on the surface of the lagoon. He retaliated by fanning his arm over the surface in an arch, which fired a wave of water at the Mermaid. Another snuck up underneath him and blew air bubbles up his back. This tickled him to no end. He shrieked.

The Mermaids rarely encountered Pan's new recruits before he turned them into Lost Boys. They tried hard to quickly gain their trust and take them away. It was an impossible goal, but they had to try something.

"Good job, boys!" Peter shouted, partly as encouragement, partly to get the attention of the Pirates that were creeping up behind them. "Now bring one to shore!"

The pirates crept through bushes and tall grass up to the rim of the beach. They were just close enough to hear Peter and Wendy talking. One of the pirates snuck over a rock to get a better look. During his crawl one of his fingers cracked. A shock of tension swept through the Lost Boys and they looked to Peter for a clue as to their response, but the calm on Pan's face returned them to their childlike act.

"Do you know what I'm afraid of, Wendy?" Peter asked, baiting the pirates.

Touched by the possibility of such a confession from Peter Pan, Wendy turned to face him and moved in closer.

"What?"

The pirates leaned in closer too, aching to hear about The Pan's weakness.

"Nothing! I'm not afraid of anything," Pan shouted and leapt to his feet, "No one can beat me by blade and no beast can lay a claw on me. I challenge lions and they bow to me. I challenge pirates and they fall beneath my sword. My crow sends shivers down every spine that hears. COCK-A-DOODLE-DOO!"

As promised, the pirate's necks pricked up with shivers. Wendy got shivers too, but they weren't from fear. Something deep inside her squealed and her chest tightened ever so slightly.

"The only thing that could ever bring me down would be poison," he declared. "That's why all I ever drink stays inside my tree and all I ever eat I've killed and cooked myself."

"But how can you be afraid of that?" Toodles asked, "You never eat or drink-"

"Was anyone speaking to *you*, Toodles? I said I wasn't afraid of *anything!* And I never eat or drink anything that isn't inside of our tree or I've not killed and cooked. You understand?"

Toodles, who never seemed part of the group, didn't understand but he nodded nonetheless in an attempt to fit in. The pirates crept back to their boats, eager to share their new discovery with Hook. Peter, hearing their departure, smiled.

That should keep them out of my way until these kids are ready.

"Alright, boys, that's enough. We should show you where you'll be staying."

"But we're not done playing yet," Michael pouted. A few of the Mermaids were pulling on his arm, trying to get him to swim away with them.

"We can come back again, don't worry. But we've got a big feast to prepare for tonight. We need to celebrate the three of you properly. C'mon now."

"Yeah, let's go, Michael. We can come back. Let's see what else is here," John comforted his brother.

But when they tried to leave, the Mermaids swarmed. They seemed desperate for some reason, and they were trying to herd the boys back deeper into the water. Pan crowed again, and fixed the Mermaids with a dark look. They reluctantly backed away, leaving John and Michael with Pan.

The brothers swam to the edge of a rock and hoisted themselves out. Michael turned and waved goodbye to his new friends. They waved back, some with their hands, others with their tails. When Michael finally turned his back on the lagoon the Lost Boy twins fell into line behind them. When he reached the edge of the forest, Peter turned around and smiled at the twins, coupled with a curt nod. The boys in back returned to the lagoon. One of them untied a wide net from his back, the other slipped club out from his belt.

"Let's see about getting you guys settled in, shall we?" Pan said to John and threw an arm around his shoulder.

"Sounds good, Peter. We should dry off, too," John said. Pan's arm was hot on the back of John's neck.

...

"He's got some kids with 'im Cap'n. They seem new to the place. All of 'is focus is on 'em. 'e didn't even catch sense of us there 'e was so caught up. 'e says that the only ting 'e's afraid of is poison 'cause 'e can't see it comin'.''

"How many children?"

"Three, sir."

A thick cloud managed to fight its way in front of the Sun, casting a much-appreciated shadow over the deck.

"How long do you figure they've been here?"

"I'm not so good for figurin', sir, but I'd guess maybe a day or two, sir."

"Hmm…it's possible they still remember, then. Maybe they remember how to get out."

"What's 'at Cap'n?"

"Nothing. Very good. You're dismissed."

"Thank you, sir."

The scout left Captain Hook's side, leaving him alone with his thoughts on the upper deck. Smee crept over to his uncle, wringing his hands.

"Jimmy," he said.

"What is it, Smee? I've got some things to figure out here."

"I just…I just heard you say to Rusty that you wanted to know the way out. Are we going home, Jimmy?"

The Sun finally defeated its intruder and resumed shining brightly on the cursed ship. A bead of sweat ran down the Captain's long face. Hook dabbed the pus and blood from his wound onto his red coat, widening the already present dark stain. "We are home, Smee. I've told you before."

"Why do you keep saying that?" Smee shouted, on the verge of tears. "Part of you remembers. I know part of you remembers, otherwise you wouldn't talk like you do sometimes!"

"Smee! I don't know what you are talking about and I will not hear any more about it. We've always lived here, so don't start!"

"But she said I had to keep trying no matter what, even though it can't possibly work I have to try, in case."

"Who said, Smee? Which 'she'? One of the Mermaids? Smee, I've told you not to talk to them. They're dangerous. Now please, I need some quiet time to think."

A sad and defeated Smee moved to descend the ladder onto the main deck, but when he passed the doorway to Captain Hook's quarters his face melted from hurt to hopeful. He pushed the door open slowly and slipped inside.

Extreme measures to keep the Sun out of the room made it as dark as a cave. Enough light from the open door helped Smee find a candle on the writing desk. He struck a nearby match and sat down at the chair. Then, as if opening an ancient Bible, Smee turned the pages in Captain Cooper's log. His fingers traced over the words as he read them, as if touching them would make the memory of home more real.

When he got to the first blank page he picked up the quill and began writing.

...

Sum day yule read this and yule no I did my best to tell the way out. Sum day yule read this. Sum day yule see it. *Go into the fog and then go backwards until morning. Sum day yule read this. I know it. I love you.*

...

He put the quill down and left the book open on the desk, unsheathed his knife and set to work.

"... Wendy and Michael fit their trees at the first try, but John had to be altered a little."

- J. M. Barrie, *Peter and Wendy*

"...when new lost children arrive at his underground home PETER *finds new trees for them to go up and down by, and instead of fitting the tree to them he makes them fit the tree. Sometimes it can be done by adding or removing garments, but if you are bumpy, or the tree is an odd shape, he has things done to you with a roller, and after that you fit."*

- J. M. Barrie, *Peter Pan or The Boy Who Would Not Grow Up*

The Tree Assigning

The longer John trod on dry land the more uncomfortable he felt; as if everything he saw was wearing a mask, which had ever so slightly slipped. Once he could have sworn the Sun gave him the kind of wink that someone gives before doing something horrible, but when he glanced again it was acting like it didn't notice John at all. There were also undertones in every glance and gesture between Peter and the Lost Boys. They were in on some joke, or knew something that they were deliberately keeping from John and his siblings. Another problem danced on the outskirts of John's mind, deftly dodging all of his attempts to grab it and make it coherent. The colors were too vivid, maybe? Or perhaps it was the way the air smelled? Or maybe it was just John over thinking everything again and he should relax.

The ground beneath him seemed to breathe slow, deep breaths, and with each exhale John thought he heard someone whispering. He strained to find a meaning in the sound, but it stubbornly remained unclear.

The Darlings entered the Lost Boy camp and were struck by how non-magical it appeared. There was a clearing and in the center of it was a long, thick wooden table. What once were tall trees were now stumps, only slightly taller than John, surrounding the perimeter of the camp. The leaf-covered ground was hard and red like dark, rich clay. Larger trees surrounded the stumps, and the canopy of those trees did a nice job of shading the table. Ropes were tied to strong limbs between trees or simply hung down to the ground. The fire pit was rather long, almost running the entire length of the thick dark table.

Perhaps the only mystical thing about the Lost Boy camp was one tree that seemed out of place. It was a squat, powerful tree with a girth so wide it would have taken more than a dozen Lost Boys joined hand in hand to completely encircle it. It was as dark as the table and sprouted no leaves. The tree had died several lifetimes ago, and it was clear to everyone what killed it. The signs were entirely too visible. What used to be healthy bark was cracked and curling, black as soot. There was a gigantic hole just a few feet off the ground where the lowest limb had grown.

"Welcome to the Lost Boy camp," Peter said, beaming at how wonderful it all was.

"Peter, it's lovely!" Wendy said, eyes wide.

"Er, yeah. It's pretty cool, Peter," John said, trying not to seem rude while still feeling a little disappointed. He wasn't exactly sure what he was expecting, but after learning how to fly and playing with

Mermaids all morning this wasn't what he anticipated. This didn't seem any different than any park he could see at home, minus all the rope.

Michael was standing beside Slightly, who had a cut above his eye and wore a bone horn around his neck.

"Woah!" Michael said. "You guys are smart! The Pirates will never find you here! They think this is one of the places you eat, but they don't know you live underground, do they?"

Peter was more than surprised, and didn't bother hiding it. All immediate signs pointed to them living up in the trees.

"How do you know that, Michael?"

"I don't know. It just makes sense. You use the trees to get underground and the ropes and stuff to see if people are coming, right?"

"Yes, exactly. Maybe we need to change the way we do things if you can tell all that right away."

"Do we each get a tree, Peter?"

"Yes, you do. You each will have your own tree and it will be your way in and out of the underground. It will also nourish you while you sleep for the first few nights. New Lost Boys can't come underground until they've slept in their tree for a few nights. It helps you get used to the Island."

John thought that sounded foolish. Something was wrong; there was that look again! Peter wasn't telling them something and John knew it. But Michael and Wendy hugged one another and jumped up and down with anticipation when Peter began selecting their tree.

"You guys wait here, I'm going to go pick out trees for you. I'll be back."

"Don't have an adventure without us, Peter," Michael called after him.

Peter ventured off into the surrounding woods and Atlan, one of the biggest Lost Boys followed after him.

"We're going to have our own tree, Wendy!" Michael cheered.

"I know, isn't Peter wonderful? We're going to have such a good time here, I can feel it."

"I don't ever want to leave, Wendy. Can we stay forever?"

"No, Michael. Don't say that," John butted in. He leaned in close and whispered, "Doesn't it seem a little strange to anyone else? Do either of you feel weird about this whole thing?"

"Lighten up, John. Have fun for once in your life," Wendy shot back.

Toodles came over and John straightened up, flashing an oversized fake smile.

"Come here," he blurted with childlike urgency, "I'll show you how we get up and down the trees so fast!" Toodles all but dislocated Wendy's arm as he yanked her over to one of the ropes hanging near a tree trunk. Then, quick as a cat, Toodles crawled up the rope, walking up the side of the tree to a high branch.

"Wow, Toodles, that was fast!" Wendy said, encouraging the little boy as he beamed.

"Now you try!" he said.

Michael stepped up to the rope and copied Toodle's moves nearly identically and he ascended the rope with ease.

"That was so cool! John, you have to try it!"

"Why don't you just fly up there?" he asked, inspecting the ropes.

Toodles and Michael laughed in unison.

"We do! That's the trick! The ropes are just to get invaders to look up above when we're all down below. Diversion, Johnny boy. Diversion."

"Oh, how clever you are, Toodles!" Wendy called.

...

"Sir," Atlan called to Peter, who was puzzling over which tree to give to each Darling.

"What is it, Atlan? I'm sort of busy right now."

"I want to know what you think you're doing with these new recruits?"

"What do you mean, Atlan?" The darkness in Pan's tone was thick.

"I mean John is too old for this, he'll never turn, and if he does it will take a long time and he won't fit in, and if he doesn't fit in we will all turn on him and eat his heart. It's a lost cause and you know it. Why even bring him here? Also, why all the special treatment toward the Wendy Lady? Toodles killed her fair and square. *She* didn't make it, *he* killed her, *he* gets to have her, *that's* the rules. I mean, I'm sad to say it was Toodles and not someone more deserving, but it was. And now you're picking out a tree for *her*?" Atlan broke off a branch next to Peter's face and threw it hard to the ground.

"Why aren't you turning her into the tree for one of them instead? That's how we do things here. Why waste one of our few extra ones if you don't have to? Changing course leads to nothing but trouble, Pan, and I want to know if it's worth the risk."

"I know what I'm doing, Atlan, and that's all you need to know. Now leave me alone. Go back to the camp."

"We're not your slaves, Pan, or have you forgotten that too? If your plans are leading me toward disaster I want to know why. And if you aren't going to tell me then I want bigger spoils."

Peter turned to face Atlan for the first time, and there was a spark of fire in his eyes, a single ember of the blaze it could have been.

"You're such the brave soldier, aren't you?" Pan asked with daggers in his voice, "Coming here all alone and talking with such disrespect to me. You're right, Atlan, you are not my slave. But it would do you well to remember your place. You want bigger spoils? *Earn* them. Next time don't let *Toodles* beat you to the punch … if you can.

"As for this, it's all just a game, Boy. Let me do the thinking and you can do the other parts that you love so much."

Atlan glared at Peter, but Peter, who was finished with the confrontation, turned his back on the Lost Boy. Atlan's options were limited, and now was not the time to pick a fight with the King of Boys. It would take all of Neverland to take down Pan, or at least some more support from the Lost Boys. Instead of attacking, he turned away and stalked deeper into the woods.

…

"I've found them, come quick!" Peter's voice rang throughout the camp startling everyone, for no one had seen him return.

"Welcome back, Peter, I've missed you so much," swooned Wendy, rushing to link her arm with his. There was a quiet, high-pitched squeal that came from her within her chest, like a wheeze, and then was gone again. She cleared her throat and the pair turned away. Michael swooped down from the tree, alighting beside John.

"Does she seem strange to you, John?" Michael asked.

John looked at his brother. Finally, someone else noticed that something was wrong. "Yes. Thank God you've noticed, too."

"Are you two coming? These trees can't come to you, you know," Peter called from the woods ahead.

"We'll talk about this later, Michael. For now let's just try to fit in."

"Okay. I do wanna see my tree," Michael said with a youthful excitement.

The brothers went off after Peter and Wendy, followed closely by Slightly and Curly. As the Darlings were exiting camp, the Twins returned from the opposite direction with their catch from the Mermaid's Lagoon dragging limply in the net behind them, unseen by either Darling boy.

The trees through which Peter was leading the Darlings reminded Michael of a Christmas tree lot, where he could claim the most beautiful one for himself.

"This one is your tree, Michael," Pan offered. Michael's tree was only slightly taller than himself. He climbed up to the top and looked down the hollow neck that led into the underworld. It was dark inside, and he could not see the bottom.

"I can't see the bottom, Peter."

"It is blocked off. You have to stay in the tree for a few nights before we can let you into our home underground."

"Why?"

"You're new. You need to be fixed up, you know? Let the Island change you a bit until you're ready to see what's down there."

"But I wanna see it now, Peter," Michael whined, overcome with excitement.

"You will, Michael, you will. But the underworld is a privilege that you must earn. You will have to prove yourself and part of that is sleeping in there for a couple of nights. But if you don't think you can do it...if you think you're too much of a little baby that you can't do what each other Lost Boy has done, then I should send you home right now."

Slightly smirked.

"No, I can do it. I can do anything you can do, Peter," Michael said, and he climbed down into the tree. It was snug, but he slipped in fairly easily. "It's wet in here!" he yelled out to them.

"It's supposed to be. That's how the tree works. Still think you can do it?"

"It's fine," Michael quickly said.

"Good. Now you, John. This is yours," Pan said as he patted the slim waist of a tree nearby. Inside his tree Michael felt the weight of sleep pressing on him and before he could stop himself he slipped off into a deep, warm sleep.

"That looks too small for me, Peter. Isn't there a larger one I can have?"

"I'm sorry, John, but this one is *your* tree. There's nothing I can do. Try it on."

John hoisted himself up over the open mouth that led into the ground. He could see that perhaps his legs and hips could slip in, but he would never be able to get his chest or shoulders through.

"But why is it *my* tree? There's a larger one over there. I can't fit through here."

"Why not?"

"My chest and shoulders are too big, I can tell already."

"You're sure?"

"Yes, Peter. I'm sure. Look at it, it's so small."

"Slightly. Curly. Make his shoulders and chest fit his tree, would you?"

Curly smiled cruelly and pulled two tools out from under his shirt. One of them John thought looked like a rolling pin. The other was a hefty mallet. Slightly's face hardly changed at all. He flew up to John, plowing into him like a football player and toppling him over the side of the tree. The two fell four feet to the ground with Slightly landing on top. A stone pounded John in the solar plexus, knocking the wind out of him, which silenced and distracted him while Slightly pulled John's arms behind his back.

Curly approached John with the Mallet in his hands.

"Stop! Peter, what are you doing?!" Wendy shouted, looking panicked. "You can't hurt him like this!" She started to run to her brother but Peter caught her arm.

"Don't worry, Wendy. It's just fun and games. This will help him fit the tree. It won't hurt him; he'll be fine," he said this in his usual boyhood confidence.

John gasped and he tried to clear the tears that had welled in his eyes. He saw something then, perhaps it was the tears in his eyes blurring his vision, but the thought the ground in front of his face was smiling up at him. But when Curly's foot stepped right beside John's face, he turned away from the earth to look at Curly, who was lifting the mallet high over his head.

"No!" Wendy squealed.

Why aren't you listening to me?

I control you now!

"Wendy!" Pan shouted, turning her face toward his. "John is going to be fine," he said as he pressed his hot forehead against hers and stared hard into her eyes. There was a quiet, high-pitched squeal that came from her within her chest, like a wheeze, and then was gone again. She cleared her throat and smiled.

Peter was so lovely. Of course John would be all right, Peter would take care of everything. He'd never let anything bad happen to John, or to Wendy, which was very fine with her.

John felt his ribcage crush as the hammer smashed down on him. Slightly got off of him, because where would he go now? How could he stand now? John's diaphragm was set free with the first hammer strike and he took a deep breath, but before he could yell out Slightly clamped a hand in front of John's mouth and rolled him over. He crouched down low and leaned over John's face. There still was no expression on Slightly's face, and his bright green eyes were more scrutinizing than excited. Slightly was studying exactly how the torture was affecting John.

John tried to yell, but fainted before he could try. He took three more hammer strikes before Curly mounted John's chest and set to work smoothing things out with the roller.

"They're almost done, John. Aren't you excited?" Wendy asked, unaware of his unconscious state.

Peter brought Tink out of her itchy, rotten pouch. "Hello, Tink. You know what to do," he said to her when the rolling was complete.

"Wendy, you're just going to let him do this to John?" Tinkerbell asked as she zipped in front of Wendy's face.

"John's going to be okay. All the Lost Boys do it. Peter will make sure he's fine," Wendy replied.

"Go on, Tink. The poor boy's suffering," Pan smiled.

"No."

"You will heal him, Tinkerbell. Despite all of our history you still honestly *care*. And watching you try to fight it is just so entertaining."

"You're sick, Peter."

"Just fix him and get it over with."

Reluctantly Tinkerbell turned toward John's body. What other choice did she have? John was necessary even if Wendy was in Pan's pocket. John was still an Element, and maybe she could find a way to rescue Wendy. Tinkerbell was just glad Michael didn't see any of this. She whistled for more Fairies to help her, and they came in droves.

Before John opened his eyes he could smell a delicious fish fillet cooking over an open fire. His stomach grumbled and his eyes fluttered open. The canopy above him swayed in the cool breeze and his chest and back hurt. His raspy cough broke a very thick silence.

"Oh," he groaned. "What happened?"

"There's going to be a little soreness for a couple days, but that'll pass. How do you feel?"

"Well, I feel sore. What happened?"

"You didn't fit your tree, John, so Slightly and Curly did some things to you and now you'll find that you fit perfectly. They're very good, been doing it for ages now."

John's memory filled in the gaps with what Peter was telling him. He remembered hovering over the gaping hole of the tree, and then he remembered Slightly helping him down. Slightly and Curly gave him a big bear hug, squeezing him very hard, and then he remembered waking up.

"Did I faint from the bear hug?"

"Yes," Peter said with a big smile on his face as he put out his hand to help John up. When their hands touched John thought he saw Peter's face change. It grew a little longer than normal and had hard angles, like a bird's beak where his mouth should have been. Then he remembered a more violent version of the story.

He was pinned down and beaten. Slightly enjoyed watching the torture happen and Curly...Curly killed John with a huge mallet. He crushed him to death and Peter did something to Wendy to keep her silent. One minute she cried out to him, and the next she was silent. Whatever was going on, he couldn't let on. He had to fit in. There was no choice.

"Can we go eat? Whatever it is it smells delicious."

"Oh, it is. It always is."

They woke Michael up and went back to the camp, the air tasting better with each step back to camp.

Their places were already set at the long dark table in the center of camp. A long iridescent fish tail was still over the fire, pierced on a spit. The meat on the table was steaming and seasoned with a spice rub. It looked delicious and was unlike any fish the Darlings had ever tasted before. It was sweet and tender, but not flaky, and with each bite John's memory erased any violence and reverted to the sweet and tender story he had been fed earlier.

Several times throughout the meal, morsels intended for his mouth fell into his lap, as his mouth was noticeably further from where his arms were accustomed to delivering food.

"Or we could tell of that cake the pirates cooked so that the boys might eat it and perish…"

-J. M. Barrie, *Peter and Wendy*

John Meets the Goblins

John sat uncomfortably far from his tree in the late morning sun. He still hadn't been told why it was *his* tree, though he'd asked more than once. Each time John tried to go up and down the tube he would get covered in a thin, viscous sap. It never stained him, and within mere minutes it would evaporate or be absorbed or whatever it was that was happening. John wasn't one for taking a nap, but every time he passed the center of his tree he needed to battle through a deep-seeded exhaustion.

It wasn't fair. Michael fit his tree perfectly, and Wendy didn't even get assigned to one! She got to use the big main tree right there in camp. She used Pan's tree to get in and out and no one said a word about it.

She's a girl. Peter says, as if that answers every question.

It's not *fair!* John threw a stone at nothing in particular and winced. The tree assigning had happened days ago and he was still sore. He picked up a stick and took out the knife he had been given and began to whittle.

This whole place is wrong; John couldn't help thinking, but still couldn't say why exactly.

That sun keeps looking at me. And the Lost Boys... do they bark at each other when we aren't looking? No. Not bark, I guess. But there's growling in there, for sure. Whatever. It's not English.

It's a wonderful place. Pan told us so. Magic is everywhere. We flew. He fixed Wendy. Didn't he? Did Wendy die? They love Michael. They adore Wendy. Mom. Me...why do I feel so weird? Why can't I fit in like Mike and Wendy? How come I was the only one who needed to be worked over with those rollers and...bear hugs? How did I get to be so alone?

John's increasing discomfort with the Lost Boys and Peter Pan had forced him to seek solitude more and more often. Peter kept trying to pull him into whatever violent or stupid activity they were doing, but John couldn't commit.

His lack of commitment enticed the Lost Boys.

"Come on, Peter," Omnes pleaded one night after John wandered off alone again. "When the new recruits don't work out, you turn them over to us. Let us have him, Sir."

"No, Omnes. No one kills John. He'll come around."

"It's taking an awfully long time, Sir. Same with Michael. Sure, Michael fits in. No one wants to lay a finger on him, but neither of them has changed yet. There is whispering, Pan. They say you're losing your touch."

"Do they? And who says that, Omnes? What do they say, exactly?" The look in Pan's eye cautioned him. He was treading on thin ice and now Peter wanted a name. Omnes wouldn't burn for anyone else's treason; he knew how pointless that gesture would be.

"It's a few, but mostly Atlan. He says that it took you a long time to change the Pirates, and now Michael and John are proving difficult as well. And there's the whole situation with Wendy, which is none of my business."

"Smart boy. Michael is special, Omnes. I think he could be useful in more ways than we've seen before. I am still testing him. And John will come around. No one kills him, you understand me?"

"But sir, we haven't had a single adventure since the Pirates arrived. It's been so long, and now you're just letting them come to the Island unchecked. It's insulting."

"No, Omnes, it's strategy."

"Letting us have John would go a long way for morale is all I'm saying."

Peter would have been willing to let the Lost Boys slaughter John. Strategically it was the right thing to do. It would allow the Lost Boys to blow off some necessary steam and eliminates one small undependable element. It was Wendy who stayed his hand, however. His control over her seemed to wane as John and Michael waded further into danger. If John needed to be killed, it would have to look like anyone but Lost Boys were at fault lest he lose all control over his precious mother.

"Be patient, Omnes. I promise you a grand adventure, the grandest we've ever faced. Just be patient."

...

"Just be patient," Smythe ordered Jameson.

Jameson was responsible for feeding a crew of men hell bent on destroying the evil Prince of Boys. He was charged with this task by a captain he had once loved dearly when he was Cooper and whom he now feared terrifically as Hook. And he was supposed to do this while he himself was feeling the effects of this awful and awesome place and with not so much as a grain of recognizable staple at his disposal.

Seamus Jameson was a proud man of the sea from a long line of proud men of the sea. He was Catholic; he was Irish; he was Royal Navy, in that order. He scoffed at the idea of chefs and thoroughly looked down his knobbed nose at fine dining. Anyone could make food look good on silver plates in marble halls. He could make a crew of men who'd been at sea for weeks in rolling waves and brutal conditions love his fish stew.

"I hate this place, Smythe. I truly do."

Jameson and Smythe worked their way through yet another tangle of brambles; through still more thorns that bit at their shins and low branches that slapped sharp wet leaves on their cheeks.

"I'm to feed you all with the stuff on this rock and I don't even know if half of it is deadly poisonous. Or which half at that."

Smythe had liked Jameson when they were navy men. He'd been quick with a joke and the first to help you up after a grog-induced fist had put you on the deck. Of course, it was probably his own fist that had put you there; but he was an Irishman so that was to be expected. He didn't like him as much now and that was a shame. As for Smythe himself, he'd watched his mates change under the influence of this place. He'd seen them twist from rowdy seamen into wonton pirates. He knew there was nothing he could do about it. His captain had shifted, too, and even if he hadn't, Smythe wasn't about to address the man directly. Who was he to speak to the Captain of the Valiant? Or even the Jolly Roger? He was a wharf rat. He always had been. A man's to know his place. And Jacob Smythe's place was to go along to get along. No one needed to know that he hadn't changed. No one needed to know that the little boy who crowed had glanced askew at him more than once. Especially no one needed to know that he'd been approached about working as an agent for the Lost Boys on the deck of the Roger.

He wasn't special, no matter what the idiot boy had told him when he'd been onshore looking for more foodstuffs. He was a wharf rat. But more, he was a sailor on the greatest naval force the world had ever seen; or ever would. He was proud to be a British Sailor. That still meant something, even if not to anyone but him and Smee.

"And to top it off, the bastard's got me off looking for flour for a cake. A cake! Where the bloomin' hell are we, Piccadilly?"

This was met with a non-committal grunt.

"Oi? Wassat, Smythe?"

"I said, 'Do you know what Piccadilly is?'"

"Nah. And neither do you."

"No sir. I truly don't."

"Meh. Just find some flour. Or a suitable flour substitute, at any rate. Flea bitten dog."

Smythe smiled. Jameson had a delightfully miserable attitude about most things. They both knew it, but he wasn't going to make Smythe miserable, too. When one of these shells of men tried to drag him into their hell, he tried to smile. It didn't always work. But the effort alone usually staved them off.

"Flour's from wheat, right?'

"..."

"So I say we look for anything that may look like wheat."

"..."

"Right then…"

Half-hours swallowed minutes and hours, in turn, gnawed upon those. The day never seemed to pass on the deck, but it did here on the Island. And after they'd forced their way through a half-day's worth of jungle, they came upon a clearing. Its eerie quietness made Jameson jumpier still and Smythe all the more at ease.

"It's quiet," Jameson mumbled quietly.

Sigh. "Yeah."

"I don't like it," he whispered gruffly.

"You don't like anything."

"Gotta point there," he said in the same tone as before.

Wind dappled the high grass while the sun swept it along in waves. Peace filled both men; but only one of them was stilled by it. Smythe saw the silent faces in the forest on the perimeter of the field. They were letting him see them: just as they weren't letting the cook.

"This grass looks a lot like wheat. D'ya'think so, lad?"

Jameson responded, "It do. 'Tis enough to look like it, I think."

...

Standing in front of his meager stove in the dark hold of the ship, Jameson did his level best to not lose his temper and beat yet another shipmate. Right after they'd arrived at that awful place, he'd been lashed to the mast and whipped for that very thing. It had been at the start of the transformation and many more than him had tasted the whip then. They were all doled out for different reasons. It was the transition from Royal Navy- when discipline was a matter of course- to Pirate Horde- where discipline was capricious and delivered by the Captain alone.

"Anyway, it looks like a cake. In a manner of speaking," Jameson said hopefully after spreading the venom-laden excuse for icing evenly over the pathetic mound.

"If you squint," Smythe quipped.

The statement was a risk that few men would have taken. Those few men, and Smythe was on the list, could still bring at least a smile to Jameson's face, but when things got as they were at that moment, prudence suggested restraint.

It worked. The cook laughed out loud for the first time in a hundred years.

"Aye, lad. A squint helps, to be sure. Let's see what the Cap'n says."

...

"Pathetic…"

A pair of hearts, and dozens of surrounding eyes, fell with this one word.

A large collection of dark clouds shifted in front of the sun and Hook could suddenly sense how important this endeavor had been, not only to the two men who'd undertaken it, but also to the crew as a whole. So he relished what he'd known he'd say from the first time he'd seen the blob.

"Excellent work!"

Natural confusion emanated out from Smythe and Jameson and infected all who heard the dreaded leader.

"Um… sir?"

"You men have done terrible work, but I set you on an almost impossible task. In this damned place, you were lucky to find ingredients close enough to cobble together this thing.

"That you managed this mess of a thing- as pathetic as it is," he punctuated this last with another smile, "shows me that you both took the chore to heart and showed the kind of innovative thinking that makes a great Pirate."

The paddy Jameson didn't even bristle at the offense. He beamed, along with his mate.

"Jameson and Smythe is it? Smee! Double helping of grog for these fine men. And shore leave for three days once we get to port."

The offer was more a symbol than a vacation. No one could remember the last time they saw a port, let alone the last time they had been able to take shore leave. But the statement had been a gold star for the pair and they appreciated it humbly.

"Aye, Captain." Smee winked at Smythe.

"Now, get that cake to the Island and let those wretched children eat as much as they can before death finds them."

...

A three-leafed mostly white flower sprung up from the soil next to John's tree. It was average in every way. No one who's ever spent time in any forest would have given it a second thought. And yet there was Peter, crouched down on his haunches, hands folded between his legs. He couldn't take his eyes off of the flower.

The leaves of the flower drove to delicate points at their tips, which gently folded back over and curled under slightly. There was a single stamen up from the middle, dappled with yellow spots on its end. Each leaf tinged a different color as it extended; one tan, one green and one a muddled gray. They were subtle tints that varied depending on the angle from which they were viewed.

It was not possible that the flower could be there for a couple of reasons. Neverland was Pan's home; more so than just because he lived there, and this wasn't one of his flowers. Its uniqueness Peter found odd, but that wasn't the oddest thing by a mile. That was the location. Nothing grew at the base of the trees in and around the Lost Boys camp. Nothing. The nature of the trees' work prevented it.

Then how could that be? Did Johnny's tree seem to be a different color than before? Why was there no movement toward turning these little boys into Boys? It was sure to be something Tinkerbell did. He'd get to the bottom of it eventually. The matter of the flower needed to be addressed first.

"Johnny! Come here for a second, would ya'?"

John was not comfortable. The glimpses he'd seen behind the façade necessarily meant that something was wrong. He just didn't know if the problem lay within him, or was something with Neverland itself. This little boy, this leader of the Lost Boys, this Peter, wasn't everything he was presenting himself as. Until he knew more, though, John was loath to tip his hand.

He got up; leaving the stick he had been whittling behind, and strode past a group of Lost Boys dragging a carcass into the camp. He walked past Wendy, coming out of the large tree with a bundle of laundry, and past Tinkerbell who looked him right in the eye. Just then a thought forced its way into his head.

He's going to want something,

but he won't ask for it.

Make him ask for it, John.

"What's up, Peter?" He did his best to appear casual.

"Are you feeling good, John? You haven't been happy much since we got here. I want you to be happy. Do you believe me?"

John's eyes fell to the ground, "Sure, Peter. I believe…" With his eyes down, John couldn't see the flash of annoyance that crossed Peter's face.

"Good. Wendy seems happy, right? And Mikey? Do you think it's me? Did I do something wrong? You? Did you think happy thoughts as you flew here?"

"Yeah. That's what you told us to do."

"I think we need to go flying, just you and me. And just Mike and me, too. But later for that. I want you to see this place and how cool it is. You wanna' do that?"

A slow pool of panic started to rise in John. Pan could smell it, and loved it. "I think I should stay here. Mom would want me to keep an eye on Michael."

"That's our Johnny. Always looking out for his family. I hope if you decide to stay, you'll protect the rest of us that much," a gentle chuckle followed, allowing John to relax slightly. "Do you think it's better if we work together to keep them safe?" It was a calculated risk, but Peter didn't feel like it was a huge one.

"Hey, that might be a good idea."

"Sure. You keep an eye on Wendy for the time that I'm gone with Mike," he could feel, but plowed right through, John's resistance. "We'll be okay and we won't be gone long. I still want to go flying with you, but we'll wait until we're all more comfortable. Sound good?"

An actual smile graced his lips, "Yeah, Peter. Really good."

...

Mike felt a little different than he did the last time he was this far off the ground. Last time there was surprise and soaring ecstasy and whimsy and more than a little bit of fear. This time, though, there was strength and more than a touch of aggressiveness. The power of it all pumped adrenaline into him so much that he couldn't help laughing a little. He could feel his teeth clench together and his fists tighten. He couldn't clamp them hard enough; and eventually he had to shout to let the world below him feel his presence, and if it desired, cower beneath his power.

Peter was careful to show a carefree and gleeful face. If Michael knew how special he was then Pan wasn't about to let on that he, too, had discovered Michael's secret. Even though Michael never carried himself as someone who knew his station in the world was a little higher than most, it was hard for Peter to believe that he didn't have some inkling to his own power. To most it appeared to be innocence or the confidence of knowing you're loved, but Pan had seen enough of so many worlds that he knew what he was seeing. The specifics of Michael eluded Peter, but he had seen many unusually gifted beings in his lifetime, and Michael was clearly one of them.

"Try a corkscrew, Mikey! They're the best. Now do a loop... now try both."

Michael couldn't always do what Peter told him right away. Occasionally it took Peter showing him one time first – but only ever once, and as they progressed, Michael needed less and less instruction."

As they danced on thermals and shot through clouds, leaving wisps of twisting cotton in their wakes, Peter saw so many things. This young one had nearly limitless potential. He was so raw, but that just meant that he could be molded: was being molded even as they played.

The force with which he drove up through the overhanging clouds was tremendous, leaving substantial rings behind. When they played hide-and-seek, Peter couldn't find Michael for several minutes, even in a wide-open, three-dimensional, cloud free space. And the whole time Mike had fallen in behind Peter, acting as his autonomous shadow. Every action was copied precisely, as if it were a rehearsed routine.

Once, Michael dive-bombed Peter, coming in directly in front of the sun. Peter would be instantly prepared to tell anyone in the camp how Michael almost caught him off guard: which was almost true. In truth, Peter almost evaded Michael, but didn't quite make it.

All of this power sat buzzing right in Peter's hands, dancing like a leaf in an autumn wind. And all The Pan had to do to unleash it was to make the little one believe that these new tricks would make his dear older brother happy and proud.

Far below them, hiding beneath thick canopy branches, a lone Pirate braved the Island to strategically place the mound of "cake" close by the Lost Boy camp. He trembled so much that he needed to carry his cutlass in his hand, lest it rattle in its scabbard.

"Can you see him, Michael?" Pan asked.

"Yes, of course," Michael replied, adopting Pan's motives as well as his skill. Without another word, the pair plummeted out of the sky, both crowing as loud as possible. The poor sailor dropped the cake where he stood and sprinted out of the woods and didn't stop until he reached his boat, but even then his arms and back mimicked the sprint all the way to the Jolly Roger, where he collapsed onto the deck exhausted.

"What a coward he was," Pan thought but Michael said aloud. "And he dropped his cake. Why did he–"

"It was a trap, no doubt. We must not eat it. It's best if we take it with us, make them think we're stupid."

"Of course. We should never show our hand if we don't have to."

...

"Wendy, wait up."

Tinkerbell flew to Wendy with a few articles that managed to fall off the pile of laundry Wendy was carrying.

"Oh, thank you, Tink."

"Let me help you with this," Tink offered. Tinkerbell was not ready to give up on Wendy just yet. Part of Wendy still existed and Tink was certain that it was fighting to get out again.

The two got to a stream and Wendy laid the pile of clothes on a rock nearby.

"Life is really great here, Tink. I'm so glad we got to come."

"Yeah, it's okay," Tink mused, "but it's not perfect."

"Oh yes it is. It's everything you could want. We can fly, there are adventures here, and everything is just so pretty, it reminds me of back home when –"

A high pitched whistle, weak and quiet, came from deep within Wendy and Tinkerbell's face flashed worry. She had not heard that sound, or something very similar to that sound, since Peter had taken control of a Lost Boy many ages ago. He became Peter's most dedicated supporter until he vanished in the forest one bright afternoon.

"Peter is just so wonderful," Wendy finished.

When did he do this to you, and why?
You were already enamored with him,
he wouldn't have to do this.

Maybe I heard it wrong.
Maybe that wasn't the sound.

"Wendy, you don't think that sometimes Peter can play a little too rough? That sometimes the life here is too violent?"

"Well, boys will be boys. You know? And Peter spoils them, always bringing home treats. I never want to leave."

Wendy picked a vest out of the pile. It was threadbare and looked like it had once belonged in the Old West. She plunged it into the river and rubbed it vigorously on itself, the way she'd seen women do it on period TV shows.

"Wendy, do you remember your home? Do you remember feeling different? Free?"

"I am free, Tink. What are you saying? I've never been happier."

Tinkerbell took in her surroundings. There had to be some way she could reach that strong, powerful girl she saw through the window. There has to be some connection still open to the girl she used to be.

"What about John and Michael, Wendy? Do you think they're happy here?"

"Well, Michael is having the time of his life. He's off with Peter right now. I bet Peter is showing Michael some of the most wonderful things. They're probably having a grand adventure." The girl turned, smiling broadly, toward the Fairie. "I can't wait to hear about it!" she squealed.

"And what about John?"

The smile faded from Wendy's face and she turned back toward the task-at-hand.

"John always ruins everything," she said. "He's so proper all the time, he can't relax and just have fun. He's always thinking and analyzing."

It was the first negative thing Tink had heard her say in a long time, so she decided to pursue that route.

"Yeah, John will probably never fit in. It would probably be best if he just left. Let us have our fun, right?"

"Exactly! Oh, it's so good to hear someone else say that. I thought I was the only one who felt like this."

Great. Just a little further.

"Yeah. I certainly do, too. I think we should just give him a sword and send him off to face the Pirates. Maybe he'll hurt one or two of them and they will finish him off for us. It'll be the best use of him for us."

"No! Don't you dare suggest that, Tinkerbell." Her words were strong and direct. There was no hint of the nauseating lilt that her voice had adopted as of late. These words belonged to a different Wendy, a Wendy that slept deep below the surface of this outer shell.

That's why Peter put this spell on you.

Simply charming you couldn't break

your ties to your brothers.

He needed something stronger,

something inside you to keep you in check.

"Come on, Wendy," Tink pushed, "He's no good to us like he is. If anything he'll be the death of us all. I already know that Peter is planning something special for him. If you and I have thought of this, then imagine what the great Peter Pan has cooked up for the little brat."

Wendy's eyes went wide and her jaw clenched. She spiked a wad of cloth into the stream like a football and charged at the Fairie.

"No one will touch him or Michael! I won't let it – " The high pitched whistle chirped from within her chest again and she barked out a thick raspy cough. "–happen!"

Tinkerbell retreated, backpedaling through the air, avoiding the reach of the wild girl grasping for her.

Stay with it, girl.

Come on, a few more good

coughs and it's out.

Reach for it, push it!

"The Lost Boys will probably tear him apart and leave you to sweep up the blood."

Wendy's barking cough repeated and it checked her advance while she choked and struggled for air. Another cough and her hand went to her throat while she focused more intently on her body, rather than the idea of her kin getting hurt.

No, stay with me.

Don't let it win!

You're almost there!

If anyone can do it, it's you, girl.

Keep struggling and you'll break it loose!

Tink tried to keep the pressure on, but it was too late.

"His entrails will be cast to the corners of this place!"

Wendy's head was down and her wild hair hid her face, but Tink knew the expression it held as she spoke. The voice was not her own, but another familiar tone.

"Nice try, Tink, but this one's mine. She's too important to lose and she likes me too much to get rid of me that easily," Peter's voice spoke out of Wendy's throat.

The girl looked up and it was Peter that looked through her eyes at Tink for a second, and then both he and Wendy were gone. Tink was left with the creature that looked like, sounded like, and thought it was Wendy.

"Yeah, he'll come around, though. He just needs time to figure out how things work here, then he'll strategically put himself in the right position and join the group. He always does that," Wendy waded out into the stream to retrieve the cloth drifting slowly away in the current. "Shy at first, loud by the end. That's John."

"That's what I thought. You aren't as strong as I thought you would be," Tink said as her hopes for freedom slipped away.

"Oh, no. Sorry to disappoint. I'm not very strong. Not like Peter is, anyway."

"You're only going to be as strong as he lets you be, and you'll take the scraps from his table and treat them like treasures! You're a joke," Tink jeered, letting her frustrations crash on this husk of a girl, and flew up over the canopy to get back to camp. She needed solitude and her cage would be nice and quiet this time of the afternoon.

...

John stood up from his tree stump and wandered off into the woods. It was the one respite he allowed himself. The rest of his time was spent searching for some way to escape back home and keeping his brother and sister safe, but Wendy was off with Tink and Michael was flying around with Peter and there was nothing to be done for either of them.

Be patient, John.

Be patient and pay attention.

An answer will come.

It has to.

A glint from the corner of his vision mercifully interrupted John's thoughts. The Sun shimmered off of something metal.

Or water?

Maybe a firefly?

In the middle of the day?

One of those glowy little Fairies?

Yeah, that's it.

A shadow passed over the oblivious John Darling as he tracked down the Fairies that were playing with him. The being to which it belonged watched intently. A dollop of foamy white something fell to the ground just behind John's last step. A tandem pair of Fairies tracked the drooling monster's path, with far less friendly intentions than the ones John was following.

"Oh. Here you are. What are you two up to?"

John smiled. It felt like the first time he had done that sincerely since he had gotten here. The two Fairies, Mushroomcap and Heilia turned their backs to John and covered their eyes. They traded off counting out loud.

"One."

"Two."

"Three."

The shadow loomed. "I don't believe in Fairies." It was a whisper and barely even that. It lilted on the breeze that almost wasn't there; playing lazily in the stirring leaves. John heard something else in that voice. It was a glimpse of a secret.

John had glanced up with the whispered distraction and when he looked down again, something was wrong. Helia looked hurt.

Worse than hurt was a thought he didn't let in. Mushroomcap looked at him with terror in his eyes. Looked through him, or past him.

A shadow flashed over a branch directly above them.

"Clap!" the Fairie ordered.

Who knew a little thing like that

could make such a big noise?

"Clap, I said!" Mushroomcap was quickly turning from the flash-bang yellow of afraid to the smoldering orange of agitated to the fire-red of angry. He moved toward John aggressively causing John to retreat instinctively.

The Fairie shot a look skyward, catching movement. It was from something so dangerous that Mushroomcap was now the one cowering. He backed away, slowly but then with increasing urgency.

For the first time, John looked up. Really looked. Above him, in the darkest shadow he'd ever seen, teemed malignant life. It was impossible for the shadow to exist above him and yet somehow not on the ground. It was a dark ink stain on the clear day. It was incomprehensible. And yet... here John was, on a magic island, being hunted, looking from winged glowing men only a few inches tall to an unlikely shadow, removed from any possible context. On this fake rock, in this land that could never be, his demise churned above him like... what? Like... metaphors had abandoned him.

"Run." It was a small but urgent voice, either in the back of his head or from where he was just looking. It didn't threaten anymore. But it did urge.

"Go. Now"

"Yes, pet. Run," answered the ten, the hundred, the thousand million horrors above him.

Too terrified to take his eyes off of the thing above him, he managed - through sheer force of will - to look down at where his friend stood. It would've seemed funny to him, but for his current situation, that he had backed away from this tiny threat... and toward that horror behind him.

His heart stopped. He was alone with a dead Fairie at his knees and Black Death over his shoulder in this land that could never be. In this land he could never leave, another glint about a yard away. It was the Fairie, the living one, trying to get his attention.

Run.

He froze.

He ran.

He never moved.

He sprinted after his Fairie friend as quickly as his young legs and lungs and the rough terrain would let him.

The whole Island shook with gleeful laughter from behind him. A chase.

He'd fallen for it. They'd wanted him to run. The Fairie, the black cloud and the Island.

But Mushroomcap waited. He was more scared than John. In a way he thought that could never be true, but he knew it had to be.

"Come on," Mushroomcap called to him.

The cancer behind him hadn't moved, just growled with hunger. But it hadn't moved, of that John was certain. He was just as certain that he was the mouse to the evilest cat that ever stalked.

Over branches. Under some more.

I just want to leave.

To be home.

Brambles caught and scraped his calves and shins, his knees and thighs. Small tiny branches whipped his face and arms and chest. He couldn't look, but he knew there were a million little cuts. He tried to fly, but the weight of his situation was far too heavy for such a novice flier.

Now it moved. Now the horror moved on legs covered in mottled hair. Feet with razor claws. A thousand mottled legs, a thousand razor claws and two thousand eyes, green as absinthe or maybe red like Satan's, lazily pursued him.

There were four goblins after him. Only four. Slightly, Omnes, Curly, and Maggle.

Peter had forbidden the Lost Boys from killing the children. But there's a lot you can do with prey short of killing it, and they were intent on finding out how much of that he could endure.

The Fairie led Jonathan as quickly as he could. They were close to safety. If Mushroomcap could just get John to his home, they'd be safe. Pan didn't allow his cronies into the Fairies' domain without him present.

Just a little further. A feint to the left. The little winged one danced and darted, not watching Jonathan's face or path, just the vicious dirty things behind him as they lunged. John followed as Mushroomcap hoped he would.

They missed.

Almost there.

Just a few more –

He didn't make it. He tripped, or was tripped. In either case John fell.

Grimy claws snatched him up after they'd let him bleed on sharp rocks.

He was lifted.

He was spun.

He was pinned against a tree.

He was hurt.

But it was nothing yet.

A face met his, a dark parody. The eyes were at the same height, but cloudy and wild. The nose met his, more or less, as well. But it was smashed into the horrid face. A scar cut deep from the cheek, across the bridge of his nose, and ended just to the right of the eye. It crossed another one there, running vertically and much newer. Angrier.

Claws tore at his shirt, exposing tender innocence, to be made less innocent soon.

"Hello, boy," Maggle said. "You ought not wander too far from the camp by yourself. You may fall and hurt yourself."

A claw dug into his shoulder and sliced over to the clavicle.

"Aye," added Curly, the timber of his voice as inhumane as possible, "Or a pirate might find you and run you through."

Teeth clamped down so hard on his forearm that the bones snapped in two like kindling and the arm below dangled from the rest by sinew and skin. He looked down at his mangled arm and screamed. Not from pain, because he felt none yet. The adrenaline was flowing too quickly, but rather from his dismemberment and in anticipation of the pain to come.

Maggle approximated a smile as he continued, "There are beasties out here, too, child."

Two claws now. They ran from knee to hip, through the meat effortlessly, tracing the line of young bone. He bled so hard that the goblin had to reset his footing.

John felt faint, but was no longer painless. Now it was painful in the truest sense of the word. His leg and arm fought for dominance in his forebrain. Which one hurt more? They were both winning. His body burned at the wounds. He felt the poison of the bite enter his blood stream. It was the most awesomely painful liquid ever created, like liquid razor blades. His synapses exploded. His brain tried to shut down, but the poison wouldn't let it. He was going to feel all of this, like it or not. His head chimed in. It throbbed from the crack he had sustained when he was slammed against the tree. More sticky and warm life trickled down his neck and pooled around his collar.

A needle claw ran softly into his belly and swirled around, twining his intestines like a kitten with yarn.

"Don't worry, young Johnny," the goblin smiled as if doing him a favor. "You won't die." The smile turned to sneer.

The pain spread as the hooked finger left his middle. If it wasn't poisoned as well, they had found a way to make a conventional wound worse than imaginable.

The other two goblins, Slightly and Omnes, returned now, a flitting Mushroomcap in two greasy fingers as the sneering Maggle pulled its claw out of John's belly and thrust it into his mouth. John tasted iron and fear; his own blood and his own death.

"It's almost done now, lad." He couldn't tell which one spoke because he finally started to fade from consciousness. Before he did, he heard the leader growl an order to the Fairie.

"Fix him, sprite, but not totally. Let him remember some of this."

...

John awoke surrounded by concerned faces. Wendy, Michael and Pan were there. The Lost Boys, too.

"John! Are you okay, John?" Michael was frantic. John's shirt and pants were torn and there was blood everywhere.

"Yeah, Mikey. I think so." John grabbed his head as he rose. It throbbed, front and back. He had a goose egg on the back of his head and he winced in agony. Wendy was unable to speak, panic in her eyes.

"You ought not wander too far from the camp by yourself. You may fall and hurt yourself," Pan said earnestly. "Or a pirate might find you and run you through. There are beasties out there, too, John. What happened to you out there? Do you remember anything?"

"Well, I met… some… thing. Or someone. A monster maybe. I'm not really sure."

"Umm, Peter," a boy spoke up, "we found him at the bottom of a hill. We don't know, but it looks like he may have fought with something and fell. We found a Fairie to fix him as soon as we could. It was Mushroomcap, I think."

"Very good, Omnes. You saved John Darling's life today."

The Lost Boys who saved John were the kings of the camp for their quick action. Peter even gave them a treat.

"The three of you get to share this cake for your quick thinking and actions today!" he said and the camp erupted into cheers.

Some of the Lost Boys looked vaguely familiar to John as he rubbed his stomach and limped on an apparently perfect leg.

"'Don't go,' they called in pity. 'I must,' he answered, shaking, 'I am so afraid of Peter.'"

-J. M. Barrie, *Peter and Wendy*

John Leaves the Camp

Wendy insisted that Maggle, Slightly, and Omnes be built a room because they had all suddenly come down with a fever, nausea, swelling, and pain in their joints. Peter stopped in to see how they were feeling.

"You understand that when I say things like 'No one kills the Darlings,' that I mean it, even if I'm away, right?"

Omnes vomited while Slightly shook beneath his blanket. "We didn't kill him. He's still alive, isn't he?"

"You are all wonderfully violent," Peter smiled. "I wouldn't have my Lost Boys any other way. But you did go against the spirit of my decree, don't you agree? You could say that you tortured John to the brink of death, only to revive him at the last moment, right? And I think that's precisely the kind of thing I said not to do."

"Sir–" Omnes began, but Peter cut him off.

"And so now you will be tortured to the brink of death only to have me bring you back at the last possible second. Understand? You Boys disappoint me. Enjoy your punishment and be grateful that I am in a good mood. Pray I stay in that good mood or I may not be so willing to follow through on the last part of my promise."

Maggle let out a cry of pain as he felt his body spasm and his arms bent in an unnatural direction. Treating this like the final period of the conversation, Peter exited their room.

...

Things became good for John at camp. In fact, they'd started off downright fantastic. Wendy paid more attention to him while he was recovering. The Lost Boys were more careful with him in their rough housing. At first, it felt like he was a sort of mascot or something. The Boys cheered him on as he healed. Even Peter was more solicitous toward him. He offered him extra portions at meals, saying more food would help him heal faster. In one instance, he mercilessly beat a Boy he'd seen as being too harsh with Johnny until Wendy first begged, and then ordered, him to stop.

Just as he started to become comfortable falling asleep in his tree the nightmares came. He was often forced to will himself awake, silent in panic, out of breath and covered in a thick viscous residue that permeated from the tree. The fear would sink away and John would be left with either heart-wrenching sorrow or teeth-grinding rage. Either way, he could not calm down without exiting his tree to dry off and stalk about the perimeter of the camp. Echoes from his dreams would still whisper terrible orders in his mind until he was rid of the clear sap, and it was everything John could do to stay his hand from doing terrible things.

In these nightmares he would get chewed on or clawed open. He dreamed his own death in ways that were so vivid and alien. They were violent dreams in which many goblins gleefully cut him apart while he was pinned to a tree. His fear and his paranoia played tag in his head.

He dreamed of other things, as well. He saw the future; he was sure of it: Wendy as a husk of a human being; a frail old spinster, pining after the Pan with no chance of securing him. She'd destroyed her bonds with family and had no friends. She sat in silence as often as not, her life crumbled around her, in fractions and splinters just like the visions themselves.

Not so with Michael Darling. Jonathan's visions of him were worse by miles. He was a terrifyingly awesome thing. He was to Pan what Pan was to Jonathan. He burned from the inside with a fire. He was covered head to toe in caked dirt, with violent windstorms whipping around is feet while he moved hurricanes above his head. He controlled all he saw. His face was terrible and fierce and sad and lonely. He was a boy in the body of a warrior; he was lost innocence made human. John only ever saw these things in glimpses; in dreams or fragments of dreams.

The savagery of the creatures in Neverland overwhelmed him. He'd faced his death there. He'd died there. Pan had seen to it. Hadn't Pan been the reason? He knew it in his core.

John knew that Pan was set apart from the rabble. The Lost Boys were no more Pan's equal than John himself was. But even with that, he felt like there was something bigger happening than his torture and death at these beasts' hands. Their underlying violence and growls were the least of it. Pan had bigger plans in mind than toying with him alone. Things were happening with more intensity now. There was an underlying sense of urgency and the Darling children were either the reason or the cure. John had been forced to pretend that he didn't notice, but he couldn't pretend anymore, and that meant something horrible.

It was why he'd left, why he'd stolen away from the camp as often as he could again. At first he'd been taken back in. It seemed like his time away was only about recovering and now that he was back, he had been being treated very well. It wasn't long, however, that these Lost Boys were trying to make him feel like an outsider again, and worse. He felt increasing pressure to decide whether or not he'd be a Lost Boy all the way. He knew that he didn't know what was out there in the forest, but he couldn't imagine how it could be worse. It was in that frame of mind that John wandered the woods, afraid to go back, afraid to go forward. Maybe there was something out there that could help him and his family. He needed so many things to be different. He didn't know where to start. So he chose to sit down on a fallen log and collect his thoughts.

What do I need?

More importantly, what do I need first?

Ok. I need to be away from Pan and his monsters. So far so good on that one.

I need to get us all off of this island and back home.
Definitely that.
If that's not the first thing I need, it's got to be the most important.

What else?

I need to stop those dreams
from coming true.

But they may
not be trying
to predict the
future. They
may just be
the things
you're afraid
of happening
and you're
telling
yourself that
they're
dreams.

Well, if that's the case, I need
to figure out a way to stop them
from being in my head.
That probably means leaving here.

If that's true
then we are
fixing two
problems at
once.

How do I do all of these things
when I'm so alone?
I have nothing.

Where do I start?

He had no water and no food. He had no shelter, no weapon; no protection from the elements of any type but for the pajamas he wore, which Wendy had mended for him after he was attacked. He knew it would pour down freezing rain at any moment; but the nice weather held.

Wendy worried when they first discovered John's absence. She hated the thought of a pirate or a bear taking him in the night. Peter dismissed the possibility. He looked sad in his own right, although not worried. Wendy didn't know what that meant. She had sensed that John didn't fit in here on the island, but had never seen Peter concerned by that. Maybe that look meant that he was beginning to care about her brother, or maybe it meant something else. That last thought played on the edges of her mind. She never let it in to take up residence in her consciousness and soon enough it went away on its own.

That seemed easier lately than ever before, and so she used the technique as often as she could. If she stopped worrying about something for even a few moments it ceased to be an issue at all.

The finality and certainty with which Peter allayed her fears soon made her angry. Not at Peter or herself, but with John. Why did he have to ruin everything all the time? She knew that he didn't like it here. He'd told her as much. He'd said that he didn't trust Peter or the Lost Boys. He didn't trust them or their motives. But how could he say that when they saved his life and treated them all so well? Why was he being so impossible?

. . .

He was hungry and tired. He was cold even in the temperate weather that seemed so permanent here. He soon came to think that it was stress – and the hunger and the exhaustion. He'd tempted fate with a few handfuls of berries and now they were gone. He'd heard plenty of animals around, but knew that he'd never catch any of them.

Even if you do catch one,

what would you do with it?

Nothing.

He prayed for relief. He dreamed of home, where his mother had made his dinner and his bed. His sleep was better that night.

…

After a second day passed with no sign of John, Peter called a small group of Lost Boys to his side and whispered to them quietly.

"Find a sign of him. I want to know where he is. If he's dead when you find him, so be it, but if any of you harm him I will do the same to you tenfold. Understand?"

"But, sir," Toodles began to ask, "don't you know where everything is on Neverland? Can't you just tell us where he is and we can go get 'im?"

Atlan and a few of the other Lost Boys that overheard Toodles exchanged curious glances with dark undertones.

"Toodles, I can't do everything for you. Otherwise you'll grow fatter and stupider than you already are," then he turned his focus back to the general group. "Tenfold. Understand me?"

"Yes, sir," they grunted disappointingly.

Peter turned to Wendy and smiled.

"It's okay, Wendy. I'm going to have them find him and bring him back. What a grand story he will have. He's been on this adventure for two days, I'm sure he will have a lot to tell us."

Wendy was relieved that Peter was finding John for her, and that Tinkerbell had taken Mike away from the discussion and was playing with him. She seemed to love Mike and knew that nothing good would come from scaring him about his brother.

Tinkerbell didn't want Michael to worry, and she did care for him more than any of the other children she had brought to Neverland, but she knew that John was okay. John was an Element, and he needed to be on his own to discover what that meant. First he would have to overcome his fear, and then he would have to quiet himself and listen to the world around him.

Tink stole away with Michael as often as possible these days. She had begun to notice the potential that the boy carried, and she ran experiments disguised as playing to figure him out, much the same way that Pan did. It was easier for Tinkerbell to see Michael when other people were around him, but there were the rare times when he wasn't moving that she would skip over him completely.

When he was with Pan he would fill with Fire, and with John he would become Earth. He was unlike anything she had ever seen. He could copy her perfectly only after a moment of watching her perform a task, and he would do it with everyone who came near him.

Later that evening the Lost Boy came back with no news of John and a flash of concern darkened Peter's face. Panic welled once more in Wendy, but was soon quelled when Peter announced to the camp that he was going out to locate John himself... and Wendy loved him all the more for it.

John definitely heard noises around him now and they were growing in both number and intensity. They really could only be those things that worked for Pan, either the Lost Boys or a large brutal animal. Peter ran this Island. What else could be stalking him so completely?

Not knowing whether to duck for cover or to run away screaming his head off, he froze. He well knew from all of the nature shows that most animals had keener senses than people. And common sense told him that he'd never outrun anything in these woods, Pan's minion or otherwise. He wasn't very fast; nor was he designed to flow swiftly through a forest; nor was he at all familiar with his surroundings.

The hairs on his arms were standing straight up. By the time he realized that his feet were shifting his weight back and forth wildly, he had already been doing it for quite a while. The time had come and a breaking point had been reached.

A shock of brown hair dashed across his periphery. When he turned to face what he was sure was a Lost Boy, he found himself staring at a child's back and a whirling sword. There was an uproar of predators' howls, all of them outmatched by Pan's crow.

A bear's head and another's claw soon fell at John's feet. His terror had numbed him so completely and fear of his host had filled him so totally that he found it impossible to process what he was seeing. When he finally did grasp it, all of his reasons for leaving melted away. His heart soared with hope and joy and the warmth of acceptance. Peter was finally welcoming him into the group. He wouldn't be so scared, so lonely… so desperately scared and so terribly lonely. He could feel at home at last.

As the red spray from the bears subsided and the fur settled to the ground, Pan turned to John. He smiled broadly and winked at him.

"Hello, John. It's a good thing I found you. The Boys have been looking for you everywhere. I promised Wendy that I'd find you. She'd be pretty mad at both of us if a bear'd eaten you. I'd be sad, as well. Want to keep a paw?"

John hugged Peter in an embrace as strong and sincere as any he'd ever given. He just then realized exactly how much he'd needed this feeling.

"Oh yes, Peter! I'll take a claw. I'd love to. Maybe you can show me how to make a belt like yours and we can put it on there."

"Of course. It would be your first trophy. And we'll get others, too. You can come hunting with us… if you want to," Peter lowered his head with this last suggestion, playing up a humble persona .

"Can I?"

"Certainly. But for now, let's go home. You're sister's pretty upset, but when I tell her how bravely you fought off those bears while you were out gathering food for us this whole time, I'm sure she'll forget all about that and you'll be fine. Everyone gets a little turned around out here once in awhile, especially if they're by themselves. Except for me, of course. I know everything about this place. Let's go have some bear stew."

"Alright," was all John could say thorough the smile of love and tears of gratitude. With a fresh sprinkling of fairie dust he flew as easily back to the camp as Peter ever had.

Everything was different for John then. He did go hunting with the Lost Boys. He even went with Peter, just themselves, occasionally. Maybe even a little more than Michael. But Michael wasn't jealous. He was so happy that his heroic brother was back that he beamed with joy and pride just to see John so happy. Wendy felt the occasional chill of envy when she saw John and Peter growing closer. However, even she felt calm that her trouble-making brother was back home where he belonged and had stopped being such a problem.

John's trophy collection grew strong. Tiger paws and bear claws teemed from his belt to the point that there were soon too many to wear. They were forced to run a line between two trees to house them all. With each new one, the Lost Boys and their leader would crow a mighty roar of appreciation for him. He always joined at the top of his lungs.

" 'There's a pirate asleep in the pampas just beneath us,' Peter told John, 'If you like, we'll go down there and kill him.' "
-J. M. Barrie, *Peter and Wendy*

Childhood Lost

"Your sister really likes it here," Pan said one day, as they sat on a small boulder overlooking the rest of the camp. It sounded like more than a question to John.

"Yeah. I suppose so," he replied.

"Mike too," John added, with a hint of regret in voice. He hoped that none of it had leaked up into his throat and stuck to his words.

"Not you though," Peter's voice seemed as full of loss as John felt.

"It's not that. Really. It's just. I just spent so much time... I dunno'. It just feels like I'm trying to catch up with them, that's all."

"No. I know. It was hard on you. I still wish you'd have come to me, John. Right? I'm Peter Pan. If you're afraid of us, of me, well then I'm lost."

"It looks like it was all in my head. Maybe I just, like, just... maybe I just came here scared in the first place. You know, from the beginning? Maybe I was ready to hate this place right from the beginning, and so I did."

"Hmm." The noise was oddly grown up sounding coming from such a young boy. No, not grown up. Old. Old like a river, not like a grandpa. More like a forest taking the first winter snow than a house settling. Everything older than twenty years is ancient to an eight-year-old. But this one heard the real difference, if only briefly.

"Peter? How long have you been here? In Neverland?"

John thought he sensed Peter tense just a little, but it may have been John himself.

"I don't know, honestly. Why?"

"Was there a Neverland before you were here? Did you create it?"

"Create Neverland? No. I'm a Lost Boy, a boy who was lost. I got here the same way we all did. I got forgotten."

"Who was here when you got here? Is there anyone left? What happened to them? Did the pirates, you know…?"

"Kill them?" the finality of the phrase landed on both of them with heavy boots, weighing them down. "Yeah. Hook killed all of them. I hate that Captain. We'd leave him alone if he would just leave us alone. I wish he'd just leave. Neverland would be so perfect if he wasn't here. Him and his stupid pirates."

"Yeah… I think I hate him, too…you know." Jonathan was more than a little surprised with himself.

"Yeah?" Peter was clearly excited.

"Yup. He should just leave. Why doesn't he?" John stood up on the rock and screamed toward the bay, "Just leave. Stupid… fucking Hook!" The word shot so quickly out of his mouth, the way any word does when one is testing the waters. "Just go and take those damn pirates with you!"

When John finally sat down things seemed to settle some. Peter leaned over to him and said in a lower voice, "His hook. He thinks I made a crocodile eat his hand. He blames me for him having it. He hates us. Can you believe that? Yeah, like I made some stupid crocodile eat his stupid hand."

"You remember him without his hook?" John was openly astonished.

"No! That's what I mean. He always had it. I don't remember him without it, anyway. You want to go find one of them and kill him?" The shift in tone and energy startled John a little.

"Umm... Okay. I guess. I've never killed a pirate before."

"It's easy," Peter said, and then with a sly grin he added, "and fun. We'll take the head back to Wendy." With that, Peter was off, and John reluctantly followed.

It took some searching, but they found a couple of Hook's men at a small river, getting fresh water and cleaning up. Peter whispered that he thought there were almost always some pirates here. John didn't know if he meant here like at this spot, or here like on the island generally. He also thought it sounded like a sort of invitation.

The pirates were murmuring and looking around a lot. John thought they looked exactly like he did when he knew he might get caught doing something really awful and he just wanted to get it over with. He began to hate these men.

If they know they shouldn't be here,
why don't they just go back to the ship?
Or, better yet, why not just
leave Neverland completely?

He'd have to remember to ask Peter why the pirates didn't just kill Hook and take the ship and go home.

Several tiny silvery eyes watched the pair watching the pirates. They had been following the two for quite a while and knew they were still safely hidden.

"Should we maybe crow?" John knew the fright in his voice had more than merely leaked out now. It was raining on his words like a summer shower as they left his throat.

"No. That would call the other Lost Boys," Peter was stalking them now, only half paying John any attention. This was his natural element. "Why share the fun? We can take care of these two, easy."

"Okay," came the less than completely courageous reply.

Peter skulked low then. He moved left along the edge of the small clearing holding the pirates, his shoulders hunched. Fire glinted in his eyes. His blade moved up and down as his arm tensed and relaxed. His feet were silent pads of a puma, a jaguar. The small breeze stilled.

The two scouts looked up and around now, even more nervously. They seemed to pay even more attention to the sky now, like they had reason to look there for bad things to happen.

Peter looked back at John, smiling. He motioned with his head toward their prey. John swallowed hard and faked a smile of his own. He nodded, his hands thick with sweat.

Two pair of silvery eyes broke from their group and darted away.

All at once, Peter jumped out of the clearing and screamed with glee. He swung hard with an overhead blow at the first man.

Several things happened all at once. It was impossible to know how to order the events. There was just a frenzy of attacks and parries by Peter.

Maybe the first pirate turned quickly first. His hand went to his scabbard in the same motion and the cutlass swept up to the block. There was no anger on the man's face or in his eyes: only absolute terror.

John didn't see either of the men react, in fact. This was because he was too involved with the complicated act of moving his limbs forward when all they wanted to do was to stay still. Compound this with the fact that his own blade had slipped from his hand and been kicked forward, resulting in its final lodging between a firm branch and a large root. John bent down to loosen the blade and so missed the second pirate reeling back in horror, tripping on some water casks and catching a rock to the back of his head.

Peter's roar, the first Pirate's fearful screams and the second's pained ones filled John's ears.

Finally, several silvery eyes blinked at once, some in surprise, and some in tears. But there was one pair that just arrived that looked on in anger. The pair in front of the group seethed with rage.

Cuts were attempted and landed, counter blows missed. Peter danced around the man he was fighting. Both fighters knew the poor fellow didn't have a chance. But it was as though this gave him a choice. If fight and die or surrender and die are the only options, fighting becomes the only option.

John stumbled out of the forest, his legs moving, but his arms stuck to the stubborn sword. The sword pivoted in his grip but refused to let go of the root. John reached the end of his range and the sword snapped back. He fell back, butt first, in the foliage. The snap had freed the sword, and John scrambled to retrieve it. Then, waving the cutlass over his head, John gave a wild, but very weak howl. He charged into the newly finished fight. The second pirate slumped to the ground.

"Curse you, foul beasts. Just leave us be. Why can't you?" The question came in gasped and tortured breaths. Peter stood over his quarry, triumphant.

"You want to take his head, or shall I?"

The second man stirred and moaned in agony. They looked over to him in tandem. Peter took his foot off of the first man's chest and loped playfully to the second one.

"Are we awake, dog?" Pan's depth of age hit John again. "John, come here."

John obeyed, but his feet were reluctant. He trudged over to the scene.

"Take him."

John looked into Peter's eyes with fright.

"I know the first time is very hard. It was for me, too. And you shouldn't be embarrassed about not fighting. Everybody's scared."

"Not you."

"Well, not me. No."

"I don't know if I can."

"If you can't; alright. But will you be able to if they attack us, or we have to go to the ship and fight them?"

John didn't answer, the blade bobbing nervously in his jittering hand.

Several voices filled John's head, shouting, "No," in unison as he pushed his blade awkwardly down into the defeated pirate.

He killed a person, another human being.

"Let's take their heads and go home."

Peter raised his bloody sword over his head when a crashing sound and voices came from the forest. Their eyes darted to the noise.

"More! Follow me!" Peter's smile was back. He bounded through the woods himself.

John thought about not joining him. He looked down at his handiwork and then Peter's.

A group of Fairies flitted out into the clearing, a furious Tinkerbell in the lead. The rest jittered to the corpses, but Tink came to hover right in front of John's eyes.

"We can undo this. But you never can," Tinkerbell said, "You will have always killed a man. Human's don't forget."

"But he won't stay dead?" John asked tamely.

"No. But you didn't know that when you did it. Now go. Go to your new best friend. He thinks he has more killing for you. It's how he starts turning you into one of them. Go do his bidding. I had greater hopes for you Darlings, but now I see I was a fool just like you are, Jonathan. You have held out for the longest of anyone I've seen, but you are changing too, just like Cooper did."

Tinkerbell hovered sadly in the air over his first victim.

"Who's Cooper?" he managed to ask through his shame.

"Johnny, what are you doing?" came the call from a moderate distance through the woods.

With Tinkerbell's admonition fresh in mind and heavy in heart, John found himself enjoying his time in Peter's graces just a little less than before. Even in this seemingly whimsical place, the sense of the inevitability John felt toward the prospect of losing his new friendship with Peter grew. Only slightly at first, the anxiety of the event and the guilt over his meeting with the Fairie fed each other until the sense of loss grew from a kernel to a ball; from a ball to a rock.

Before he'd let it go any further John took his concerns to Peter, just as directed before. Sensing exactly how risky that could be, he tried as hard as he could to approach his friend delicately. He didn't want to expose Tinkerbell as the one who planted the seed of his discomfort, as he was fairly certain that she wasn't everything she seemed to be. Jonathan tucked that certainty away; assuring himself that it might be useful later.

He'd seen how Peter Pan dealt with those who failed to see or execute his vision properly. He might dismiss a Lost Boy from his presence with the flick of a wrist, or he might stare a moment or two too long at another. Either way, the Boy went away.

Often they were gone for a considerable time, John thought. And some he never saw again and Wendy didn't seem to remember them ever being there at all. There were enough Lost Boys, and he himself was unacquainted enough until then, that he told himself any number of stories to explain these occasions. Even with those justifications in mind, John treaded lightly with the boss.

"Peter?"

"Yes Johnny."

"I was just thinking… remember the pirates from the other day, the ones we killed?"

"Yeah!" Peter's face lit up at the mention of the event, but as to whether it was because it was their first real thrill together, or for some other reason, John couldn't tell. "That was superb, Johnny. I wasn't sure you had it in you, but you showed me. I was gonna say, too, John, how much fun I've had with you the last few days. I was worried that you weren't enjoying yourself here. You are, aren't you? Now, I mean?"

"Oh, sure. Yes, for real," John did a reasonable job pretending to smile and laugh. "I just was thinking that, uh... you know. Those two weren't really... Did they seem really scared to you? Like, maybe, way more than a Pirate should be? I don't know. You know? Just asking."

Peter didn't need supernatural intuition to see how uncomfortable John was, but his demonic nature did enjoy it. He raised an eyebrow just far enough past imperceptible for John to notice and take more alarm and asked, "Yeah, why? What're you saying?"

"No, no, no! I'm not saying anything. I'm just saying that did you think that maybe, ah..." John struggled, but only for a moment, "maybe Hook has men that don't really want to be Pirates. Maybe he kidnapped them. Or tricked them. Maybe he tricked them into coming here, so he could make them fight in this war with you."

"Yeah, maybe," Peter shrugged, "I guess that could be true. Why? Does it matter?"

"No. Yeah. I mean, no. I don't think it maybe matters that much, but could we use that, you think?"

"I like the way you think, John," Peter turned to face John. He'd known from the beginning of the conversation what John was thinking, and why. He decided to try something to see how John would react. "Stupid Captain Hook has everybody on that boat scared of him, right?" He never lets them go anywhere without permission.

They have to do everything he says. They can't ever screw up, you know? I've seen it. He just kicks them away. And they have to go under the deck, into the ship. I watch him a lot.

"Kind of like when you thought you had to watch us from the outside. I saw you. Of course I did. It just made me sad because I couldn't do anything to show you how to be by us; couldn't say anything. I guess it just seemed like we never… I don't know. But we're okay now, right Johnny? It would make Mike and Wendy really happy if you'd stay. Me, too.

"Anyway. Hook. He's a jerk. He hunts us. Sometimes he just leaves his ship, and comes here to hunts us. He really wants me, though. He hates me. But it's like he needs me. I dream sometimes, I know, I know, I'm not supposed to dream. That's what they say. I just tell the Boys that I don't sleep or dream 'cause it sounds good. But I do. And sometimes I dream that I became a Lost Boy because he wanted me here. I don't know about why me, though. Why not any other boy? But then again, maybe I am just any boy to him. I don't know. I do know he hates me, though. Maybe that's why he made us come here. So he'd have somebody to hate and fight with. I think that sometimes.

"But those Pirates. They weren't scared, John. They looked surprised. But they weren't scared. They're all liars, you know, right? You do know that, don't you? They all seem like regular Pirates. But I've seen them. I don't think they're men. I think I've seen other… stuff about them. Like sometimes I'll see their faces, but they'll be different. They'll look like some mean animal. They don't know I've seen them like that. He probably does. Hook, I mean. That stinking Captain probably knows everything that happens to this Island. Our

Island. He probably knows where I go to be alone, away from these guys. I bet he even knows when I go. He wants Mike and Wendy, John. Do you know that? He wants Wendy. I don't know why. Probably for some stupid grown-up thing. He wants Michael, too. But Mike's special, isn't he? I can't figure out why, but he is. And Hook wants him. That's why he doesn't want you by him. You're special too, John. I can see that. I've gotten that one figured out, for sure. But Hook wants to keep you away from your brother and sister. He thinks he can get to them easier if you aren't there to protect them.

"I'll protect them, though, John. You can believe me. I won't let anyone near them but me. And you. Of course, you, too. I think he's got a plan for you, too. But I'll protect you. As long as you're here in Neverland, you'll never be out of sight of a Lost Boy. Promise.

"You'll never be anywhere I can't get to you in just a flash. If you need me. Just call. I promise, John, I'll never leave you alone. Even when you think you're so far away, I can get to you in a heartbeat. I run this Island and everything on it."

Pan looked into John's eyes intently. He smiled and John felt a small shiver creep down his spine. And just like that, John had every fear confirmed. He swallowed hard and nodded.

"Th-thanks, Peter. I feel better now." He turned around and went back to his siblings.

Pan smiled deeply as though he was enamored. His shoulders heaved. He strode past the solitary audience to his intimidating speech, his slave. She dangled in the air with less frivolity now. As he passed her he mumbled, "Nice try, bug. But afraid is the same as friend with that one, try anything like that "Voice in the back of the head" nonsense again and you'll watch us enjoy a Darling dinner."

"The boys on the island vary, of course, according as they get killed and so on; and when they seem to be growing up, which is against the rules, Peter thins them out."
-J. M. Barrie, *Peter and Wendy*

Sentencing John

For the next several days, Jonathan smiled and played and ran and chased and laughed on the outside. He was just like the rest of the group. He even managed to stop the nearly silent tears every night as moonlight sparkled on his wet cheeks during his dreams, which not only were of his own death, but also the death of an innocent man in a river.

But to Pan, John was becoming a liability. Michael complied with every suggestion without hesitation or question despite not changing into one of the Lost Boys. Wendy was deep within Peter's pocket. John, on the other hand, still did not fit in, had begun questioning things, and simply refused to accept the Lost Boy way of life, clinging steadfast to his humanity like a toddler to a security blanket. John needed to be dealt with before he could swing Michael away from Peter, or break Wendy free from her charm. Plus, he was distracting Peter from any work he might be doing against the Pirates.

He needed to seek out more information, and no more time could be dedicated to coddling the whimpering babe. But Peter couldn't simply destroy John without having devastating effects on his grip on Wendy; and Wendy could not be risked so late in the game.

A day had passed since the revelation Pan had shown to John, and Peter called to him from across the camp.

"Johnny Pirateslayer, come here!" The mood was light and airy. The moniker made John wince.

Fairies flitted about in the air around the camp. They chased and danced as always. Tinkerbell was among them, but hearing the tone of Pan's voice, she went into action. She would disappear with a few fairies at a time and then return alone. Pan's focused on higher fare today, and he didn't notice the Fairies slowly trickling away.

"Lost Boys! Michael and Wendy please come over. Johnny is the new boy here. I told you all how he saved us both when we were ambushed by some of those vicious pirates."

"They're the worst!" came a voice from the throng. Pan laughed.

"Who was that? Toodles? No? Agen, huh? Yeah, Agen. They're the worst. But as our new Neverland hero Johnny Pirateslayer is going to go on the hunt! Tonight!" He waited theatrically for the excitement to settle. Michael beamed at his hero. John had always been this way, but Mike was glad everyone else saw it now, too. Wendy looked more than a little worried, but tried to keep in the spirit of the event. John was mortified.

When the roar settled to a murmur, Pan erupted again, with a flourish, "Alone!" The Lost Boys exploded in cheers. John was led through the seemingly endless crowd of children, who stank of hate and evil, returning all of their smiles and good wishes in turn. A bow was thrust into his hand and arrows slung onto his back. Someone gave him a short iron blade. It was dinged and chipped and very out of balance.

The crowd opened up to Peter, who stood beaming, his own smile as wide as Mike's. His hands were on his hips and he was floating a couple of inches off the ground. He grabbed John by both shoulders and crowed, turned him toward a path and gave him a small shrug of encouragement.

John stumbled out of camp and down the path. The bow fumbled in his hands and the sling of arrows slid off his shoulders. The pathetic blade in his right hand got even more in the way.

He found a rock and sat down on it hard. He winced and shifted. Setting the bow down at his feet he tried to wriggle out of the tangle of the sling, but the blade kept getting in the way. Eventually, he paused, took a deep breath to calm his emotions, and let the air out slowly. Like his father had taught him, and for the first time since he'd been in Neverland, he took time to breathe in and out deliberately as he counted to ten. Thinking of his father made his chin sink into his chest and he began to sob deep, soul-bred and unstoppable tears. These were silent, but for their intensity, not for their crier's need for privacy.

He only let himself have this indulgence for a few minutes, fearing that whatever Peter had in mind for him wasn't going to wait too long to happen.

When he looked up, it was dark. The mocking moon was overhead and the stars shone extra brightly.

Have I slept?

> *Of course not.*
> *I couldn't have slept for*
> *hours here, like this.*

Okay, then.

Why is it the middle of the night?

Who knows?

Maybe Pan made it into night.

Yeah, that's probably it.
It's not likely that you dozed
from a week without sleep.
Not that you've been close
to falling over from stress
and exhaustion for days.
No.
Pan probably made it night.

Well, I have been pretty tired.

He looked around himself and once he got his bearings he
realized that he even knew where he was. Vaguely. These last several
days, first as an actual member of the group and then again as a
stranger among them, had afforded him the chance to get to know what
increasingly seemed likely to be his home for the rest of time.

He picked up the bow and arrows and positioned them properly
on himself. He retrieved the blade. Now, though, he looked at it with
disgust and contempt and tossed it aside, into the woods. The trail
ended slightly downward and in a gradual leftward arc. It ran roughly
parallel to the beach, although quite a distance from it.

As he came around a sharper bend in the curvy road, the path
lit up in front of him in an unearthly green light. Instinctively, John
looked up for the cause.

"Down here, John!" Tinkerbell called.

John started, recovered quickly, and squatted down to speak with the Fairie Princess. Under the low hanging forest brush were a couple dozen Fairies with their leader in front.

"John, he's sending one of them out here for you."

"I figured he'd kill me tonight. I'm sort of relieved, actually."

"What? You can't say that. You're the one to help us all get out of here."

"You want to leave here, too?"

"Of course, don't be dense. But to do that, the first step is to get you through tonight and then someplace where he can't find you."

"But no place like that exists."

"I know. He tells everyone that. It's amazing what people will believe when they say or hear it. But he doesn't know as much about everything as he'd have you believe."

A small spark of hope glowed in John. Suddenly there was a chance that he could survive.

A weak spot in his armor.

"So, what's happening to me tonight?"

"He's sent out a goblin to attack and torture you. They are almost silent when they want to be and Pan made it dark far earlier than normal tonight. It's not really night. He can't control the time here on Neverland. That's part of the rules. But he did send the sun away, so the beast is probably after you right now. Don't panic, though. Keep calm. We'll help you. We can start to get you to safety now. I've sent Goosedown ahead a little ways. She'll blink twice every minute or so, to show you the way. Be alert. We can't stay lit for too long, or he'll see us."

"You're leaving me?" John's calm started to give way to panic again in his voice and throat. He didn't want to be alone.

"Of course not dear," Tink offered soothingly, "Now come. Let's get you somewhere you can sleep in peace and without fear of anyone. One place like this exists. We can get you there tonight in the dark; but that's it. After that you have to remember for yourself how to get there."

They moved hesitatingly along the path toward the safe place, or "The Rock" as Tink called it. She explained things to Jonathan on the way.

"Many of the things I tell you will probably be forgotten before too long. That's how Neverland works. In fact, you may well forget our help here tonight."

"How can I? You're saving my life," John said, in earnest, "I can't ever forget that."

"That would be nice, Jonathan. Try to remember as much as you can. You do seem to be less affected than most, but Neverland is a powerful place."

The path they were heading down turned, but they continued heading straight and ventured deeper into the wilderness

"Okay, so what is this place?"

"It's first and most exactly what it calls itself. It is a never land. You never age here. You can never leave here. And if he doesn't want you to, you can never get back here. That's rare, however. He never lets you human folk leave once you've arrived.

"When the Earth was much younger than today, my folk lived in Pixie. It was a beautiful place. There were more animals on our peninsula than exist in the world today."

"Hold on a minute. Pixie was a real place, like, on Earth?"

"Pixie was real, yes. In the time of the magicks, Fairae was a powerful kingdom. Fauns and nymphs, naiads and elves and dwarfs all lived under the kind hand of the Pixie King. But others lived with us, as well. Darker ones. Poachers and killers. Ogres and trolls and goblins."

"Lost Boys?"

"Indeed. The Lost Boys are goblins, except for you and Michael. He changes children to serve his purpose when he brings them here. He changes the girls into trees, and each boy is assigned to one of them. Over time, after sapping almost all of the life's energy from the trees the boys change into goblins that replenish Pan's army."

"Wendy!" John panicked, his mind fluttering. He spun, as if to go back to camp, but realized quickly that he had no idea where he was. The woods had swallowed him and in the dark every direction looked the same. "What happens to the trees after they – Was my tree once a – Was I killing her? Is that what the sap–"

"Don't worry, I don't think he plans to change Wendy. He's treating her differently. He won't hurt her. Come along, we have a bit more walking to do."

John and the group of Faeries pushed onward through the thick underbrush.

"Why goblins? Why not something worse, like ogres or trolls or something? Why not something bigger?"

"In our land, the only real enemies we had were goblins. Ogres were mean, but stupid and easily tricked. Trolls were a greedy and jealous lot. They would stake claim on a meager pile of land and never leave it. They were only trouble if you couldn't pay their fee when you stumbled into their land. But they were myopic and slow. An occasional lesser animal got careless and became lunch, but even after that loss, we'd be blessed, as the troll would then lie still for a while.

"But the goblins. The goblins were truly the worst lot. They were smart - smarter, in any case - and vicious. They stole what they hadn't reaped or hunted. They ate what they hadn't prepared. And they killed, whenever they felt the urge, whatever they didn't like, which was everything."

"That does sound like the Lost Boys."

"We would skirmish with them. Mostly when something of great import was to occur. We'd condition them for a week or two. Prepare them by engaging them in an off site spot, well away from the coming event. They never learned. Smarter than ogres, but not very.

"On one of the many diversions, I led a band of one hundred Fairies out to the Great Marsh. We'd tacked and swung around to allow them to be between us and Fairie's main house and its catapults. There was a risk there, but less than you may imagine. We were a distance from the house and they were stupid enough. They always assume we'd get directly between them and our home so as to protect it, so they often forgot to check their backs. It was a tactic we used from time to time and it never failed. As we set up one particular fight, a dense red and black fog surrounded both groups."

"You and the ogres."

"The goblins," Tink corrected. "Ourselves and the goblins."

"Sorry."

"Not at all. It was so murky that there should have been no fight, but there was regardless. It was clumsy and brutal. If a target was spotted they would be mercilessly attacked because you never could tell where the next brute was. When the fog cleared, we found ourselves in this place. Never to age as we should, and never to leave. We were in our Neverland.

"We Fairies were doubly cursed, however. After Pan recruited and pressed the goblins into his service, I saw no way out of our predicament. We'd be more or less free here, but unable to leave. We all had families in Pixie and were eager to see them again. So I led an attack. We staged an incursion to capture Pan and force him to release us. We are tiny, but filled with powerful magic. Clearly, we failed. Most of us who didn't perish were captured. Around eighty of us in all. When he learned who was responsible, he made me his personal slave, his toy."

"What is Peter Pan, then? He's not a Goblin, and he's not a Faerie."

"He was first a bird, as all humans once were." John's face showed his confusion, but Tinkerbell pushed on. "Then he was a human, but not completely. Then he was abandoned by his mother and became an orphan. He flew off to find another family to love him. What he found must have been much worse than any bird or human. A family that taught him grown up tricks like magic, cruelty, and pain. And he uses all of the tricks they taught him whenever he can.

"But, he reached too far; got too ambitious and is now trapped here forever. Neverland is a playground-prison for him. And I have been here with him since his sentence began."

"How can you be here right now helping me then? That must have been ages ago."

"It's true, we all live within time, even Pan. But from Neverland we can go to anyplace in any time. That's how you are here now with sailors from a few hundred years before your time. Although you are mistaken about time, you are correct about how long we have been here. And while we've been here, not one of us has died of old age. It has forced us to be careful and observant, and patient. After 10,000 years he has become arrogant, and that is making him sloppy."

"You've been here for 10,000 years?"

John was so immersed in the story that Hollyhock, one of the Fairies traveling in the group, pulled on John's sleeve to direct him out of the way of a low hanging branch.

"As more punishment, he took away our ability to forget. I remember every single day, every single torture, death, and revival at his hands, but most importantly I remember every mistake he's made."

They came to a fork, one road clearly disused. It was almost over grown with ferns and weeds.

"Now Jonathan, listen. The Rock only protects you if you leave something of yourself there, a memory or emotion. You can't disguise yourself there. The Island changes with each life that touches it. Pan has incredible control over it because he is just so much more powerful that it reacts stronger for him, but all of us have our own small influence. So many children have come here, many who have felt the way you do. I send the brave ones who try to escape to the same spot on purpose. After so long with all of them wanting a hiding spot the Island has acquiesced. It's how you can escape his notice, Jonathan. It has become a blind spot for him. Remember, leave a part of yourself there."

A flash of matted fur and another with sharpened claws flew from the woods at the front of the split in the road. The goblin tackled and rolled over John. John could barely see it raise a gnarled hand to slice his belly in the darkness. But just before it tore into him the goblin was attacked by a score of angry lights. Foul tempered flashbulbs from very belligerent cameras blinded it.

The goblin swiped with closed eyes at the swarm. John wasn't able to witness any of this at all only because when he'd seen the claw rise, he'd closed his eyes. But even through his eyelids the light had been strong enough to shrink his pupils some. Now with eyes open he saw the luminated battle.

"Stand aside, Jonathan. We'll handle this," Tinkerbell was downright ecstatic.

John pushed back with his hands and legs, scooting himself backwards. When he put enough distance between him and his attacker he asked, "Shouldn't I help?"

Tink turned to him and he saw a look of bloodlust on her beautiful face.

"Oh, no, boy! He's ours now!"

The flashes of light disappeared one at a time, into the beast. Through its skin John could see them squirming in it's flesh, occasionally coming close enough to the surface to cast a horrific glow from inside. It clawed at its own skin in an attempt to ease the pain beneath. As it tried to howl, the scream caught in its throat. With a spurt of green blood, ten Fairies launched from its mouth with the contents of its throat. It looked at John with a real panic in its eyes. Somehow, impossibly, John felt a twinge of sympathy for it. The pain it felt was clear and yet unimaginable to him. Very, very slowly it seemed to implode before him. It kept its mass, but it seemed to lose all of its structure. Only its filthy skull remained intact, sans eyes and nose, however.

Almost as quickly as it began, it was over and there were Fairies sat joyously cleaning each other of its gore.

"How many dead," Tinkerbell called out, with a voice very much like a military leader.

"Five. Hollyhock, Junebug, Sprytak, Babysbreath and… Tinkerbell…"

"What is it?"

"Sleighbell. We lost your brother."

She seemed to fold in on herself for a moment.

"No we didn't. Use Junebug for dust and you four gather the other bodies. The rest of you! To the boy!"

"But, Tinkerbell, he's finally at rest. You know our rules about–"

"I know the rules! But the end is closer than we think and we have our role to play. We can't afford five losses. Not now. Get John!"

Caught completely on his heels, Jonathan found himself under sudden attack. He tried to back up, but managed to succeed only in tangling himself up in his feet and falling on his back.

The Fairies crawled all over him. His skin buzzed at first and he feared he was about to find out what the goblin experienced first hand.

But it never came. All he felt was a slight, then rapidly expanding tickling. He burst out laughing. It was uncomfortable. The lights climbing all over him flared until he was covered with daylight.

A few injured Fairies went from dim to nova instantly. And the four tiny, dead winged, people leapt from their resting spots glowing with life.

Not that John saw any of this. Not with his eyes nailed shut in laughter, and desperately trying to hold back his tears.

As the pleasure-pain of the tickling subsided, and John sat up, hands bracing himself up from behind, he saw the whole troupe of his saviors perched on him. One or two relaxed in the creases of his pajama legs here and there; and a few on each knee. Their smiles were as big as his.

"Whew. Well my lad. It's time for you to go. Remember how to get there. And promise me you'll try to remember the feeling that's in your heart right now every time you think of us."

"I'll never forget. I promise."

John reluctantly rose, dusting himself off.

"Oh! Johnny, I nearly forgot! One last thing before I leave you... or before you leave us, anyway."

Tinkerbell deftly swept herself up along John's neck, tickling him as she went. In one motion she twisted her body through his hair while grabbing small locks. She pulled away all at once. The sting was unexpected and he nearly swatted Tinkerbell like a mosquito. Her quick reflexes saved her as she dodged his attack.

"I'm sorry, John. I need to take some of you."

"Why? That hurt!"

"Oh, dear one. What you've been through..." Jonathan could hear the sarcasm in her voice. "If Pan is going to believe me long enough for you to effectively escape his notice, I need to convince him that you've been actually killed; that our poor friend at your feet was successful in his attack. Here, spit on the ground."

John did as he was ordered. He watched Tink swirl some dirt in his spit and then she worked in the hair she had stolen. In front of his eyes the tufts of hair grew and morphed into the greater part of a skull. His skull. He recognized his head, or what was left of it. It was a gruesome sight. There was every reason to think this terrible artifact in Tink's hand was, in fact, once part of his head.

"Now I'll take this to 'the boss' and we'll see exactly how convincing my skills actually are." She danced over to John and lightly kissed him on the cheek.

"You're very brave, my dear one. Very brave. Never forget that."

He gently stepped over the puddle of goblin and made his way up the disused path. He looked back once or twice and waved.

Tinkerbell smiled when he looked, even knowing he couldn't see their faces from that distance.

But she was sad, even forlorn. She knew deep inside that this Island and that demon would make an enemy out of this friend before long.

"Shall I after him, Captain," asked pathetic Smee, "and tickle him with Johnny Corkscrew?" Smee had pleasant names for everything and his cutlass was Johnny Corkscrew, because he wriggled it in the wound. One could mention many lovable traits in Smee. For instance, after a kill it was his spectacles he wiped instead of his weapon."
-J.M. Barrie, *Peter and Wendy*

Pan Meets Smee

The clang of the ship's bell vibrated over the Jolly Roger, summoning all who were able to congregate on the deck. Smythe pushed his way toward the front of the group as several were trying to push back as far away from the Captain's Quarters as possible. Hook stood smiling, adopting his newly derived pose of dabbing off the weeping stump of his arm on his coat. The red around his front pocket was now stained a dappled dark brown.

"I'll make this short so we can get out of this blasted heat. Four of you need to go ashore to get water and food. As you know, our last pair that went out for water has never returned. I will send four of you now for safety and I want the volunteers to step forward now."

Not one boot twitched. Every pair of eyes shifted from their captain to anything around them that may have ever been interesting.

"Now, now, someone needs to come forward or I might have to get cranky. You don't want me to get cranky, do you?" Hook asked as he drew his pistol from his belt.

"On three. One," He pointed the gun at the crowd in front of him. "Two," the gun began to casually pass from one side of the crowd to the other.

"I'll go," said Smythe, stepping forward.

"Good! You see? There's one. Anyone else? I only need three," the gun fired a bullet straight into the crowd, striking the foul Gentleman Starkey in the chest. "more volunteers," Hook finished while the echo from the pistol rang out over the water.

Starkey's body hit the floor and three other sailors came forward: The Handsome Cecco, Morgan Skylights, and Noodler, whose hands were fixed on backward.

"Excellent. Get back before sundown with as much water as your boats will haul and enough game to feed us for the week. Take two boats, fill them to the brim or don't return."

The meeting was over as quickly as it had started. The body of The Gentleman Starkey passed Smythe as his boat was lowered into the water below. Its splash sprayed water all the way up to Smythe and got onto his face. The crew above rolled with laughter and shouted out jeers and taunts to Smythe on his descent.

"Even in death he smites us!" they shouted. "You gonna take that from a corpse, Smythe, you yellow son of a gun?" An overwhelming part of Smythe wished, in that moment, that Peter had not chosen him. Ignorance was bliss, and right now Smythe would have given anything to have either.

Once on the Island, Smythe knew he was being watched. It was a foolish thought, but he wanted to stay with the sailors as long as possible because he hoped it would help them to stay alive. If he could inform on them and keep them safe at the same time he would try.

Eventually, though, after filling six casks of water and loading them onto the boats, Smythe knew that he must leave his comrades.

"I've gotta go fill the bog, mate," he called to Noodler.

"Don't be too long, the others should be back soon with the meat. Watch out for the poison oak."

Smythe ventured off alone, sure that it wouldn't be long until Pan found him, and he was right.

"Well, well, well. If it isn't my loyal subject."

"Hello, Sir," Smythe replied, bowing low, "how can I be of service?"

"Nothing too harmful, I expect. Tell me about Captain Hook," Peter demanded, circling his kneeling spy.

"What kind of information do you want, Sir?"

Pan smiled, "All of it. This is what makes the game fun. The more I know the more tailored I can build my attack. What kind of man is he?"

"He is a good man, when he's not burdened by this place. He seems to be slipping further and further away from his original self, though. Shot a man today for no reason."

"Did he? Friend of yours?"

Smythe knew his place in this relationship. He knew what he was, a low-down, miserable turncoat. But he still had his pride and whatever honor he still held on to would not be mocked.

"At one point, yes, you arrogant little dog. He was a friend of mine."

"Aw," Peter teased, "I'm sorry that happened to you. That must be very sad for you. Tell me, does Hook have any friends on board the ship any longer, or has he killed them all by now?"

Smythe weighed his options. Either he would have to tell Pan about Smee and Cooper's relationship, or he would try to lie about it, which was something Smythe was never very good at. He never had to cultivate the talent. He was never someone with a secret that needed hiding. Born on a ship, raised on a ship, lived on a ship, that was Smythe's life, and aboard a ship no one had any secrets to lie about.

"No. He's ruined all past relationships," said Smythe's mouth, but his eyes and face told another story.

"Now, Smythe," Pan said, stalking. "This only works if you hold up your end of the bargain. You're hardly worth anything to me if you go on lying like this," he warned, letting his façade slip enough to frighten the truth out of Smythe, but he held fast to his friendship with Smee and held his tongue.

"Fine, have it your way. I'll just get one of those others here on the Island to tell me," and he drew his sword quickly and kicked the kneeling Smythe onto his hands and knees. Fearing death and unable to think any clearer Smythe blurted out the truth.

"Smee!" he yelled. "Smee is the Captain's one strong relation on the ship. He's Hook's nephew. Somehow Hook still remembers, and despite the occasional short fuse between them they still support one another."

"This Smee, you will bring him here."

"What will you do to him?"

"That is none of your business. You will bring him here and what happens after that will be between him and me."

"Don't kill him. Please, I beg you, don't kill him!"

"Now this is interesting. You don't have a soft spot for Smee, too, do you?" Pan smiled, enjoying this new revelation. Smythe said nothing, but Peter saw the tear that fell from Smythe to the dirt below his face.

"Bring Smee here. You don't think that being a Pirate is the worst thing I can do to you, do you? Bring Smee or you will find out the worst I can do," he lifted Smythe's face to look into his own, showing Smythe his glowing ember eyes and sharp baby teeth. "Understand?"

"Yes, Sir," Smythe managed to utter when he finally caught his breath.

"Good. Now get off my Island before I reconsider allowing you to take that food and water."

Smythe scrambled to his feet and ran back to the stream where he rejoined the Handsome Cecco, Morgan Skylights and Noodler. He was just in time to help load in the last lion carcass and row back to The Jolly Roger.

...

Aboard the ship, Smythe attacked the situation like removing a bandage. He sought out Smee quickly and set to work getting him to Neverland.

"I just think we ought to go now, 's'all, laddie." The sheepish manner that Smythe had adopted confused and frustrated Hook's nephew. He tried to focus on the situation at hand, but as was customary for Smee, another thought pushed its way into his mind.

Message, he thought. Then, *No! It's not your turn, yet. I'm thinkin' of somethin'!* But by now his original thought had vanished, pushed to the back of the line by that rude, interrupting "message" thought. Smee looked around, trying to find his way back to the original thought. It was Smythe's face that reeled Smee back around to the correct path.

"Why're you actin' like that? What's a'matter with you'?" Smee asked his friend.

"How do you mean?"

"Yer fidgety and I don't like it. Not a bit."

It was unusual for Smee to be so assertive; almost aggressive; unusual, but not unheard of. On bad days Smee's thoughts would wrestle one another in a huge battle royal. One could find Smee in those moments in a terrible mood, throwing tantrums and flailing, making no sense as he spoke. It was everything Smee could do not to leave Smythe where he stood in exchange for a good, cleansing running and yelling episode, which usually left Smee too exhausted to think about much of anything.

When he did adopt a more direct attitude, more in keeping with the Cooper name, the sailors knew they'd better watch themselves. No one wanted Smee to blow up at him. It was always an awkward experience, as he could neither fight back completely, nor convince Smee that he was in the wrong. Smythe had to tread that ground very carefully. The guilt swelled inside his heart.

Get to the Island, Smee could not help thinking

"You'd said you needed to go back. Right…"

Find the boy.

"… Smee?"

Message.

"Quiet, Smythe. I'm thinkin'."

What was it I needed to do?

Was it Jimmy told me to?

No.

"'M juss sayin-"

"Shuddup! It's hard enough me thinkin' without you interruptin' me."

...

                                               Dear one...

It was mommy told me to.

Peace crept in.

                              You have a message to deliver, Sweet.

"Well, let's go then," Smee resolved. His conflict had ceased, and just as quickly as the answer came to him, his mood relaxed as well.

...

Smythe enlisted his trusted friend O'Neill to help he and Smee silently load a boat. They didn't need much. Moonlight glanced off of the hammer of a pistol as Smythe tried to hand it to Smee. Smee refused it, but did accept the sword and dagger offered by O'Neill.

Smee's brain hurt. The entire day had been filled with one thought after another without any clarity or resolution from any of them. He had been spinning in one place for days. But aside from his headache he felt a deep-rooted excitement as well. Maybe it was just the change of scenery that made him feel better, but he felt he was finally going to solve some problem.

His body remembered. It could recall the symmetry it once achieved the last time he stepped foot on the Island. It ached to return, and the impending freedom weighed down on him, causing more trembling and distraction than normal. Smee was jumbled, but could not recall the last time he had smiled so wide.

He held out hope that his confusion was not permanent. It was relentless on the ship, though, and he could not remember if it had always been that way, or if that had only started when they'd arrived there in Hell. He thought he could remember a moment when he was whole, but the details were foggy. What he did know was that he hated, with passion, every moment that he was not in control of himself.

The boat slid ashore with a soft landing and Smee smiled at his fellows. It was gone. There were no more broken bridges, and his thought waited patiently in a line, one after another without pushing or fighting. O'Neil managed to break thought the nerves and fear that showed on his face just long enough to return the heartfelt smile to Smee. But Smee's smile failed him when he saw Smythe's face. Where nerves and fear blanketed O'Neill, only guilt and torment was found on Smythe. Smee's newly borrowed clarity revealed the truth.

"What do you think you've done, Jacob?"

There was a new authority in Smee's voice then.

"Sir?"

"Jacob, look at me. Look. Good. You're washed in guilt, man?"

"I… mm… I don't know what you mean, Smee."

Smee paused. There was no one around, he could feel it, so as subtly as he could manage, he sent O'Neill out to secure a tight perimeter so he could face Smythe alone.

"You're an awful liar. Always have been Jacob Smythe. Even I know that. What happened? Come now, be honest and lay down your guilty heart."

There was nothing else for Smythe to do but confess, and Smee deserved to know the truth. They were friends, and Smythe had betrayed him. "I'm supposed to deliver you here. To him," he said with a single tear, the weight of his sin crushing down on him.

Smee raised an eyebrow. "Is that all? Relax, sailor. You did well. I needed to speak with our host anyway. You've done nothing more or less than exactly what you were supposed to. Had you not lured me away I may have completely forgotten my task, or snuck here on my own. Fate saw to it that you guide me back here. At least now I know I have a friend nearby."

That only made it worse. Thoughts of Brutus and Judas danced in Smythe's brain. He knew no solace could be had from, "I was only doing my job."

"Besides, Smitty," the impish grin they all loved flashed again, "when we get back, I won't remember anyway."

A short way down the shore Smee found a narrow path inland. It partially cut through a mild natural beam, which served him well. Cover was essential for as long as he could afford it, and so he laid on his belly and crawled up a hill, using the tall grass to hide himself. He easily maneuvered over the rise, so close to the ground that he could smell the soft pleasantness, the rich loamy earth. But like everything in this place, the beauty of nature was infected and corrupted by the Pan's evilness. It had an odor that was tangible. It clung in the nose and throat, oily like the smoke from a grease fire. It hung in his lungs. Smee knew that he would never get rid of the stench, no matter how this ended.

He rose to his knees, distancing himself slightly from the worst of it, and then to bent leg, he crept along the inside edge of the trail, using the greenery as cover while it lasted. The saber hung loosely and agilely in his right hand, but his tension revealed itself with how tightly he clenched to the dagger in his left. His forearm flexed instinctively, shifting the pressure he put on the handle up and down its length. He trod lightly on the worn path, barely making a sound. Unnaturals would even have had a hard time knowing he was there.

The first Goblin Smee encountered didn't even twitch at Smee's arrival. The Lost Boy crouched on his haunches, his back to Smee, carelessly playing with some unfortunate bit of prey, unaware of the impending stroke of irony. Smee's dagger found its way around the neck and snuggled up nicely to the filthy throat. His saber found even more purchase, sinking easily three inches into a soft side.

"Crow for your master, Boy," Smee growled softly. He scared himself a little bit, never having heard this kind of ferocity from himself before. "I need to speak with him."

"He's not my-" was all that escaped the goblin before the dagger drew a small trickle of green blood and the saber slid a little more. Fear and hatred mixed in equal measure in the miasma around them. "Alright." He cawed tentatively at first, but Smee encouraged him to give subsequent efforts more vigor.

"What's you name, child?" asked Smee, with his newfound menacing voice.

"Boy? Child? Don't you know who you're dealing with, Pirate? Thatle's my name, and Thatle's the name that dines on your bones before the sun rises again."

"I know what you are, foulness. I'm simply playing the same game you do. You pretend to be a boy, and so I will be as afraid of you as I am a toddler. And you'll have no meal tonight, my lad." With that, the dagger finished the job it had started as enthusiastically as the saber.

This foray onto the Island, let alone by himself, seemed to bring about a change in Smee. It was only on this Island at this time that Smee finally understood his nature, his place in the world and in this drama. He felt new and important.

As he marinated in this new clarity, he heard Pan swoop in, full of sound and fury, trailing three of his soldiers behind. They crashed a mighty roar through the woods.

As the first one crested the hill Smee had just descended, Smee flung his dagger to meet him. It hit the Lost Boy unceremoniously, in his left eye, to the hilt. He fell before Smee's arm was through the sweep of the throw. The body served as impediment enough to cause the next goblin to stumble and that led, in turn, to the hold-up of the last.

As Smee recovered from his strong throw, the second beast righted himself, arms out, only to lose his equilibrium along with his right arm at the elbow. Smee had flashed his saber, and took off the Goblin's arm easily, silver and green reflecting in what little moonlight there was.

Pan looked on, infinitely amused.

Doubtless to his relief, the goblin didn't feel the pain of the lost limb for long, as his head land neatly next to the arm and the jade pool, newly formed, at his feet.

Pan's little smile fell just slightly, along with the head of his crony.

The last of the Lost Boys could proudly lay claim on the fact that he actually placed a claw on Smee, but not for long. The hand was calmly and efficiently removed at the wrist in the same swooping motion that buried the saber in the clavicle. As the Goblin glanced to his new wound, Smee bent down and wrenched his dagger out of the first Goblin's eye and drove it home up through the last Lost Boy's jaw and into its brain.

Pan's smile now played lightly in the wispy clouds, miles from his face.

Smee looked down at the carnage, more in disgust than pride, until he found a shred of cloth to clean his hands and glasses. A splatter of green mist remained diagonal on his face. Disgust morphed to amusement and then to glee as his gaze rose to meet Pan's eyes. Pan seemed less angry than Smee expected him to be. He looked more annoyed than anything.

"Send more, djinn. I like the practice."

"What do you want, half-wit?" Pan spat.

"Come down and we'll talk about that."

"Have a care, mortal. I'm not so easily dispatched as the fodder at your feet."

"I have no wish to kill you, demon. And we both know I don't have the means. But I do have a message. Just for you, and that's the only reason I'm here. But I do truly thank you for the gifts."

As Pan lightly floated down on the thermals and then on the lower breezes, he seemed to regain his confidence. He lit on a narrow branch, folding his arms in a futile attempt to retain his "carefree child" characteristics.

"The message then."

"My mother and I spoke before we ever left the port in Barbados. I told her that I didn't want to come here, that I didn't want to have to face you alone if we found ourselves here, but we both knew I'd have to. She wanted me to tell you first that although you don't know her now, you soon will. And then she said I was to warn you that it would be your hubris that killed you. She told me that warning you was pointless, but she rather insisted I do it anyway. Thirdly, I am to tell you that you will receive a 'special gift' for harming the Darling girl."

Pan swallowed hard now. His affectation vanished for good now.

"Hmmm… interesting. Anything else I'm to know, simpleton?"

"Yes, dear Pan, one last thing. Mother says that the last thing you'll ever know in the depths of what you call your heart is the terror of dying beneath her feet."

And then, while Pan seethed and flared his fiery eyes, Smee turned on his heels and strode away confidently. Back to the life of a mascot; of a half-brained fool.

It never even occurred to Pan to strike him down.

…

- 209 -

John could barely make out his arms in front of him as he trudged through the forest. The canopy above him blocked out all of the moonlight and so he was forced to creep slowly for the last hour in these conditions. His only relief from the blackness was the occasional blink of light from the Fairie ahead of him, guiding him to a secret safe place hidden from Peter's gaze.

In the darkness, John focused his attention on what he smelled and heard. The rich smell of the rotting forest floor invaded his nose. He noticed how loud his own breath sounded in the air around him and made an effort to quieting down. Then he noticed his footfalls on the thick forest carpet beneath him and before long he had figured out how to place his feet down with near silence.

Halfway through his journey, John became a silent and invisible intruder passing through without leaving a hint of himself behind. His breathing slowed, his steps were deliberate, and a new awareness awakened inside him. The earth beneath him seemed familiar. He could sense where his footfalls should land to keep his feet safe. The ground had become an extension of his body.

John was soon reminded of an old blessing he had read somewhere and one part of it bounced around in his head.

> On the day when the weight
> deadens on your shoulders
> and you stumble
> May the clay dance to balance you...
> May the nourishment of the Earth be yours...

The thought repeated over and over and he soon felt the downward slope of the forest. He saw a quick succession of three blinks ahead and then the world was back to black. A few steps further revealed slivers of moonlight up ahead and finally he emerged from the darkness in view of a steep slope of rock jutting up higher than the woods through which he had just passed.

There was no path up the slope, but John could see as plain as day the easiest route to the top. On his way up the massive rock, John noticed there was no hillside in the forest he had just come through and he wondered exactly how shallow that final downward slope had been, if it was there at all.

Atop the rock John found he could see almost the entirety of Neverland. He saw the rock monolith where…

…where what?

Something happened to
Wendy near there.

What happened to her, though?

Something awful.

He could almost make out the lagoon where he and Michael played with the Mermaids. He could see the Jolly Roger rotting out in the water. As John slowly turned to take it all in, he noticed more island he had not been to yet, and he saw snow nearby. It encompassed a small corner of the Island and John thought he could see great wandering things in the moonlight that may have been polar bears.

A small lean-to had been crudely built on the corner of the rock. There was a cot under a small tilted roof of bark and branches. Beside the lean-to stood a small barrel. John pried the lid off and found a stew of trinkets and treasures within. There was a whittling knife, a baseball cap, and identity bracelet belonging to Anthony Paul, a long white feather, a few smooth stones, a bag of marbles and many more trinkets and treasures.

The moon was waning when John noticed the first hints of sunrise giving everything around him a tint of blue. Exhaustion overcame him as he realized he was safe. The whole night had been spent maneuvering through the dark and his mind and body ached. John rolled onto the cot and buried himself in sleep.

"Instant obedience was the only safe thing. Slightly got a dozen for looking perplexed when told to take soundings."
-J. M. Barrie, *Peter and Wendy*

Pan Quells Rebellion.

Lulls bring boredom, even with unnaturals. Longs lulls can only be worse. Pan had kept his Lost Boys at bay, resisting the urge, the need to unleash his horde on his prized nemesis, the captain. This was no more an accident than it was a courtesy. It was a single example of the multitudes of strategic forethought on Pan's part. Starve a dog long enough and it will kill anything you want it to. But you can't starve it too much, or it will quit or die. Through thousands of years of honing this art, Pan had the skill down fairly well. Usually. He also did not want to go charging into a trap. That simpleton may have been some kind of bait. Pan was impulsive, spontaneous, and carefree, except when he smelled a possible trap. Then he was his own opposite.

Some of the goblins hunted lesser beasts for sport or food. Some fought each other, from restlessness or from a slight, real or perceived. Some eyed the rotting vessel anchored out in the bay, just waiting for the word to attack.

But a few of them, just a few, whispered words of treachery. Of mutiny and rebellion. They weren't slaves to this monster, after all. Thus, when sunset brought inevitable respite for those pirates every night, it only managed to stoke even more rage and disgust in the ranks of Pan's army. Howls of frustration over lost opportunities grew more frequent.

On one of these nights, under the watchful eye of the paper moon hanging low in the night sky, as yet another chance to tear and bite and kill and eat and revel slipped away, the threat of the tension breaking was more real than ever. In the flickering green-blue light of the fire burning the bones of years of prey, moments stretched and bent and twisted. Edges began to fray. Ends snapped and senses heightened. Any newness was good after so much of the same. Usually.

But the recent newness, the visit from that one pirate, bravely coming to shore and leaving again unharmed was too much to bear. He single-handedly slaughtered several of the scare. That, however, wasn't the problem. Those slugs were too slow and deserved what they had coming to them. The outrage was that he spoke to Pan about something that wasn't shared with the rest of them, and *then* the trespasser turned his back on their leader and was allowed to walk away *untouched*.

Atlan was the most vocal about rebellion. He had three of his most trusted allies take Pan out hunting so that he might speak more freely to the remaining members of the scare. The boy Michael had accompanied the hunting party. He was to kill a menagerie of beasts as a formal way to join the Lost Boys for good: a kind of test. He still had not changed, but it was clear that no one had ever adapted to their way of life better. The girl was preparing for sleep, and John was still missing, so no one could rat them out before plans were in motion and the Lost Boys were unified.

...

Michael pushed a large frond out of his field of vision. A tiger was laying flat in the tall grass, its tail flicking from left to right. It was examining every twitch and breath in Michael's body. Michael knew that he shouldn't be here. There was no way for him to be able to avoid this fight. The trees couldn't protect him, and he couldn't get far enough away to be safe.

He felt the comforting weight of his sword and knew that Peter Pan and three of the Lost Boys were with him. This was his fight, though. This was his chance to join the tribe for good. It would be his first big game killing. He locked eyes with the tiger, and in those eyes he saw how fiercely and quickly it could tear him apart. Fear tried to give way to clarity, because he knew that none of the other Lost Boys were ever afraid when they hunted. But Michael's six-year-old mind raced and panicked, hunting for a way out. That gold and black cut right through him and made his hands shake.

Just when Michael began feeling the tears in his eyes and a lump in his throat the tiger's eyes darted off to the right and a second later it lunged at another target.

"You should be more careful, traitor!" Peter shouted as he pushed Agen out into the open grass and ferocious jaws of the great tiger. Michael watched in horror at the body that wasn't his being torn to pieces. His friends Traw and Bolgra soon joined Agen's shouts of surprise and pain. Traw had his arm taken off by a quick flash of Peter's golden sword, and while he contemplated the loss Bolgra's stomach split and its contents disappeared in the fern patch below.

Traw did his best to escape, but the tiger was attracted by his clumsy movements and finished him off with little effort. Michael shook with fear, assuming he would be the next to fall under Peter's wrath. He got down as small as he could, trying to hide in the tall ferns. He saw Peter walk out into the grass and stare down the great tiger. Michael thought he could hear Peter say something, but the words dispersed before he could make them out. The tiger growled and backed away one step at a time, not letting its guard down before it was far enough away to turn and run.

Then Peter turned to Michael, sheathing his sword he said, "It's okay, Michael. You can come out. It's all over."

Michael waited in the fronds in case it was a trick. He had played many games of hide-and-seek, and that was a classic maneuver to coax someone out of their hiding spot. But when he noticed Peter inspecting the recently deceased and not looking for him he crept out slowly, always ready to run.

"Peter?" he asked, quivering, "What happened?"

"It's okay, Michael. I'm not going to hurt you, buddy. These three were trying to trick me. But I found out about it and got the jump on them. You're not trying to trick me, are you Michael?"

"No! Trick you how?"

"Well good. Then you have nothing to worry about. Come on. This hunting trip was part of the trick. I need to get back to the camp before it gets worse. Alright?"

"Okay, Peter."

...

"Lost Boys… to the fire!" the shout was unmistakable. Pan's call was unique unto itself already. An angry Pan wielded his voice like a scythe.

The camp sprang to life in an instant. An angry boss might very well mean an attack on the Jolly Roger was nigh. He never needed a pretext to fight, but his minions knew that from time to time he liked to invent some offense to further angry up his blood.

Another possibility, of course, was that this ire was inward turned. Rarely did a goblin misstep on this Island anymore. Too many had paid with their stinking, squalid lives for the rest to not have learned some lesson. Usually.

Once gathered, they sat in silence, the sapphire and jade light dancing on the dirt, the teeth, the scars, and the matted hair.

A comet of red streaked into their midst and exploded on impact, revealing Pan standing in its small crater. Danger certainly lay ahead now. Pan only used the dramatic entrances when he was flexing. There might well be one fewer in their numbers before sunrise.

"I want names," Pan roared, "of all of all of the betrayers! Give them up or green blood runs. You'll feed on goblin flesh tonight, I promise."

This vow was not as pleasant as it may seem. It was true that goblins loved a good meal made of their fellows, but only one fairly won. When forced past their lips, the beasts found the meal foul and ashen. Taking food is one thing; cannibalism has its own rules.

"Hold your tongue, Puck." It was Atlan who spoke now, spitting out Pan's most hated nickname, no fear to be found in his voice. "Remember that we are here by choice, sprite. Your power, what power you have, is wrought with our claws, won with our blood, cut from the Pirates, the Cowboys, the Indians, and the Fairies with our blades. You would be well served to act less the king. You lead by our leave."

"And you, my dear agitator, would be well-served to count your strength before you play your hand," Pan purred. The purr was never a good sign for whomever it was meant.

"We know what you are. We aren't frightened by you, nymph," said the still fearless creature, taunting.

" 'We'… 'We'… Observe your precious 'we,' Atlan, and understand that I know your worth," Pan said slowly. He slung a bag filled with the heads of Atlan's conspirators in a lazy arc over the heads of the assembly, landing neatly at his feet. Agen's head rolled out of the bag and stopped at Atlan's feet. But Atlan wasn't one to be unnerved. Usually.

"Hm. Yes. Well, you are still outnumbered here, Pan," Atlan sputtered, less powerful than before. "And we are still not your slaves."

"Indeed, Atlan, indeed. It's true that you aren't slaves. Any of you," he offered, turning to his audience theatrically. "It's true that you can leave at any time you wish."

He continued, "Who here would join brave *young* Atlan on his bold new adventure?" Not one head moved. Not one gnarled finger twitched.

"Lovely Atlan. I believe we have just seen your numbers. But go as you would. We have no quarrel, you and I."

"I will go," Atlan answered, not at all confident now, but trying not to be cowed either. "I'll handle the morsels on that wreck myself."

"The pirates?" Pan asked, trying but utterly failing to either feign surprise or contain his glee. He looked toward the ship in the distance and closed his eyes, drawing slow breaths. "No. I'm afraid I can't let you do that. You see there is a plan in motion. My plan. An attack on the Pirates would incite a quarrel between us. Understand?"

Pan turned back to face Atlan, but now his eyes were glowing coals set in his twisted, cracked face. Without warning, tears of green blood stained Atlan's cheeks. His life sweated from his pores, too. Soon his greasy hair burst into flames, his twisted legs gave way. His distant stare spoke, as his dead lips couldn't.

The hotter the fire, the faster the fuel is consumed, and burning his fire that hot took its toll on Peter Pan. No goblins saw the effort it took for Pan to cast his spell, nor how destroyed it left him. Neither would any of them know how safe they were at that very moment. How easy it would have been to follow through with Atlan's threats. How close Pan had come to mortality.

He staggered a turn now, taking advantage of his still awestruck soldiers reeling and staring at their fallen brother.

"Tink, I need you," he whispered.

Shortly his faithful Fairie arrived at his side, successful in her attempt to hide her hatred of him.

"Enjoy your dinner, fellows," Pan called back over his shoulder.

He knew Atlan was right, they were not his slaves. Further, he knew the rest of the goblins were too stupid to figure that out.

Using that much magic could be dangerous for Peter and rest was vital. Already Peter's body was screaming in protest to each footfall. His eyeballs seared in his head, demanding that he close his lids immediately. He hobbled over the threshold of the burned out tree.

Tink could feel the intense heat of the demon wash over her. He stank of sulfur and desperation.

He collapsed onto the leafy bed in the corner, eyes closed, clamped rather. The leaves curled and browned beneath him. Tink's contempt for him, interplaying with his rank odor revealed his weakness in bold relief. Reluctantly she set to work making him healthy again, for although he was weakened he was still more than she could defeat right now.

Pan fell fast into dreaming, and in it the words mocked him.

Imp.

Nymph.

Puck.

"An awful sense of peril came upon Maime…she heard the murmur of an angry multitude [of Fairies]; she saw a thousand swords flashing for her blood, and she uttered a cry of terror and fled."
-J. M. Barrie, *Peter Pan in Kensington Gardens*

John Meets Outcasts and Fairies

A day came and went while John slept. He awoke for the first time in a long time feeling refreshed. While walking the perimeter of the camp, shaking sleep from his mind, the smells of the Island wafted to him: salt, fish, rotting wood, flowers, pine, maple and animals. He could see the Sun rising on the horizon and a rumbling in his belly forced him down from his invisible fort.

The connection between John and the ground beneath him continued to show him the way. Before long he found a chicken scratching along a ridge of ice that had begun to form. He was near the border of the snow-laden corner of Neverland. As John approached, creeping slowly, ready to spring, he caught sight of a small string tied around the chicken's foot that lead to a steak sunk into the ground a few yards away. It was a trap that John didn't want to bother, but it was too late. He heard low growling behind him.

Three large, hungry wolves were focused on Jonathan and slowly stalking closer to him. His only choice was to run into the snow, which he did. The ice severed the connection he had with the ground beneath him and sent John careening into the air, landing hard on his back. His head hit the ice and he saw stars, immediately enveloped by darkness.

He woke up surrounded by blue light. His head felt like it was on fire, but that quickly eased as the pain pulled into a tighter focus on a lump on the back of his head. He scanned the area around him and couldn't make sense of which end was up or down. Was he standing, or lying down? Why was everything blue?

"Are you alright?" Jonathan heard someone ask. "Why don't you sit up and drink this. It's water."

John sat up and suddenly the room made sense. The air was cold, but his body was warm. He was covered in a thick, light colored fur blanket and the large cavern around him was made of ice, explaining the blue hue. John turned for the cup of water, but his hand never made it to the handle. Instead it recoiled in shock. The person holding the cup was a grown man.

"Ah!" Jonathan's scream bounced around the room and he skittered backwards, sliding out from under his blanket. He got to his feet, hands jittering about, his mind reaching out for a weapon to use against one of the Pirates that had captured him.

But the Pirate just smiled at him and laughed a little. He offered out the cup again and said, "It's okay. You're safe here. Have some water. What's your name?"

John kept his back to the icy wall, his mind still searching for a way out. More Pirates appeared to him milling about the rest of this immense ice cavern.

"You're safe, I said. We're not pirates or anything. We're just like you. My name is Joe."

"How did I get here?"

"We brought you here. We were hunting and you got in the way of one of our traps. The wolves were coming and so we saved you. But don't worry, we got the wolves, too."

"Who are you? What are you doing here? Where is this place?"

"Calm down. We're outcasts. We were once Lost Boys like you and we escaped here, to Winter, where you are now." Joe could see John was still nervous. "We just live here. But if you come with me I'll show you something. There's hope now," Joe said, putting the cup of water down and extending his hand in a peaceful gesture.

John slowly stepped away from the wall back into the room.

"My name is Jonathan Darling. Do you know how to get out of Neverland?"

"Oh, no. There's no way back. But there's choices. We get to live here fairly peacefully."

Joe walked John through the icy compound. They first passed through the dormitories. Furs hung in many places in the hallways they passed through, but in each individual room the furs covered every inch of ice and actually made the rooms a fairly comfortable temperature. John counted thirty rooms.

As they walked, Joe explained how they came to be there. Tinkerbell had sent all of them to the rock. With so many people wishing for a place to hide, the Island eventually expanded the safe place from just the Rock to the place Joe referred to as Winter.

"We think he used to be able to see this land, but the snow and ice now outline an area he just can't see or feel anymore. We're able to survive patiently here."

"But how did you grow up? I thought that didn't happen here."

"We decided to. It was as simple as that. You have to see that those children, the Lost Boys are so terrible that we wanted nothing to do with them. We didn't want any of the other Islanders to mistake us for them, so as a way to protect ourselves, we grew to grown-ups."

"Other Islanders? What other Islanders are there?"

"There are the Indians. They're pretty quiet, though. They keep to themselves, and don't seem interested in sharing anything. And there's the Fairies."

"But the Fairies are in Peter's pocket. He's got Tinkerbell and she commands the rest of them. Doesn't she?"

"Yes, she does. But there's a fraction of them who have retreated to this side of the Island. They're our allies. We help them when we can and they help us back. We're trying to use the Island to help us get rid of Peter Pan, but it is taking a long time."

By now Joe and John were outside. There was a small valley between two hills that was crowded with smaller igloos. John saw the three wolves hanging upside-down in front of one of them, which must have been a butcher's hut. There were igloos dedicated to housing chickens and even some that held frozen fruits and vegetables gathered from parts of the Island not encompassed by Winter.

"How are you using the Island to get rid of Peter?"

"We all meet every day at the same spot and wish as hard as we can for the same thing: a way to beat Peter Pan. After many years the Island has begun to answer our wishes."

"How?"

"An elixir began to drip from the ceiling about a hundred years ago. One drop every couple of years."

"What does it do?"

"I don't know, exactly. The Fairies know more about magic that we do, so we let them deal with that. I think it gives someone power, or breaks Pan's power on someone. Something like that. They've tried it once or twice but there wasn't enough to have it work completely."

The pair crested a hill and John could see the green of the Island at the foot of the other side.

"This is what is so exciting!" Joe said, jogging ahead. "I think Winter is growing. That must mean that we're gaining more control over his portion. See this?" Joe said, crouching down beside a rod that had been jammed into the ground a few inches within the edge of the snow.

"I put this rod here several years ago to mark the very edge of our snow. And now look at this! We've gained nearly five inches of ground here."

"How many years have you been here, Joe?"

"I don't really remember. Long enough to grow this old and see five more inches of snow gained on Peter Pan's land."

A tall lean man slid down the side of the hill and slipped next to Joe.

"Joe! The Fairie emissary is here. He knows about John being here and would like to meet him," he huffed.

"Are you feeling alright, John? How's your head?"

"I'm alright. I'm very hungry, though."

"Max, tell him we are going to feed our guest and then he can speak with him."

Max nodded and then charged back up the hill and disappeared behind the other side.

"Come on, then. Let's get some food in you," Joe said and clapping John on the shoulder he guided him toward the valley they passed through earlier.

John had a delicious meal of seared wolf meat with various unknown spices in a thick sauce and a medley of vegetables, some of which John recognized from home, and others he had only seen in the Lost Boy camp. It smelled rich and smoky and tasted wonderful. He didn't want to stop eating after he cleared his plate, but his manners prevented him from asking for more.

Instead, he washed his hands with some fresh snow and rubbed his wet cold hands on his face to rid it of any sign of the meal. He then followed Max through the hills to another section of Winter, where a handful of Faeries sat waiting on a flatly ground boulder used as a table.

"Hello, John," one of the Fairies stepped forward and extended his hand. "My name is Reed. I am the emissary to the royal family of the Fairies," he said, smiling.

"Pleased to meet you," John said.

"Do you know why we're here, John?"

"I assume you meet everyone who comes into Winter."

"No, Jonathan. Winter is not our responsibility. We are friends with the Outcasts, but they govern and manage themselves. We have come here to check out a few rumors that we've heard."

"What kind of rumors?" John asked.

"I will tell you after I ask you a few questions. I don't want you to base your answers on my expectations. With your permission I would like to begin asking you a few questions."

"Sure. I guess so. Go ahead."

"Thank you. Clearly you are one of the newest arrivals to the Island.

"Yes."

"Tell me, what do you think it means when I say the word 'Elemental'?"

The question caught John off guard. He'd heard of Elementals before, but only in stories and he could not understand what they had to do with anything. "I don't know. Aren't those creatures that are made of an element? Like fire or water?"

"Excellent. Yes. You have two siblings that have come with you, isn't that true?"

"Yes, that's true."

"And how are they taking to the Island?"

"What do you mean?"

"Well, for example, you are having a hard time accepting your host and that has caused you to run away to the rock for refuge. How are the other two adapting?"

"My sister Wendy has fallen head over heels for Peter. It's like she sees him do no harm. She's always staring off, dreaming, or hovering around him. And my brother Michael has reacted the same way he always does. He just adjusts himself to fit in with whoever is around."

The Fairies exchanged glances. Reed's eyebrows raised in a surprised look, which John noticed. The crowd around them seemed to creep in closer. John realized that he, too, was holding his breath with the rest of them.

"Describe what you mean, please," Reed urged.

"Well, when he's with me he is still the same Mikey I knew back home. He's smart and fun and logical. But when he's with Peter he acts just like Peter. It's as if he has been here forever, side by side, with Peter Pan. He's fearless and agile and ruthless just like Peter when he's around. But when he's with Tinkerbell I can see how gentile and clever he is. He just adapts his personality to match whomever he's nearest, but that's not because of being here. He's always done that."

"Have you ever seen him adjust not only his personality, but his physical ability as well? Can he see things differently when Tink is around? Is he faster when he's by Peter Pan?"

"I don't know if he sees any differently. And, yes, he's fast when Peter Pan is around, but he doesn't have any reason to be that fast when he's not by Peter. Why? What does that mean?"

"John, I'd like to bring you back to our village, if you'd be willing. I think our leader would like to see you."

Reed could see the distrust and questions in John's face, so she revealed a bit more of her hand to put him at ease.

"I think Peter has cast a spell over your brother and we may be able to give you something that would break the spell. It would give Michael back his own free will while simultaneously taking a potential weapon away from Pan. Michael would be able to see Peter for what he really is, the way you see him. But first our leader will need to speak with you."

"How are you and your Fairies related to Tinkerbell?" John asked with a little defiance in his voice.

"Tinkerbell is the daughter of our king. We are the same tribe as Tinkerbell."

"Tinkerbell is my friend. She saved my life."

"Of course. Then allow me to take you there under her honor. We will treat you as if you were her guest, not mine," Reed lifted up into the air and nodded his farewell to Joe and the rest of the Outcasts. "I will see you tonight at the wishing spot. Until then."

Reed turned back to John and motioned for him to follow her. John shook Joe's hand, an action much more adult than either participant felt they had achieved, but neither thought of a better way to say goodbye.

"Thank you, Joe."

"Take care, John."

" 'I forget them after I kill them,' he replied carelessly."
-J. M. Barrie, *Peter and Wendy*

Stories

Peter emerged from his tree after a long night's sleep. There was still a slight visible shake left in his arms, and anyone who dared to look closely would notice his feet fell a bit heavier today. Pain grinded in his joints with every step, and his eyes still stung. If aspirin were available on Neverland, Peter would have taken an unhealthy dose and collapsed back into restless sleep.

But as things were, there was no aspirin. Instead, Peter had access to everfruit, which strengthened and healed. There was one, and only one, Everfruit Tree on Neverland and it too used its own fruit to grow strong, fast, and healthy. Its limbs groaned under the weight of the fruit it hoarded; yet coaxing the fruit away from the tree was still quite a task.

Peter would need help retrieving his treatment, but due to his performance last night, the Lost Boys would be too afraid of him to focus on anything as dangerous and important as the Everfruit Tree. He would need someone who was strong and who still looked up to him. Someone who was not at the bonfire last night. Someone who was eager to be tested. Someone whose last test was interrupted by treasonous acts.

Someone like Michael.

...

John had never seen anything quite like it. When he walked into the Fairie camp, he was immediately struck with a sense of otherworldliness. He had no context for the feeling. If he'd been older he might have recognized it as intoxication. As it was, he just knew that the feeling scared him and exhilarated him all at once.

The village appeared haphazardly arranged at first, but on closer inspection he saw that there was a definite order to it. It was an order that his healthy human mind, craving right angles, didn't see right away. The flow was regimented and almost severe in its execution, but still remained organic.

A tiered system of sentries kept the village safe from intruders. Each level of defenders handed an interloper off to the next seamlessly. It was a great and effective way to keep an eye on everything while remaining hidden. As such, there was never a time when John didn't feel many eyes on him, so he was extra careful where he placed his steps. He saw what a pack of these things could do to a goblin, and he didn't want to tempt them into showing him what they could do to him.

Despite the great deal of security and the ever-present watchful eyes, he somehow felt like he was immediately a part of the community. The Fairies not on sentry detail treated him with curios openness. While his blatant awe must have been evident to all of them, they were not at all shy or insulted. The closer he got to the center of the small town, and what he could only assume was his destination, the more he felt at home.

"I'm going to announce your arrival. You are safe here. I'll be back to escort you to her soon."

"Umm… sure. Right. Of course."

The emissary smiled and disappeared into a small but elegant hut. John had just enough time to look up and see beams of light shine through the intricate architecture. He was close to deciphering images, like inverted shadow puppets, cast upon the wall when Reed emerged.

"She'll see you now."

John was struck with a sudden sense of himself. His clothes were rags, torn and filthy dirty. He felt downright ugly surrounded by such delicate beauty. A quick attempt to smooth out his clothes failed, and he looked back at Reed with worry on his face.

"I'm nervous."

"Of course you are. Have you ever met royalty before?" Reed asked, already knowing the answer.

"I don't think so."

"Jonathan," Reed looked up at him with gentle amusement, "if you had, you'd know it."

John was speechless, a condition to which he'd grown accustomed recently. The already impossibly disorienting world of Neverland had become more impossible and more disorienting by the day since he'd escaped the Pan. He did his best to smooth his hair down, and then went with Reed.

He led John past a tall wall and into a small room on the other side. The wall completely surrounded the room, and it had a half a dozen ledges that ran along it upon which many Fairies sat watching. Atop the wall were perched more Fairie guards. As John stood there he saw more and more Fairies flying in over the top and taking a seat along the various ledges. Feathers adorned the wall in front of him, creating the only smooth, soft surface in the entire room. Reed motioned for him to stay still, and then moved one of the feathers aside.

Jonathan sat before the royal Fairie named Fern. She came out from behind the feather curtain, and was not at all what John expected. She was a Fairie, but other than that, there was nothing more remarkable about her than anyone else he'd seen that day. Her clothes were lovely, but they fit in with every other Fairie's. She had no crown, and she had no robe. She was just another Fairie. The only way he could distinguish her from the others is that everyone bowed their head when she entered, so John did as well.

"You poor boy," she said to him when she saw the confusion on his face. "So much is happening to you that you can't possibly understand. There is so much history at work here, and you've been flung right into the middle of it all."

John's mind opened up at that moment. He had never considered the terrible chain of events that could have possibly resulted in this very moment. He suddenly felt so selfish. This was so far beyond him, and here he was, feeling sorry for himself after only a few weeks.

He found himself hungry to learn Neverland's history.

"Perhaps understanding more of where you are will help you. We Fairie were created when the first child laughed. That laugh broke into a thousand pieces, which became Fairies. We live according to that laugh, and do all we can to spread and protect that joy. Each new Fairie takes with them a small shard of the first laugh from their parents, and when a Fairie dies, their shard reunites with the rest.

When we run our course and are wiped from the earth the laugh will become whole again and skip about until it fades away forever."

John then heard every Fairie around him make a sound in unison. It was the echoing sound of laughter that faded away slowly. After five skips of laughter, it was gone completely, and all the Fairies looked upward and clapped once.

The ritual, if done by a single Fairie would have looked ridiculous, but in unison the sound was humbling. John held his breath for the duration of the moment, afraid that if he moved or made a peep the powerful notion would shatter and the world would be left mundane again.

After a moment of silence, with the wind blowing through the trees Fern continued her story.

"Our life here on Neverland began several millennia ago. Tinkerbell's father was the crown of the Bell clan. He set out on his own as a young Fairie, as is customary of our royalty. His mission was to establish his own kingdom, which he did in a very humid land that was teeming with wildlife, both friendly and unfriendly.

"The King, his Queen, and his family put down roots, cultivated the land, and spread joy to all that came near. All except for a few, who neither wanted nor deserved it.

"Tinkerbell and her brothers, like all of us, were rambunctious youth. A parent tolerates what he or she must and the King and Queen were no different. They realized that the best way for their children to learn was to let them learn. And so they did just that. Tinkerbell and her brothers often found themselves in trouble, but it was rarely serious."

As interested as John was with their history, he could not help but turn his eyes to a pair of Faeries slightly behind Fern. They seemed to be twins, or maybe it was just because they were dressed the same and had their hair pulled back in the exact same manner. Their embroidered shirts were an iridescent blue and green design that caught the sunlight just enough to pull John's attention back to them time and again.

"There came a time when other powerful entities made moves on the territory the King had carved for himself and his subjects," Fern continued. "He had no wish to fight with anyone. This is not to say that he was a coward. Like I said, we defend our joy with a fierce heart. He was simply prudent and realized that while other races may have needed enough space to warrant border wars, he and his Fairies were of small stature and appetite.

"He sent his children out to assess the need for confrontation and the possibility of a peaceful coexistence. They'd not been gone long when he received a package."

Fern noticed John's eyes wandering and yanked his attention back to the story.

"It is vitally important at this point for you to grasp just what a corporeal form means to a Fairie, John. It dictates so much of how we Fairies have acted here on Neverland. You humans have something within you that lives on after you die. In many ways, your body is no more than a vessel. This realm, like any other, is but a stage in your journey.

"We have no such luxury. This is all that we are and we keep this in the front of our minds absolutely. When we die, our souls rejoin the broken pieces of that first laugh that created us. There is no afterlife, just a return to our true form. And when all of us are dead, that first laugh will be whole again, be heard, and then be gone forever."

All around him, every Fairie enacted their ritual again. They all made the same laughing sound, and then they clapped when it was all over.

After a moment of silence, with the wind blowing through the trees Fern picked up her tale.

"In this state of mind, we exist in the very moment. We must. And we live a long time, by any measure, and in this place we have lived beyond any length we otherwise would have.

"So when I tell you that the King received a package of severed Fairie heads with a heavy heart, it is imperative upon you to grasp the true nature of my meaning. Such things had to that point been unheard of. Many among the search party were his own offspring, shards of laughter broken off of his own, thus making the tragedy all the more complete. He searched franticly for his most beloved son and daughter among the sacrificed and felt a guilty relief to not find them.

"A short time later, he received a dispatch as to the nature of their new enemies. It was written, with much hatred, by his stout-hearted daughter."

"The note read very simply, 'Have encountered foul beasts. Will dispatch. Reply unnecessary."

The chill of her tone sent a shiver up John's spine. Even after thousands of years, and filtered through another person's words, the letter still carried its cold, steely weight.

"With eight words, his daughter had told him everything he needed to know – about the beasts and about her. Where his tastes trended to politics hers trended toward the light, flexible and effective stinger sword.

"A person ought never feel one, and few have, but foul beasts often experienced the unique joy of a hundred simultaneous wounds. They weren't exactly swords as a person might recognize that word. As weapons of brutal efficacy, however, they were always quick to be identified. Their attack can do both physical and psychological damage.

"The King always held out hope that any current foe could be a future friend and knew that, left to her own devices, his daughter would thoroughly prevent that either by alienating the enemy beyond thoughts of reconciliation or butchering them beyond possibility of recognition. He summoned her back to him at once.

"No sooner did she enter the kingdom than the sentries sounded the alarm. Several goblins were charging the castle. They had followed her, and were rushing in fast.

"Goblins were the one constant enemy of us Fairie. They had limited magical abilities, and were easily tricked. But their cruelty needed to be respected.

"Our army was quickly raised, and the King's daughter turned right around to lead us. The King donned his armor and flew out by her side. They took their soldiers out to meet the oncoming goblin scare. He refused to proceed too hastily but his daughter held no such reservations and hurried in. What could he do but follow?

"Just before they clashed with the Goblins, a red and black mist covered them like a blanket. The Fairie soldiers immediately looked to the King's daughter for direction. Without consulting the King, she threw out orders.

"We were to turn the enemy around, place the goblins between the castle walls and Fairie soldiers, and not to blink. The lights would only be good for the enemy to see by. It would just make them a target. The King tried to protest, but before he could the fog thickened and swallowed us all."

John's heart was racing. Everything Fern said about the fight with the Goblins and the strange mist bloomed so vividly in his mind as she spoke. He could hear the snarling Goblins, and his hair stood on end as he heard the Fairie Princess call out her orders.

"The fight was brutal. Any enemy found in the thick mist was hastily and violently destroyed. You never knew where the next brute would come from, and so had to make quick work of the ones you found.

"When the fog lifted we were here in this awful arena. As such, awful things will doubtless need to happen to get us all home. Good people may have to do things they know they'd rather not do."

The storyteller took her time at this point to make absolutely certain that Jonathan was paying complete attention. It was critical that he knew what she just said was true.

"You understand, dear boy, that is true, don't you?"

"Yes ma'am. I do. Sometimes good people have to do bad things so that worse doesn't happen later."

"Good lad. You're a very good and smart boy."

"No ma'am. I'm a coward and I ran away and left my brother and sister behind to deal with that thing by themselves."

"Sweet child. They're not so alone as you might fear. You're here now, aren't you? You came to see me today with Reed and that's a very brave thing to do. You don't know us. You've no real reason to trust us. All you've seen only shows that we hate the Pan as much as you do. For many people, that wouldn't be enough for them to find themselves standing where you are."

He bowed his head, as much in humility as gratitude, "Thank you, ma'am. You're very nice."

"Hmm," she half-grunted her acknowledgement. "Well then, it seems as though we've reached the end of the useful part of the story. I hope that you take the right lessons from it. The Princess is a proud and noble thing. And while some of us may disagree with her on some things, even important ones, she's still our leader and we're proud of her."

She could see he was not quite grasping the subtlety of her point.

"You do know who the Princess is, do you not?"

"I think so, ma'am."

"Good. I'd like to speak to you about your brother, now. I'm told that he and Pan are growing close, and that when Michael is near Pan he shows signs of absorbing parts of his personality."

"Yes. But it's not like that's anything new. Michael has always been that way. He just adapts to the situation."

"We have reason to believe that that may not be the case. We think that Pan may have Michael under his control and is grooming him to become something greater than the Lost Boys. This could be catastrophic for us, and I'm sure it would be upsetting for you if Michael became tethered to Pan."

"Absolutely."

"If we told you that we had a way to release Michael from Pan's grasp, would you be interested in accepting our help?"

"Yes, of course."

"Good. We have an elixir that has been painstakingly collected. It is incredibly rare and important. You need to make sure that he drinks it all." Fern nodded to one of the other Fairies in the room, which left, only to return a moment later with a glass vile filled with a milky liquid.

"You're sure this won't hurt him?" John asked.

"I will not lie to you. When the tie is broken he will feel ill, but that will pass."

John hesitated.

"You know, John, sometimes good people –"

"Have to do bad things for the greater good," John finished. He put out his hand and the Fairie laid the vile on his palm.

"Make sure he drinks it all."

"I will. Thank you."

"You must keep yourself safe as well. You, and you alone hold the key to breaking Pan's hold. That is why I am giving this to you as a gift. It will protect you."

Fern unclasped a charm from around her neck.

"My lady," Reed interjected.

"It's alright, Reed. It will serve him until the transfer is made and then come back to me. We've already discussed it in private and that is the agreement," Fern interrupted.

"How can you trust it? It is sworn to you, and giving it up could doom us all."

"We are doomed if this fails. We've discussed things in private. That is the agreement," she said in a tone that implied the end of the discussion.

The tiny chain fit snugly around the first knuckle on John's pinky finger. The charm was a small black circle. When the light hit it just right it reflected greens, yellows and reds.

John needed to say something, but there was so much to comment on that he couldn't decide. "Thank you," was all he said.

"Good luck, Jonathan. It is time for you to return to them now. Our guides will lead you back."

...

Peter flew high up over the canopy of the forest and came loudly careening into the clearing of the Everfruit Tree. It would take at least two-dozen Lost Boys joining hands to completely surround the twisted and gnarled armor of the tree. It had softball-sized fruit heavily dangling from a few overburdened limbs. The fruits varied in color. Some were swirled with purple and gold. Others were white speckled red orbs, while others seemed a bit of translucent green and orange. Peter crowed loudly and the Everfruit tree shook. Leaves on the ground flung up in the air as vines unraveled from the earth.

Meanwhile Michael quietly snuck to the rim of its domain. His face was covered with black mud and sprinkled with bits of moss. Pan didn't bother telling him that the tree couldn't see. It just felt the disturbing ripples in the air. But Michael was so eager in his application of camouflage that Pan let him finish. He carried a device that consisted of a net scooper that fed into a tube with a handle. He sat waiting for Pan's signal.

The tree was doing its best to whip Peter out of the sky. At first one vine sufficed, but after a while of frustrating the tree, a second and third tried their luck. Peter was growing braver with his swoops, getting closer and closer to the branches. Just the scent of the fruit worked wonders on Peter's constitution. When he would get too close, the tree would groan a deep, chest rattling moan and its branches would curl toward him. A scar on the tree would open high on its trunk, revealing row after row of teeth. The branches tried forcing him toward the mouth but he would swoop clear and escape the quick, whipping vines.

After a few of these death-defying swoops, Peter whistled a shrill tone and Michael sprang to life. He swooped low, a few inches off of the ground toward one of the overburdened branches. A few of the vines took notice of him, forcing him off his direct course to the fruits. Peter caught a glimpse of this and dipped low to help Michael. Together they dodged and weaved and spun to safety, always an inch or two out of reach.

The frustrated tree began to growl and gnash and shake. When they passed under the great limbs of the tree, sharp leaves and needles fell on their backs. Michael, not expecting the cuts on his back, dropped his fruit collecting stick in surprise, which was quickly intercepted and broken. Michael followed the way of the collecting stick as he lost his happy thought for a stronger focus on his pain.

He tumbled to the ground and rolled. Before the vines could locate him, Peter swung himself around and charged the fruit. Vines that had lurched for Michael were quickly diverted in the interest of protecting its fruit. Michael laid on his back and watched Peter avoid the vines and branches, noticing before long that Peter was creating a pattern. The vines were tying one another up in the tree's own branches. Michael held back a laugh as he forgot about his cuts, lost in the adventure.

"Now, Michael!" Peter called, and without hesitation Michael sprung up. He took off his shirt and sped along to one row of various fruit. Holding out his shirt like a net, he scooped the entire branch. The tree roared and shook its remaining leaves and needles down on Michael, but he had built up so much speed in his attack run that only a few caught his ankles on his way out.

...

Things in the Lost Boy camp had settled into a type of lull again. It was the kind of thing that happened with some regularity as of late, small spikes of adventure surrounded by long bouts of the mundane. With Mike hanging out with Peter and Jonathan out doing who knew what, Wendy had the run of the encampment to herself. She was Mother.

Tinkerbell looked on with a great deal of interest at this new dynamic. When things were very slow, and she was fairly certain that Peter would not be sending her off on some stupid errand or another, she took chances to use some of her less commonly used magic. She needed a perch, some focus, and the right mood in camp.

Wendy filled her position as Mother in the camp, but with an underlying sense of discomfort bordering on being frantic. Her brother was gone. Her other brother was changing before her eyes and her own self was changing by the day, too. Every once in a while, depression would settle in, and then vanish again, like her body absorbed it. Each time it felt a little worse but vanished faster.

She was not a stupid girl, but she had an overpowering feeling of a blind spot. It was the feeling she had in math class when everyone else got the answer but her, and she stood at the board with everyone staring. Some looked on with interest in watching her finally understand; most, though, watched with amusement at her plight. She could feel it. Worst of all, she knew it was her fault, no one else's. She stood on the brink of quitting at any second because she knew she was not good enough to solve it. Someone or some thing dropped a veil over her and was watching with a smile as she squirmed beneath it.

Tinkerbell sent thoughts into the back of a few of the Lost Boy's minds, and then quickly established a connection with Wendy's. She needed to stay subtle. Although Wendy was under Pan's spell, she was still a strong girl and could do both of them harm if she fought Tink while she was in her head.

"Mother, tell us a story," some of the Boys said, almost smirking.

"Uh… I don't know if I know many stories."

"You're Mother. You must know some stories," they answered, toying with her.

"Okay… let's see…."

"Make it a good one," said Toodles sincerely.

She felt a real pressure to perform, as though there'd be consequences if she didn't.

"Right. Okay, then. Sure. I may have one. It's a long story, so settle in children."

What are you saying?

Doing?

This would easily have been the weirdest thing she'd ever done if she hadn't spent the last who-knows-how-long flying, watching Mermaids, running through forests and falling in love with Peter. She wasn't much for speaking in front of groups. It always felt so formal and disingenuous. She always found herself concerned with what her hands were doing. But this time the words flowed easily, and Wendy just let herself go. Tinkerbell send the words of the story into Wendy, and she spoke them. But if Tinkerbell was lucky, maybe their meaning would slip past Pan's spell and shake Wendy from its grasp.

"A long time ago in a very distant land there was a pretty young princess, and she was in love with the neighboring kingdom's prince, Jack. The two were smart and strong, and they made one another stronger. They were going to live together happily ever after."

"This is a good story so far..." Toodles said, smiling.

"Thank you, Toodles.

"One day, a powerful sorcerer came into the princess' kingdom and demanded her hand. When she denied him, he put the princess under a powerful spell. She did everything the sorcerer told her to do, including love him.

"When young Prince Jack next saw her, their love pulled on the threads of the sorcerer's spell. The princess was nearly freed herself from the sorcerer's grip, and she would have, had the sorcerer not acted quickly. He tightened down his spell, and needing the young prince out of the picture, he struck a deal with the young prince. He promised the young prince that he would let the princess go unharmed if the prince sought out a magical ring for him.

"Seeing no other way to save his love, the young prince set out to capture the ring. He was a bit naïve to believe the sorcerer, but very brave.

"The first part of his mission sent him to the dark middle of the sorcerer's kingdom, a place rarely explored by men. The sorcerer was counting on the monsters in his kingdom to kill the young prince so he could keep the princess forever."

Tinkerbell settled in comfortably, letting the story pass through her into Wendy, ever hopeful that she could free Wendy from inside the girl sitting below her.

"Jack was scared..."

"But brave!" Toodles offered.

"Yes, dear. Jack was very brave. But brave and scared can both happen together. Brave just means that you do what you know is right even though you're scared.

"So Jack was scared (but brave)," she said to Toodles with a wink, "when he entered the dark lands. The sorcerer watched Jack through his crystal ball, and was upset to see him pass through the dangerous landscape unharmed. The sorcerer then commanded his troops to go find Jack and bring him back to be tortured, for by now the spell on the young princess had been given enough time to solidify. She wouldn't break away from him anymore, even if Jack died right in front of her. The arrogant sorcerer had gotten Jack out of the way for long enough and no longer feared him.

"They found and chased Jack through the forest. When they captured him, they tortured him to near death. The sorcerer had told his soldiers to bring Jack to him alive, but he'd never told them to bring him unhurt."

The Boys stole looks at each other beneath Wendy's sight. They didn't have to bother being secretive, as Wendy had no idea of the impact of what she was saying. She continued.

"At the feet of the evil sorcerer, Jack knew that he would never escape his fate and that he would be a captive forever of this terrible man. This thought brought to him an unexpected calm and he slowly closed his eyes and took a few deep breaths. When he opened his eyes again he looked the sorcerer in the eye and said, 'I know what you are. You aren't as strong as you believe you are. You are stronger than I am, of course, but you can be defeated. And you will be.'

"With that, the young prince threw himself out a window that stood nearby. He didn't know what was on the other side, but he believed that even the unknown was better than the fate he knew he'd face here.

"A small band of birds gathered around where he was going to land and quickly caught him and slowed his fall. Jack landed heavily, and lay there for a minute in a daze, but he was still alive."

Tinkerbell sat on a vine overhead, and a bit off to the side, looking on with great interest. A quick glance at her would have betrayed nothing more than interest. However, a closer examination would have shown a mountain of concentration. She rarely broke her stare at Wendy, doing so only when she allowed the girl to pause or when Toodles interrupted her.

Tinkerbell had tried to get Wendy to spit out the spell before. By the river she described John's terrible death, and Wendy had nearly expelled the spell. But maybe Tinkerbell could get a bigger reaction from emotional pain, since physical pain hadn't worked.

"Jack took off running as fast as he could while the evil sorcerer commanded his creatures to chase him. They got together in small groups and spread out looking for him. But they didn't know that Jack had friends, too. Mostly these friends were in the form of the birds, but there were others, as well. Other creatures the Sorcerer didn't know existed.

"One by one the small groups of creatures sent out by the sorcerer disappeared. Sometimes parts of them would be returned to him as a warning to leave Jack alone. Other times there were no signs of the search parties at all. Jack didn't know these friends were helping him, either. He just kept his head down and followed his path.

"He had run to a beach where he could see a small island just off shore. The island couldn't be any worse than it had been by the Sorcerer, so he dove in to the surf and swam out to it. He was all by himself and very lonely. The kind of lonely that told him to give up, to let the evil sorcerer and his creatures and soldiers come take him back to some strange fate."

Toodles piped up in a meek voice, "Did he give up, Wendylady?"

"What do you think, sweet Toodles?" came the reply.

"I sure hope not."

"Let's find out exactly what he did.

"Now, the birds couldn't follow him out to the island, for it was far away and they were tiny. The sorcerer didn't know it was there and all of that meant that Jack had plenty of time to think about his predicament. And plenty of time to get lonelier still, which is exactly what he did. Before long he lost hope that he'd never see his home again, and he began very much to resent his young stupid Princess for making him leave. He'd told her he didn't want to go, but she'd dragged him out of the window... and, uh... and bullied him and told him he'd have fun... wheth- whether... he'd want to or not."

Wendy struggled and frowned hugely. She knew that something strange was happening to her and that this wouldn't fit in the story.

Where are these thoughts

coming from?

Where is this story

coming from?

Tinkerbell smiled as Wendy frowned and took great pleasure in the discomfort the girl was feeling. The more uncomfortable she was, the harder she would look for its cause. If she could discover the spell it could be broken.

Wendy began to compose herself. Toodles looked up at her questioningly, so Wendy pushed ahead.

"Um... he grew more impossibly lonely all the time."

Tinkerbell could see the sorrow in Wendy's eyes.

Good girl.

Keep going.

"He began to despair of ever seeing all that he loved again."

A tear welled up in Wendy's eye. Tinkerbell grinned brightly.

"It was about then that he discovered the ring. One morning he found a small ring on a rock near where he sat on the cool mornings. It was an ugly ring, but tough looking. It was made up of all sorts of materials by the look of it. There was no way of knowing just how long it had been on that rock, or on the island itself, for that matter. But it was clearly old and worn. He put it into his shirt pocket. Just having the ring on him filled him with a kind of hope. He began once again to believe that he might complete his quest and return home to all that he loved whole, and in one piece after all."

Wendy looked at the Lost Boys, hopeful.

Tinkerbell furrowed her brow. That wasn't the story she was feeding Wendy. Something was going wrong.

"It was not long after his grand discovery that he ventured off the island again to search out the rest of his quarry. While he didn't feel especially courageous, he did recognize that you often have to go places you don't want to go in order to get to places you do."

"I think I like this Jack more all the time," Toodles said.

"Me... too, I think," Wendy offered, sputtering.

A thought came to Tinkerbell from Wendy's mind, then.

Silly Fairie.

The girl will stay mine.

You cannot have her.

"The sorcerer had tried to trick Jack," the spell continued. "He'd thrown many tricks and puzzles at him while he was at the castle and even after the birds had helped him get away, too. It was still his realm, after all. And these tricks had worked for a long time before. But Jack was strong, stronger than he knew, as I've said."

Tinkerbell was not about to give up now. She tried to lock onto Wendy's mind once again. She needed to override the spell, which was currently taking over Wendy once again.

"And he made a special friend of one of the birds. She was a small thing, but powerful in many ways. She came to love Jack like he was her very own brother. Like he was a son, or the best friend she'd had in years."

- 250 -

Tink hesitated for just a moment, and the spell gripped Wendy again. Tinkerbell's sadness nearly overwhelmed her. It was the first time that thought entered her mind and she realized it was true. Not only was Jonathan her greatest chance to overthrow Peter Pan, but also he was also kind and grateful without any hidden agenda. The break in Tinkerbell's focus almost gave Wendy back to Wendy completely, but Tink caught herself in time to rededicate to the mission before she could be locked out for good.

"The sorcerer couldn't find Jack when he was on the island. And like in many other things, this coward eventually talked himself into believing that Jack was just a worthless boy and that he couldn't be troubled with such trivialities."

It had never really occurred to Tink that any of the goblins would pick up on what the story may have meant. She was just trying to reach a part of Wendy that was buried deep within her subconscious and draw her out quickly before Pan's spell could recapture her mind.

But one of the Lost Boys was beginning to piece things together. Ratch was at one time a young boy from the lower end of the island of Manhattan. His stepmother had convinced him that his father resented him for his constant presence. She'd been trying to talk him into moving in with her full-time, and nothing had worked to that point. She didn't know, or didn't want to know, that however miserable she could try to make his life at his dad's house, it couldn't touch the sadness and despair that he knew at his mom's. So when the opportunity to go with Peter Pan had presented itself he leapt at it with open arms.

He'd long since cemented his hate for women and had labeled them all as weak and manipulative. He only tolerated Wendy because of Pan's obvious affection for her. As far as he could see, girls were only good for turning into trees and being sucked dry of their life. At least that way they could do some good by helping make the Lost Boys stronger. He had grown twisted and gnarled enough that had the chance arisen to kill Wendy he would have reveled in it and taken his time. As it was, he now found a possibility to make her hurt.

As he rose to his feet to make his move, Tinkerbell saw her error. It would've been Ratch, wouldn't it? Why was he even there, with his hatred of females? Wendy was going to have to move quickly but Tink found that Wendy was momentarily paralyzed. Tink's attempts to twist Wendy around were futile. She was in check. She may have controlled Wendy's mind, but the spell had taken control of her body and held her prone in the face of the oncoming danger. Tinkerbell was forced to withdraw from Wendy to save her life. She flew down to Ratch's ear. Her position as Pan's right hand often proved useful, but she never needed to use her leverage so abruptly.

"Ratch! Peter needs you at the beach."

"But Tink-"

"Now, Ratch! Should I tell him you're too busy with this young thing and her stories to obey a direct order? How would he react to that? How would he treat you dear Ratch? I doubt well."

"You wouldn't tell him…" He was anything but certain of that.

"No," Tinkerbell offered, transparently honest. "I wouldn't ever do that to you or any of my sweet Lost Boys."

She paused for dramatic effect, and in doing so, saw Wendy scratch the back of her neck. Her paralysis was over, which meant that the spell had moved back up into her mind. Tink wouldn't be able to break back into the girl now. She had lost again.

"But how certain can you be that none of your mates here won't? Boys can be so… childish, don't you think?"

After a few short moments of heroic sized contemplation, Ratch raced from the circle and to the beach. He knew deep in his heart that it was another of her tricks, but knew that he could not take the risk. She would laugh uproariously at him on his return and when the others joined in, he would be forced to acknowledge the humor, all the while tallying more marks against both her and her alleged gender.

"Would you continue, please, Wendylady?" asked Tink. She knew she had lost Wendy, but she needed to keep trying. She needed to make sure.

"I don't think I want to, Tink. I don't feel so good."

"Aw, please. Come on now, Wendy. We were just learning about Jack and the birds. Especially the little one. Was she pretty and smart and perfect?"

"I. I don't know. She was a bird. I don't think I can say if she looked any different in my head than any other bird out there. She wasn't anything special"

"I bet she was pretty. And all of those other things, too. Don't keep the story from us," Toodles pleaded.

"I suppose I can continue," Wendy offered shakily.

"Wendylady, how did the warrior defeat the sorcerer?" Toodles asked, excitedly.

The spell gave Wendy something else to focus on. It didn't need her to accidentally stumble on Tinkerbell's solution.

Wendy realized how late it had suddenly become. There were things to do, and she didn't have time to be telling stories.

"Jack came back to land. All the time he'd spent on the island served to remind him just how much he missed home and how desperately he wanted to return. But he knew that this most important woman in his life needed him out there and that she only ever had his best interests at heart.

"When Jack got to the sorcerer, he handed over the magic ring. The sorcerer had no choice but to release the princess, and they lived happily ever after."

Tinkerbell at least had been clever in crafting her story. The spell inside her had no hand for tact, and ended the story quickly. It took everything wonderful out of the story and made it empty, boring, and predictable, the exact thing the spell was supposed to do with things that were unique and interesting.

"Alright, everyone. It's past midday and there are chores to be done. Everybody up. I need someone to clear the table and get the dishes ready for tonight while I start cooking. The rest of you need to tidy up your trees. It's beginning to look like a tornado touched down here."

Toodles sighed loudly and the rest of the lost boys grudgingly obeyed. Wendy quickly turned away from the group, moving through the actions of preparing supper.

Where did the day go?

And where are Peter and Michael?

Tinkerbell's heart broke then. Any hope she had of freeing Wendy had diminished. There was only one more chance for her to break free, and she had to do it herself. Tinkerbell couldn't help her anymore.

...

Pan and Michael sat on a small wooden pier. Their feet swung with ease just a few inches above the water. Michael felt just as thrilled while eating the everfruit as he did gathering it. Every bite gave him goose bumps, and it was all he could do to stay seated. His thoughts raced from the recent adventure with the tree to the adventures that Johnny and Peter must have had.

"I wish Johnny would come back soon."

There was something remarkable about Michael. His adaptability and natural talent at seemingly every task gave him a lot of potential. If Peter could just figure out how he did it, how he acted like a seasoned Lost Boy on his first day on Neverland, how he flew with such ease, how he defeated the Everfruit Tree on his first try with minimal damage to himself, then Peter could wield him.

But making Michael into a weapon meant Pan would have to break that tedious relationship between he and Jonathan. His mind turned quickly as it formulated a plan. The everfruit was already in Michael's system, giving him a lot of energy. He could be easily distracted.

"I know what Johnny was sent out to do, and there's no way it would take him this long to do it. He's staying away on purpose."

"No way," Michael said without thinking. "He would never stay away from us on purpose. He loves us."

"Then why do you think he hasn't come back yet?"

"He's probably having a great adventure."

"If he is, he didn't come back to find us so we could share it, did he?"

This time Michael was forced to think about the situation. He couldn't focus very well, and the ideas came and went before Michael could think about what they meant. Soon, for some unknown reason, Michael was jealous, and he didn't like it. He threw the rest of his piece of everfruit into the water and watched it sink until he couldn't see it anymore.

Silence hovered around them until Michael had to break it. He couldn't stand thinking badly about John. So what if he was having a great adventure without him? It didn't mean anything. They were still brothers, even if John was being selfish and not sharing any of his fun. Michael was sure he would share his adventures with John. He wanted to. But did John want to share? No. He was just a mean old stupid head who…

"I don't want to talk about this anymore. Tell me a story."

Peter smiled to himself. He could see the anger and agony playing on Michael's face.

It's a start.

"What kind of story?"

The everfruit coursing through Michael crammed too many ideas into his head at once, leaving him to sift through them laboriously. He wanted to just pick the first, but also couldn't stop himself from seeking out the best one.

"Tell me about one of your best enemies."

"I don't remember my enemies, Michael."

"What? How do you forget them?"

"I forget them after I kill them. I remember broad ideas about them, but not the details."

Michael sifted through more ideas until he got to the biggest, juiciest question of them all.

"How did you get here?"

The question caught Pan off guard. He had not thought of that story for a long time. Slowly, a grin appeared on Pan's face. It was perfect. Michael's reaction to the story could tell Pan a lot if he approached it right.

"When I was a much younger Peter than I am now, I tried to steal treasure from a dragon."

"A dragon?"

"Yes, with three heads. I heard that he protected a horde of treasure that would make its owner the most powerful person in the world."

"Wow."

"So I went to the dragon's territory one night, and broke into his mountain through an air vent. It was so hot in there, Michael. It made me want to just curl up and go to sleep. But I fought against it, and I came up in a room filled with treasure.

"There I found myself, Mikey, surrounded by the most beautiful weapons. There were cutting and chopping ones. There were so many different kinds of bows that I didn't recognize half of them. There was even one made of fire. The person who carried it never felt the flames, but whoever the arrows hit sure would. The same thing with the ice one."

"Wow."

"Yeah. But this part of the treasure wasn't the biggest or the best. It was just some magical weapons. There was a doorway at the far end of the room, so I grabbed a small golden sword and went through the door. That's where I found the dragon.

"He was as big as a house, and covered with heavy scales that were as black as tree bark after a strong rain. He didn't see me at first. I must have come in from the back somehow, because the dragon was facing a much bigger door and had his back to me.

"I was lucky. I could have snuck up on him easily and cut him down if I wanted to. It was just a matter of getting close enough and striking where those thick scales weren't protecting him. Unfortunately, everywhere I crept there were those thick scales, everywhere but its eyes. Eventually my luck ran out and it heard my footsteps. One gigantic head swung around to guard me while the other two scanned the room to make sure no one was coming to help me. I was stuck."

The everfruit had found something on which to focus, and it made every word of Pan's story real to Michael. It was Michael in that room with the dragon, and his heart pounded in his chest. He could feel the sword in his hand, and the sickening panic in his belly.

"Do you know what I did then?" Pan asked.

Michael began talking, as if it were his story. His panic gave way to calm calculation as he filled himself up with Pan's story.

"I realized that the people who came for the treasure were prepared to fight the dragon head on, and it wasn't used to someone running and dodging quick like a rabbit. So I stepped to the left and then sprinted to the right. The dragon breathed fire behind me. It hurt my back, but I kept going. I had to."

"Good. What next?" Peter asked.

Remarkable.

"The other two heads swung around, but couldn't come right at me because of the fire. I was able to climb up its leg. I confounded it like we did with the Everfruit Tree. The three heads were filled with three different brains, and although they all controlled the body, each head individually controlled its own neck and jaws. I'd never felt so close to death as each of them snapped at me and I narrowly escaped."

Michael's eyes flashed around him as he imagined the three-headed dragon attacking him. Pan sat still, watching Michael become enveloped in the scene.

"Two heads collided right behind me, and in the ensuing confusion I spun around with a wide slash of my sword. My luck came back. The slash sliced right across an eye. The body shuddered, and the head roared. It must not be used to pain, because it wriggled like mad, smashing itself into the ceiling, and into one of the other heads. I threw myself from the dragon and watched as it breathed fire all over the place.

"I've never been so scared."

His last phrase struck a chord within Peter. That was the first time he had ever been afraid of death, as he watched the dragon thrash, roar, and blow fire everywhere. The ceiling began to crumble as the giant beast thrashed, and Peter had been certain that he would not make it home alive.

"That's right, Michael. But I made it out. The dragon did more damage to itself than I ever could have."

The initial strength of the everfruit was beginning to subside in Michael, and he was able to start separating himself from Pan's story. His heart and his breathing slowed down, and the serene pier and water returned.

"When the dragon finally fell, I spotted two more doors behind him that looked just like the door I had come through. The first was filled with more treasure than I ever imagined could exist. Gold and jewels were piled high everywhere.

"I sent a message back to my family after I'd seen the treasure. How could I not? This was a grand adventure, Mikey. The grandest yet. I sent word by way of the birds to my brothers. I knew it would make them so crazy. I was out making a big noise, and they were stuck on the side of a mountain."

"You have brothers?"

"I had brothers, sort of. I'm a Lost Boy, remember? My mother lost me, and when she did I found another family. A better family. At one point I had six brothers, and they lived in a mountain, just like the dragon but far away. I had to let them know that I was succeeding at what they were too afraid to do. I was the smallest of them all, and they never let me forget it. But there I was, standing amongst more riches than they would ever even dream of.

"In the middle of the room was the best treasure I could have ever asked for, and I took as much of that as my heart could carry."

"Your heart?"

"Yeah, my heart. You see, the dragon's best treasure wasn't gold and money and diamonds. It collected secrets. And Mike… I love secrets."

"What was it?"

"What? The secret? Wouldn't be much of a secret if I just went around telling everyone, huh?"

This touched Michael and, being only six, he couldn't help but show it. He tried to get up and turn away before Peter noticed, but it was too late. Michael stood and stomped up the pier toward the beach. The fish that had been hiding in the shade beneath the pier scattered for safety.

"Oh alright, Baby. Don't be a baby, Baby. I'll tell you. This secret was how to make things look like I want them to look like. Anything. I can't use it too much. Dragons are way more powerful than us and it takes a lot of thinking, but I can do it sometimes."

Michael turned back around and listened to the rest of the story on his feet.

"When I went through the third and final door I looked down a corridor with a giant man standing at the end, guarding one final door. It seemed so weird. If someone would get to this man, they would have had to defeat the dragon. This was a big guy, but he was nothing compared to a dragon.

"I approached carefully. He carried a gigantic axe, and as fast as I was, I couldn't get past him into the final room. I needed to defeat him."

"Go back. Take the treasure. Take the weapons. But do not pass through this door."

"What's through that door?"

"Control, power, and destruction. It is best left alone."

"I want it."

"It is not for you. Turn back."

"I took a deep breath and walked right up to him. He was as mean and ugly as he was big. But I wasn't scared. You know what I mean, don't you Mikey? Just because they're bigger it doesn't mean we can't beat them."

Mike nodded, but had to ask, "He might have killed you, though. You could have died. Weren't you afraid of dying?"

"Death, Michael, would be a great adventure," Peter said, dreamily, the way a person talks about one day becoming a teacher or doctor or veterinarian.

"No, I wasn't afraid. I had the dragon's secret in my heart and I wanted to try it out. I walked right up to him and said, 'My, you're certainly a big one, aren't you, friend?'

"He growled at me. Something about me not passing. Something I completely ignored. I continued on with what I was saying. 'Those arms are as big as tree trunks. I bet you could crush someone like me with one branch.'

"The big oaf looked at me smugly. He flexed the big muscles in his arms.

"'My word, that's impressive; and those legs. They're not even like tree trunks. They're bigger. You could stamp me into dust. I'd become dirt and those big legs could just grow roots right in me.'

"He didn't feel it happening right away, but it'd started.

"'But what if someone also huge, not someone like me, came along and tried to charge past you? What would you do then?'

"He lifted his giant axe over his head and roared. One of his legs had already started to grow into the ground, but thankfully he hadn't tried to lift that one up when he stomped his other foot down hard. The whole mountain shook. He brought the axe down and held it with both hands. He made it clear without using words that he'd just stand his ground and not move for anyone or anything.

"'Yes, but if something *really* big came along? Then what? Certainly that wouldn't work then. Maybe those giant fingers of yours could branch out and wrap them up.'

"Mikey, I'll tell you what. At this point it was all over. This big dummy never stood a chance. Where I convinced the other idiot he was a plant, this moron actually thought himself into becoming a tree. Can you believe it?! Sometimes people are so stupid."

"What did you do then, Peter? If the man turned himself into a tree in front of the door, how'd you get past him?"

Peter waited with a sly look on his face, while Mike figured it out. An image popped into Michael's head, and awe passed over his face.

"You didn't! You didn't go past him, did you Peter?"

"Nope. I sure didn't. I took that big axe from his giant leafy hands and chopped him into little pieces. Then I took one of the bigger splinters, picked the lock on the door and walked right into my new favorite room.

"I grabbed the treasure and made it my own. It wasn't gold or silver either. It was something much better. It was an elixir, and when I drank it the whole mountain erupted around me. Fire exploded from every crevice and the walls came tumbling down. The last thing I saw was a black and red mist roaring through the door behind me. It billowed around me and I blacked out. When I came-to I was here on Neverland."

...

"Smee, I need to tell you something," Smythe said to Smee one night. Smythe could think of little else than his betrayal. The lines under his eyes betrayed his exhaustion. Nearly a week of sleepless nights spent staring at the rafters above him, listening to the snores from the men around him had given Smythe ample time to cultivate a great rock of sorrow and shame in his gut. It was time to harvest the stone inside him or let it kill him.

"You look real bad, Smythe. You sick? You should eat some fruit, it helps me feel better," Smee suggested, always helpful.

"I am sick, Smee, but unfortunately I can't get better until I tell you something."

Smee didn't understand. Sickness was when you felt nauseous or hot or cold. Talking didn't fix any of that.

"No, Smythe. We can talk later. You look terrible. Fruit and rest for you. Go see Murdy; he'll fix you right up. I was sick once and he had me better in two days. And he gave me some sweets to help me along. Tell him you don't like the medicine and he'll slip you some sweets."

"Smee, this is serious. I have something to tell you and it's very important. You have to listen to me. I've done something bad.

"Getting sick's not bad. Just take a break for a while. See Murdy and take your medicine."

This was not the first time Smythe tried to confess to Smee. He had tried on countless occasions throughout the last few days, but each time Smee would latch onto some ancillary detail or another and Smythe wouldn't be able to lay down his burden.

The stacking betrayals were eating Smythe alive from the inside; the betrayal of Smee; of Captain Cooper, or whatever it was that the Captain had become; the betrayal of his shipmates. The worst of these had been Smee. If harm came to him it was without justification. Smythe was a good Catholic boy, just like he'd been raised to be. He knew that bad things happen to people who did bad things. And everybody does bad.

Except Smee.

He'd never seen Smee hurt anyone. He didn't drink or curse or carouse. He was never malicious. He never even found humor in the malice of his shipmates toward each other, no matter how seemingly harmless. Smee was the most pure hearted person Smythe had ever known.

Smythe asked Smee to go for a walk, hoping to find another way to confess his guilt. The pair walked down into the food storage hall, which was now a sad remnant of the once bountiful trove. Rat droppings were scattered in the corners and empty crates and tipped jars and bottles were all that decorated the scarcely furnished room. Mildew permeated the humid air that at one time smelled of spices. Smythe would find the solitude he needed in this room. He kicked a crate under the low hanging chandelier and lit a few candles with his lantern. Then he sat down on the crate and motioned for Smee to do the same on another one nearby.

"Let me tell you a story, boyo."

"You tell good stories, Smitty."

"Well, you're a good listener. In this story, the main character," Smythe searched for a name. "Uh, Davey, a fair-haired happy boy learns a pretty terrible lesson for forgettin' who his friends are. Let's say he's an Ipswich lad, like myself.

"He loved his mother and he loved his dog and he loved his

friends. He did everything with him. He went on grand adventures with them. They scrapped with boys from other neighborhoods for fun, and he was happiest when he was with his friends."

Smee was getting restless already. He couldn't sit still for long stories, and this one was shaping up to be a doozy. He fidgeted with his hands and started looking around the room.

"Laddie, eyes on me. This is important. Davey had a dark secret that he never told anyone."

"What was the secret?" Smee asked, snapping back to attention at the mention of such a delicious word.

"It doesn't matter what it was. It's just important to know that he never told anyone. But one day, a strange boy named, ah, Paul, from another neighborhood came to Davey when he was alone and tried to threaten him."

Smee saw a fly land on a shelf with one plate and a half-empty jar of some yellow liquid. The fly buzzed continuously. Smee hated that sound, which grew louder and louder, quickly gaining the lion's share of his attention. He'd go kill it. Just as soon as Smitty was done.

Hurry up, Smitty.

Smythe tried hard to keep Smee's attention and keep all of the characters straight in his story.

"The stranger, Paul told Davey that he'd tell everyone his secret and none of his friends would like him anymore. He told him his mom would hate him and kick him out of his home. He even convinced the lad that his dog would leave him for a better master."

"Why was the lad afraid of this happening? Did he trust his friends? Did he think they'd abandon him so quickly?"

Smythe had to think on his feet. He knew that while Smee was slow, but one thing he grasped entirely was loyalty. He wouldn't believe that this lad's friends would just up and leave over something in the boy's past.

"First of all, it was a really dark secret. I mean to tell you, it was as tragic a thing as the child could imagine."

Smee looked at Smythe solemnly. He leaned in close and whispered what he gleaned was the boy's secret. "Smitty," his eyes narrowed, "was he part French?"

The honesty of Smee nearly broke Smythe. He almost broke out into fits of laughter, and would have had he not buried his face in his grimy hand to hide his smile and bit the inside of his cheeks.

"Yea, Smee. He was part French. On his father's side. And he'd convinced himself that if anyone ever found out, no one would stand by his side, not even a mangy dog."

"So what'd he do?'

"This strange boy told our hero that he'd tell his whole neighborhood about the boy's lineage. His father would lose his job; his friends would beat him and run away; and his dog would go, too. But not before biting him. Hard.

"All the boy had to do to avoid the shame was one very simple thing. You see, Smee, the boy's group were very good scrappers."

The fly flew up and around the small hanging candle chandelier that dangled wax like long flowing sleeves above Smythe. It was closer. The room was dark enough that it would disappear into the shadows from time to time, but he never lost that horrible noise. It was drilling deep into his brain, burrowing like a tick in his ear.

"Smee, please pay attention. The fly can wait," Smythe commanded more harshly than intended. His fatigue and desperation had sapped him of most of his patience.

"Davey and his friends always beat the boys in the surrounding areas. All our hero had to do to keep his secret safe, was keep an eye on his friends. And tell the evil stranger, Paul, when they were out and about. Not even every time. Just enough that the strange boy's crew could get their hands on the lad's friends in smaller groups. To rough 'em up in smaller groups and find out who was best friends with who. He knew what he was doing. He knew he was hurting those closest to him. He knew he was making the group weaker. And he knew the betrayal was costing him a part of his soul every time he did it"

"That's pretty low, Smitty, selling out his friends like that."

"I know, boyo. It's a tragic story. He realized he could have told Paul to go to Hell and just deal with the consequences. It would've saved his friends. But he didn't."

"Does it end well anyway?"

"No, Smee. The boy did it. He betrayed his friends and they never found out."

"But they didn't leave him. His mother didn't kick him out. His dog stayed."

"True things, all. But the boy knew. And every day until he died as an old man, he knew that he'd betrayed his closest mates. It haunted him."

"I feel bad for the boy," Smee offered with a small frown on his face.

"I knew you would, boyo. That's one of the things that makes you special, Smee."

Smythe barely managed to leave his crate and blow his nose on a rag without Smee seeing the tears pave through the dirt on his face.

"Perhaps John had not behaved very well so far, but he shone out now."

-J. M. Barrie, *Peter and Wendy*

<u>John Returns</u>

After supper was devoured and the dishes were cleaned, Peter and Wendy sat alone at the table. Michael had gone to bed for the night and the Lost Boys were off hunting. Wendy was securely wrapped in a story of Peter's heroism when Tinkerbell entered the campsite.

"Peter, Wendy. I found Jonathan."

"Oh thank heavens!" Wendy cried, "Where is he?"

Tink turned up the dramatics, taking a small amount of joy in both setting Wendy up for a hard, but also hoping that the harder she fell the harder she would fight against Pan's spell.

"I searched under every rock and asked every tree, but none had seen hide nor hair of him. I even went so far as to risk my life talking with the Indians and the Crocodiles, and it was when I was in the clutches of one of the crocodiles that one of them let slip his whereabouts."

"Where is he, Tink?" Wendy pouted.

"Yes, Tink, get on with it. Why didn't you bring him with you?"

"I did, sir. I brought back what I could."

Tinkerbell went back behind a tree close to where she entered. "What do you mean, Tink? Is he alright?"

Then, in order to get Wendy as worked up as possible Tinkerbell flung half of a skull into the camp. It rolled to a stop at Wendy's feet.

She shrieked. Her stomach flipped as her young mind searched for some way to make him better, as impossible as that was. She cried out in pain, and the squealing sound within her pierced the air as it found its way out of her. The spell inside her was fighting hard to maintain its control over the girl trapped inside. She dry heaved and coughed. Tinkerbell hoped this would be enough and silently cheered her on.

That's it, girl.

Now is the time!

Break free!

"Tinkerbell!" Pan shouted, "How could you? Go to the tree at once and don't come out! Shh, Wendy, it's alright," he consoled.

As Tinkerbell went by, Pan hugged Wendy, and over her shoulder he cast such a hot and fearsome look at Tink that she had only seen on one or two occasions before. Her skin dried out immediately and she hurried her pace to escape it.

"Shh, Wendy," he continued to say, but Wendy couldn't hear him over her own screams.

"Shh." He pulled his head back and gazed into her wild bloodshot eyes. Then, closing his own, he placed his forehead against hers and began growling deep in the back of his throat. Wendy's arms went limp at her sides and she stopped shaking. She would have collapsed if not for Peter holding her head against his own.

...

A small group of Lost Boys always patrolled the perimeter of their camp. This night, a group of four noticed a few Fairie lights blinking and a single boy creep his way into their home.

The Lost Boys, eager for game, fell in quietly behind him. A few steps of stalking their prey brought them nothing but confusion. It was as if the boy stepped behind a tree and disappeared.

"He probably got carried away by those giant ants, poor bastard. Them's worse than us. There's a mound right over there. Let's get away from it."

...

The small force of Fairie rebels led John to the outer limits of the Lost Boy camp. They hovered for a moment while John crossed the invisible border. He could hear the Lost Boys around him, sucking life from the surrounding trees. Some leaves rustled and he stopped, once again, in the dark to listen. His return to the camp would have to mimic his escape. He slowed down his breathing, and like before, could feel the Earth around him. The footsteps of several Lost Boys encroaching on him may as well have been tiptoeing on his skin. John crouched down in the shadow where he stood, hoping he would be passed by, unnoticed.

When the patrolling group came upon him he held his breath. They stood no further than an arms length away but did not see him.

One of them even looked right at him, made some comment about an anthill and then moved quickly on.

...

"Wendy, are you okay?" Peter asked her.

Wendy blinked and looked around at the surroundings. She looked bewildered until she was able to lock eyes with Peter. Then her appearance softened from fright to peace.

"Of course I am, Peter. Why?"

"Well, we were in the middle of talking when you suddenly stared off and wouldn't come back to me."

Her head burned, and the thought she remembered something, but when she tried to focus on it the image dissipated like a dream in the morning.

"Well I'm back now. What were we talking about?"

Just then Jonathan walked into the clearing.

"Is there any food left over?" he asked, startling Wendy.

"John!" Wendy cried and ran to him.

"Hello Wendy. How are you?"

"Oh my God! Where have you been?" she hugged him hard.

"I've been out hunting for bears," he said, staring over her shoulder, locking eyes with Pan.

"Michael!" Wendy shouted as she spun toward the tree in which Michael slept, eager to reunite the family.

"No, Wendy. Let him sleep. I'll see him tomorrow. Right now I'd like to eat something and get some rest."

Peter's knuckles cracked as his fists clenched tighter. Not only was John still alive, but Tinkerbell had also lied to him. He had survived this long on his own. How? Where did he find help?

"Where did you go?!" Wendy shouted at him, the fight between anger and joy bouncing inside her head. "We looked everywhere for you!"

"I guess we just kept missing one another, I was constantly moving," John lied. He stole a dangerous look at Pan to see if he noticed, which clearly he had.

The Island did not do its part
and now I'm standing here
being taunted,
insulted by this smug little kid.

"It wasn't that bad," John continued, smirking a little in Pan's direction. "I learned a lot about this place." Then, when he saw Peter's jaw clench something overtook John. "I learned a lot about you too, Peter."

What?! How?

"What it must be like here for you. How you *really* survive." John casually picked up a piece of meat from the table and tore a chunk from the bone with his teeth.

"So tell me about it, John. What was it like? Did you meet any Pirates or Indians or anything?" Wendy continued to prod her brother.

John locked eyes with Peter, searching for a clue on how far to take this, but Peter just stared back, almost daring John to continue.

"I met a few people, but for the most part I was on my own," John said solemnly, suddenly changing his tone. "They taught me some things that helped me survive. I guess I'm more like you now, Peter. The Island's population is helping me, just like they serve you, great King," the sarcasm was subtle enough for Wendy to not pick up the difference, but Peter noticed it just fine.

He knows too much.

I'll have to take matters

into my own hands before

it goes too far.

"I think I'll go to bed now. I can tell you more in the morning, Wendy. Good night, Peter." John turned away, baring his entire back to Peter as he went to his tree.

Pan picked up a bow that was leaning against the table and an arrow from the dirt nearby. The arrow was knocked and aimed just as Wendy turned back from John to look at him. Joy turned to horror on her face as Peter let the arrow go. It ripped the air right by her cheek, flinging a bit of her hair out of the way as it passed. It flew steadily for the back of Jonathan's neck, a slow but effective death.

The charm on John's finger multiplied and multiplied a thousand times over in a fraction of a second and then receded to the original disk, unnoticed. The scales covered John's skin and folded back again in the blink of an eye. John felt a sudden stiffness and then everything was normal again, like he had just been doused in cold water for an instant.

The arrow clanged against the Fairie armor and skittered to the dirt. Peter felt a chill flair up his spine as he watched the arrow bounce off of John's neck just like they had when he fought the Dragon so many lifetimes before. The mischievous King of Boys found himself wondering who Jonathan had met and what he had learned, and most importantly what he had become.

Wendy tried to let out a scream, but before she could, Peter clasped a hand over her mouth and another around the back of her head. John didn't notice the arrow, and Pan didn't need him turning around right now. John just continued to walk toward his tree while Wendy struggled silently against Peter.

Pan was in no mood to try solve the mystery of John. If he couldn't be killed, he must be sent away. Wendy was almost ready to be sent back home as well, anyway. And with Tinkerbell's apparent involvement in hiding him all this time, and the restlessness of his army, Peter did not have time to arrange for keeping Michael. He was still loyal to Jonathan, and there was no way to separate the two yet without a potentially violent backlash from the boys. He would just have to count Michael as a loss, but he didn't really need him anyway.

"Sleep!" Peter whispered harshly into Wendy's ear, his voice a hot hiss. A familiar warmth filled in Wendy's belly and expanded to the rest of her slowly. Then he sighed and pressed his head against hers once again.

"'If you believe," he shouted to them, 'clap your hands; don't let Tink die.'

Many clapped.

Some didn't.

A few little beasts hissed."

-J. M. Barrie, *Peter and Wendy*

The Poisoning

The Sun had just begun to peek over the horizon when Pan shook Wendy awake. He needed to send the Darlings away before they became too much for him to handle, so he needed to get a little more of Neverland into Wendy before she left to germinate.

"What's going on, Peter?" she asked in a groggy whisper.

"I'm going to show you Neverland, Wendy. It's important that you absorb as much of it as you can today. There's a lot to show you and I think your brother John will want to take you guys home soon. C'mon," he offered her his hand, "Let's go. We'll start with the Indians."

Wendy hurried to collect her things and meet Peter outside. This was it! Today Peter would show her the secrets to the Island. She tied up her hair and splashed a little water on her face. Then, after making sure Michael and Jonathan still slept, she went to Peter.

"I'm all set," she said eagerly. "Are the Indians friendly? Should we bring them something? Perhaps I can get some sweets together for them before we take off?"

"We're going to start things off walking today, Wendy. I want you to take in as much as you can, and flying makes things go by too fast. It's important to make this place as much a part of you as you can. I don't want you forgetting about this when you get back home," and the pair started walking hand in hand.

Across the camp and over some thorny bushes, a man with a scar across his throat and stubble on his tattooed face crawled backward on his hands and knees, praying to remain out of sight. When he felt he was out of view, he sprang up and sprinted to his skiff, hidden amongst the weeds and bushes in a small inlet. He pushed the boat deeper into the water and paddled without rest, despite the burning muscles in his back, all the way back to The Jolly Roger.

"I'd never forget this, Peter. And I'm not going home. I want to stay here with you. Let John go home if he wants. I don't ever want to leave your side."

"That's sweet of you, Wendy, but you must go home eventually. You need to grow up for me. How can you be the mother if you stay a kid forever? That doesn't make any sense."

They stepped into a clearing in the forest surrounded by long needled pine trees and in the center was a crop of what looked like a mix between flowers and mushrooms. They were yellow and white and had brown spots on the fruit, which was about the size of a golf ball. They smelled sweet, like honey and almonds and were dripping with some kind of clear nectar. Wendy's stomach groaned a bit.

"Mmmm, breakfast!" Peter said, and with true little boy's excitement he dropped Wendy's hand and ran into the cluster of plants. "Would you like some, Wendy? They're yummy. They taste just like they smell."

Wendy plucked what seemed like a ripe blossom from one of the flowers nearest her and nibbled on the edge. Flavor exploded in her mouth and she was certain she could never eat another doughnut or cinnamon roll again in her life and still be happy if she could just have these every morning.

"Oh my goodness, Peter, these are delicious! What are they?"

"We call them Eyeball Puffs because of the brown spots. We should take some with us. Have some more."

Wendy didn't need another invitation to eat them. She already had filled her hand with more and stuffed the remaining bit of the first one in her cheek. Peter was filling up a pocket on his shirt with as many as he could find. They dripped whatever nectar they had through Wendy's fingers and down her wrist.

"Alright, c'mon. We've still got a ways to go before we get to the Indians."

...

"Sir!" Bill Jukes panted to Captain Hook as soon as he got his boat securely strapped back in place. His scar burned, and his legs shook from the effort he just expelled.

"What is it, Jukes?"

"He's taken the girl, sir. They're going for a walkabout. They're far away. We've got some time now and the other boys are still asleep. The camp was still as a graveyard when I left."

Captain Hook jumped to his feet and threw off his crimson coat. He dabbed a bit of red rusty murk off of his wounded arm onto his coat, which by now had leaked through his coat and began to stain his white shirt underneath.

"Prepare me a boat, I'm going to do this myself."

"One's already prepped, Sir."

Hook flipped open the lid of a small box on his writing desk with his iron claw, sending the lid flying. Then, delicately with his left hand he removed a small glass vile stopped with a cork and filled with a foggy yellow liquid. He slipped this into his pocket and pushed his way past Jukes. He ran to the side of the ship and descended as quickly as he could, which took him much longer these days than it had...*when?*

It didn't used to take

this much effort, did it?

No, it didn't.

When was that?

He got into the awaiting boat and ordered Flint the oarsman to row as quickly as he could.

"You'll row this rotting carcass to the island as fast as you can without slowing," he shouted, spittle flying from his twisted mouth, "or you will watch as I remove your organs one at a time!"

...

"And this place," Peter proudly announced, "is where we practice killing things, like wolves and bears and Pirates. They all come here for the fresh water at this stream. It's a pretty excellent place because they *need* to come here, so we get to do whatever we want and they'll keep coming back."

"How often do you practice killing, Peter?"

"It's mostly with the new Lost Boys, but sometimes I just come here to practice on my own. It's fun! You're running around, swinging a sword, flying, confusing everyone and getting them all mixed up. That's when you know they're done for."

Wendy was looking at the clear cool stream. It was shallow, but wide across. She imagined that she could walk straight to the other side with little more than her knees getting wet.

"You should taste some, Wendy. I need you to take in as much of this place as you can. It's better than you think it could be. Here," Peter said, walking to a tin cup laying on the rocks, chained to a stick on the shore, "Try some."

After all of the eyeball puffs Wendy was very thirsty, and the water helped cool her entire body. She felt the first drink run down past her chest and into her belly. The second drink went further, though, flowing through her limbs and even up into her hair.

"My goodness, Peter, it's wonderful. I feel cooled and refreshed all over! I can feel it in my fingertips!"

"Yeah, it's pretty good, don't you think? It only tastes that good right from the stream. Whenever we carry it home it just tastes like regular water. Weird, huh?"

"Remarkable."

"Okay, let's go. We're almost to the Indian camp. We have to be careful now because they're vicious sometimes, and without warning." Peter grabbed Wendy's hand again, but this time they flew, "So we don't snap any twigs." They hovered only about a foot above the canopy and headed almost straight east. Wendy hugged Peter's arm and rested her head on his shoulder as they flew.

"Down there, do you see them?" asked Peter, slowing to a stop so Wendy could take a look.

He was pointing at a small gathering of red skinned people milling around a clearing similar to the Lost Boy camp.

Wendy nodded.

"Let's go down for a closer look. They're quite mysterious," Peter told Wendy and they descended behind some thick tall trees.

The Indians moved slowly and deliberately through the camp. She noticed they were not speaking to one another. In fact she noticed little emotional response at all among them. They reminded her of the businessmen she saw on television, milling around one another without ever making contact.

"They seem so slow and formal. And they aren't armed like everyone else here," Wendy whispered.

"They sure are slow and formal," Peter said, "But don't let it fool you; they can move fast when they want to. When I first got here they appeared out of nowhere and attacked us. They drove me and the other Lost Boys to the other coast of the Island. It was pretty brutal the way they attacked. We would be fighting and some of the Lost Boys would go missing without a trace, no blood, no dust kicked up, no screams. They would just disappear. Some kind of Indian black magic, I think."

"How did they get here?" Wendy asked.

"I'm not exactly sure, Wendy, but they're brilliant at hiding and they're very strong."

Peter could see Wendy was getting nervous.

"They can come out of nowhere, but don't worry. They only like to take those of us who have been here the longest. Only a few of the Lost Boys here are left from the original group. They should worry the most. Sometimes the originals just won't come home again."

"So, why don't you fight them like you fight the Pirates?"

Pan hesitated for a second. He knew why they didn't engage the Indians anymore, but he couldn't tell Wendy.

"Well, Wendy," he started, "we stay on our side of the Island and they stay on theirs. They pretty much keep to themselves. Besides, when we're actually fighting up front, they're boring. It's like they only fight hard when our backs are turned."

"But they take Lost Boys once and a while. Don't you want to protect them?"

"The Pirates raid our camps more often than the Indians do," he lied, "so they're a bigger threat. I can't fight a battle on two fronts, so I have picked the Pirates as my enemy for now."

"I feel nervous, Peter, like they're watching me," Wendy confessed. "Can we go?"

"Sure, as long as you remember what you saw here."

...

Wendy was right. No further than ten feet from them stood what Pan would have called one of the Indians, although he would have been incorrect. It concealed itself among a cluster of trees, which he matched effortlessly. It noticed Pan and wanted to entangle, ensnare, capture and bludgeon him to death. It wanted to restore balance to the Island, but the timing was wrong. The girl was here with him, so it would have to wait. In the meantime the "Indian" was focusing intensely on Wendy.

Its green and gold eyes had a certain look in them. It was a look one gets when solving a puzzle. The creature was trying to trace a line of what must have happened to bring this girl here. She had the same eyes and facial contours as someone it once knew, clearly a relation to That One, that one member of its family that broke the rules and thus broke the mould. It was That One that stepped out of line and went against its purpose to please itself. The one who became attached to a girl that Pan brought here. The one who didn't strive for balance, but instead let emotions run its actions. That one who saved her before it was time. That One was the one to seek out a way of escaping Neverland and took her with him.

This girl was tall for her age and slender and her face was all but identical to That One's, with a touch of the girl That One saved in her nose and lips. How had That One's daughter returned? It wanted to ask her, but the timing was wrong. Pan was here with her, so it would wait.

...

"Wait for me Flint, and keep a sharp eye," Hook ordered before he snuck quietly and carefully up the beach toward the forest. He made sure to keep himself hidden from anything that may be a spy of Pan's. His sea legs were no match for the forest, though, and anyone on shore who might have been paying attention could have found him in a second. Luckily for Hook, however, Pan's example of Atlan and his specific instructions for the rest of his Lost Boys to not engage Hook or any Pirates allowed him to enter the goblin camp unmolested.

While Hook was creeping into the camp, the Lost Boys were creeping out and regrouping on the shore. They were about one hundred meters from Hook's boat and the waiting Flint. Silently they crouched, listening for the alarm to be raised.

The Sun was taking its time rising this morning, and by the time Hook found the burned out tree it was still considerably early. He descended the stairs into Pan's lair, which was dark and musty. The tree had been long dead, not even the bugs crept within. There was one "window" that was more of a crack in the bark than a window. The bed was a wide, hollowed out log that was scorched, twisted and cracked. There was a wobbly nightstand beside it where a cup of water patiently awaited his arrival.

At first he reached into his pocket with excitement. But when he found the vile with his fingertips, he paused. One more time he scanned the room, looking up at the non-cobwebbed ceiling, searching for any sign of an ambush or trap. Assured that he was in no immediate danger Hook slowly and silently removed the cork stopper with his teeth and poured what poison he had, every drop, into the cup and quickly retreated, lest someone in the camp awoke, or a damned Fairie spy of Peter's should find him out.

A Fairie had, in fact, found him out. Tinkerbell was in her cage that Pan called her "apartment" when Hook entered. He slowly pushed the door open and when Tink saw him her heart went out to him. The man of water that she had first seen when they walked on the boardwalk in Barbados was tall, full, and confident; a waterfall flowing sure and strong. The man who entered now was so dried up he was little more than a trickling drip of melting ice. His wrists were scarcely bigger than her torso and everywhere he went, he dripped bits of himself behind. The ends of his limbs were no longer defined and powerful. Now they tapered off into nothing. He had kept himself out of the water for too long.

He's afraid, she thought,

of the crock and the Sun.

But the moment for which Tink had been awaiting finally arrived. If she drank the poison now, then she would be long dead before Pan returned. And if she could be dead long enough, then no amount of clapping would revive her. She could be free of her nightmare, free of her body, and free from the grip of that demon. So she sat waiting, and did not try to help him.

Hook crept quietly and swiftly out of the tree. He got no further than three steps before a horn blast rumbled through the forest like thunder. He turned and saw a filthy goblins up high in a nearby tree with a horn made of bone. The thing gave a horrible smile that told Hook he had fallen straight into a trap. He turned and sprinted toward the shore where his boat was waiting for him.

"Flint! Run Flint! It's a trap!" he shouted, hoping that his oarsman would hear. But it was too late. The horn blast startled Flint and he fumbled his loaded pistol into the bottom of the boat. The Lost Boys charged out of the woods toward him, shedding their childlike disguises, revealing to Flint what they really were. Their terrible forms, all claws and teeth descended on him and the boat in a flash. Then they skimmed off to the ship on the horizon, taking up their positions and waiting for Pan's arrival.

"Pirates!' [Peter] cried. The others came closer to him. A strange
smile was playing about his face, and Wendy saw it and shuddered.
While that smile was on his face no one dared address him; all they
could do was to stand ready to obey."
-J. M. Barrie, *Peter and Wendy*

The Plan Unfolds

The horn blast shook the air around them and Pan stopped in
midair. He turned and flashed a smile toward Wendy. He grabbed her
wrist harshly and rocketed off toward the Lost Boy camp, nearly
jerking her arm out of the socket. Peter offered no apology or
explanation.

"He didn't wait as long as I thought he would," was the only
thing he said.

...

Michael and Jonathan were shaken awake by Slightly, who
was armed and had a horn hanging around his neck.

"We've been attacked! Get Up! We're making a charge on
the Pirates! Let's go! Let's *go!*"

John had slept on the ground beside his tree all night, and so
was up and ready in an instant. Michael, on the other hand, climbed

out of his tree and was in the middle of brushing the tree's morning glaze from his body when he realized John had returned.

"John!" Michael cried and flung himself around John's waist. "You're home!"

John hugged Michael back, enjoying the simple, peaceful moment.

"Come on, guys! We don't have time! We're under attack! Let's go, let's go!" Slightly shouted again from within the forest.

Michael and Jonathan grappled for the weapons they had been given and clumsily charged after Slightly.

"Wait, Michael. I want you to drink this. A friend gave it to me on my trip. It'll help protect you, okay?"

"What is it, Johnny?"

"It's magic, Michael. It's going to help you. If we're going to fight the Pirates I want you as safe as possible."

Michael took the vile, said thank you, and drank it down. He could feel it drop into him like a stone. His vision blurred for a second and then righted itself. It felt like the draught dropped right through him, down past his feet and into the ground beneath him. He felt a sudden connection with the ground deep below, and the Island seemed to shrink around him. It was no longer a vast wondrous world of adventure. It was just another place that he knew backward and forward. He knew where everything was on the Island and was beginning to know all of their names.

He could hear the wind, a breeze at first then a rapid deafening wind whipping through his ears. Then the ground loosened and swallowed his feet, ankles, knees, thighs, hips, and when it hit his belly button, a wave of water crashed down on him from out of nowhere and knocked the air out of his lungs, but not the wind out of his ears. He tasted the salt from the water as it filled his lungs and belly. Then, as his eyes closed, his skin burst into flames. He could feel it bubble and crack and sting.

"Mikey!" Jonathan shouted, shaking Michael back to his body. "Are you alright? You were asleep on your feet. Are you okay? How do you feel?"

Michael felt good. The magic and wonder was returning to the Island and his moment of horror was losing its importance. His brother was here and everything was going to be all right.

"I feel fine, Johnny. I feel like I've just done a re-do. But it's fine. Let's go." The two brothers charged out into the morning sunlight to find Slightly.

"Where's Peter?" Michael asked.

"He's out with Wendy, showing her around. He'll be there, though. C'mon, let's go," Slightly answered and flew up over the canopy for a more direct route to the ship.

...

Hook broke out of the trees and onto the beach. Most of Flint's pieces were in the water and the boat shattered. The Sun was starting to rise and promised a hot day. Wasting no time Hook returned to the tree line at the top of the beach. He drew his sword and began chopping at a thick low limb. It fell with a crash, but small vines had worked their way around his feet and when he turned back to the sea he fell face first in the sand.

The Island was revolting against him and he could hear Pan's voice deep in his memory:

"*The ship is your territory*," he said, "*And the Island is me*."

Hook slashed the vines and scrambled madly toward the sea. When he got to the edge of the water he paused, but only for a moment. The pause was so slight that it was almost undetectable, a stutter step. But in that split second a throbbing pain thumped in his right arm at the rusty, bloody intersection of metal and flesh. He felt the phantom eye of a phantom crock under his thumb. And immediately following that memory Smee wandered into his thoughts. Hook bounded into the surf, carrying the heavy branch as if it were weightless. The limb kept him afloat, but the trip was still long and tiresome, and even this early in the day the sun beat down on him without mercy.

...

Peter and Wendy touched down in front of their tree.

"Wait here, Wendy, I'm going to get Tink," Peter told her.

"What's going on, Peter? Where is everyone?"

"The Pirates attacked. The Lost Boys are waiting for me to get to the Jolly Roger so we can counterattack. I'll be right back."

"But Peter," Wendy said and grabbed his hand, which was burning up, "If the Pirates attacked why isn't anything broken or on fire? I thought they always burned everything."

"Wendy, I don't know how they did it, but your brothers are at the ship, I know it. And we have to go rescue them. But before we do, I need to get Tink. I'll be right back, now let me go." Peter's eyes told Wendy that it was time to let him go. A fire seemed to burn behind them, and for a moment she thought his face stretched and wrinkled tight like leather. He looked so ugly for that moment that she didn't recognize him. She took a step back and let his hand fall back to his side.

"We'll be off in a flash. Don't worry," he said, returning to his pretty boyish self. Then he turned and dashed down the stairs into the bedroom.

"Tink! Tink, where are you! Come on, my plan is working and we need to hurry. Where are you?" He went to her apartment, which was nothing more than a modified birdcage hanging next to his bed. She wasn't inside and the door was left open. Then he noticed the empty water glass just below her hanging apartment. His mood shifted immediately and he slowed his pace. He was no longer summoning Tink like she was a duty-bound servant. Now he was stalking about the room, hunting her.

"Tink," he whispered, "I know what you're up to, Tink, and it won't work. 2+2=4 Tink. I can put two and two together. I've got your number now. I'll find you, Pixie. The only think you'll have gained will be a painful death for you and – hmm, let's see, four painful deaths for your father? That seems appropriate, don't you agree?"

Tinkerbell, who was hiding in the soot of the fireplace, tried not to move. She just focused on the fire raging in her belly, melting her from the inside out.

"Does it hurt, Tink? I'm sure it does. Hook wouldn't spare any mercy in killing me, so I can only imagine what it's doing to you right now. It might even be worse than what I've done to you so far.

That would be something, now wouldn't it? What kind of pain is it, Tink? Is it knives in your guts?"

Tink focused more on her pain and tried to shut him out. She didn't move a muscle.

"Or maybe he's freezing you. That would be a new feeling for you. How ironic that would be for you to die freezing with all the years you've spent burning by my side," he let out a crow that made Tinkerbell shiver. There was no way she could shut that sound out of her head, no matter how much she focused on the pain.

"The only thing more ironic would be that you've spent that many years burning by my side and someone else found a way to burn you to death. Now, Tink, you know I can't allow someone *else* to burn you. I'll have to save you and then avenge your pain by killing the man who did it to you. So why don't you stop this now and come out. You're just prolonging the inevitable."

Tinkerbell winced as a flare of pain boiled in her lungs. Pan stalked slowly toward the sound and crouched just beside the fireplace.

"Tink," Pan whispered, "you're just wasting my time. It's doing nothing but making me furious." The word 'furious' fell like a lead ball in the room. He started meticulously dragging his dagger sharp nails through the soot. When he sifted her out of the dust Tink was too weak to move, let alone fight back. She only looked at him with defeat in her eyes.

"What are you waiting for, Tink," growled Pan, "die. Do it. Submit to it. Let it go, slave. Die."

And that was the last thing Tinkerbell heard before the room went dark and silence rushed into her ears. Then the darkness was replaced by light. It was so bright that she could feel it pressing against her and she could hear a laugh echoing in the distance, like a train approaching from far away, but coming fast. Then the light faded and she was outside, surrounded by other Fairies like her. They were flying free all over the swamp. The wind spoke to her about which breezes would fling her fastest and when to duck, roll, or rise over obstacles. Her friends swept around her and they hugged and high-fived and laughed together. Crows bowed to her and the clouds tasted sweet. She could hear the laugh echoing around her and it was wonderful. Such unbridled mirth bouncing and rolling around her, limitlessly happy, with the voice of an innocent infant. She flew toward the sound, eager to rejoin it, and fall into nothing once more.

Then delicious full rain clouds rolled in to bathe the Earth with fresh, cool and clean water. The lightning clapped and revealed a horrible image, which stopped Tinkerbell in mid-flight.

"No," she whispered, "he can't."

But then lightning clapped again and sure enough, she saw his twisted dark face in the shadows and folds of the rain clouds. Then another bold of lightning clapped, and again it clapped, until the world around her melted and she saw Pan's shadowed face in front of her and heard his hands clapping.

"Did you have fun?" he asked in a dark tone. "Now, let's go. You're going to help me send the kids back."

Tinkerbell was more than perplexed. No one ever went back home. Angela was the only one to make it out alive, and that surely wasn't because Pan had allowed her to leave. Pan never made his mind quickly, and certainly had never changed his mind about anything. What was he up to, and how did Tinkerbell not see it coming?

"Why are we sending them home? What did you do?" she asked defiantly.

"That's none of your business and you'll help me anyway. You have quite a fondness for them and I'm sure you want them to escape, don't you?"

It had occurred to her just then that he was right. Tinkerbell, somewhere along the way, had abandoned her plan of using the children to overthrow Pan. Now all she wanted was to protect them from him. Now she understood why they hadn't changed. All this time she thought it was because they were Elementals, but that was ridiculous. Even the mighty Captain Cooper had changed into Hook when Pan willed it. And the children were still children also because Pan willed it.

"You didn't want them to change, did you? That wasn't the point, was it?"

"I did at first, Tink. But then I realized that they might be more powerful as they are. I needed more time than I have to figure them out. So now, instead of forcing it, I'm sending them away."

"What about Wendy, then? Why is she so special? You could have talked her into becoming a tree any time. She would do anything you asked her to."

"My plans aren't your business, bug," he said and he forced Tinkerbell into his rotten hip pouch, tied it shut and came outside to find Wendy.

"Are you all ready, Wendy? We're going to the ship," Peter Pan ordered.

"Me?" she asked, "But Peter, I don't fight. I've not done any killing before."

"That's true, but you've got to take in as much of Neverland as you can, remember? That's what today is all about." And that was the end of the discussion. Peter took her hand in his and they flew, not past the canopy, but zigzagging through the forest. Wendy shut her eyes.

"All traces of human weakness gone, as if a bucket of water had passed over [Hook]."

-J. M. Barrie, *Peter and Wendy*

"MICHAEL (reeling). Wendy, I've killed a pirate!
WENDY. It's awful, awful.
MICHAEL. No, it isn't, I like it, I like it."

-J. M. Barrie, *Peter Pan or The Boy Who Would Not Grow Up*

Race to the Ship

Sailors stood motionless on the deck of the Jolly Roger. The horn blast had shaken their courage, leaving an ever-sinking pit in their stomachs where that courage had once so delicately resided. Their captain was nowhere to be seen, and without him to boil their blood, it ran as ice through their veins.

Aside from the alarm raised on the Island, there was no sign of an attack. Each man stood where he belonged, armed just how they should be, yet anyone could see how unprepared they were for the oncoming battle. Their nerves were scraped raw with anticipation. Each creak of the ship, each clanking pulley and chain exploded in their minds, pushing them ever closer to the edge away from fight toward flight.

The Lost Boys were not fools, however. They skimmed the surface of the water and gave the Jolly Roger a wide berth so as to creep up on the seaside of the ship. They hovered a few feet above the waves, waiting for their signal to attack. They knew Peter was on his way because after a few minutes, waves began to slap into the ship harder and harder until there were white caps roaring across the top of the sea, the water doing its part for Peter Pan.

...

A sudden onset of waves pushed against Captain Hook on his arduous return back to his ship. They pushed him under and back toward the shore. It was as if every bit of the sea was acting against him. But the further he swam away from the Island, the longer he was in the water, the stronger he felt. His legs were able to force him further through the waves and his lungs held more and more air.

He was not sure when it happened, but somewhere during his swim Hook began to welcome the crashing waves. Each one invigorated him a little more than the last. Soon they were not a burden at all. He would rise up over the crest of each wave and slide effortlessly down the back, building up enough momentum to carry him up and over the next. The wind felt refreshing on his face and the spray of water gave him a sense of nostalgia.

This is how it should be.

This is how it used to be.

Somewhere along the swim, the tree limb he used became more of a burden than an aid, so he let it go, allowing it to drift far away.

Every time he caught a glimpse of his ship, anger swelled inside him. It motivated him to push harder. He needed to get on board. He needed to protect Smee. But what he needed most of all was to feel Peter Pan's throat crunch in his left hand while his iron right plucked out the little demon's eyes.

...

"COCK-A-DOODLE-DOO!"

It echoed over the world and crashed into the ship like a cannonball. Pirates on the deck of the ship spun around wildly looking for the source. It seemed to come from all directions, and simultaneously nowhere at all.

...

The Captain heard the crow's call, Pan's war cry. His anger multiplied and he kicked harder against the waves. He could feel his familiar swimming rhythm and before long his entire body was working in unison and his kicks sent him further still. The waves also stopped pushing him back. They split in front of him, allowing him to pass through with ease.

But even at this pace, James knew that he would arrive at the battle just in time to see his last sailor fall dead on the deck and Pan's army flying off, leaving him alone in this harsh, rotten world. Sorrow pulled him down for just a second before he shook it out of his head and pushed on with greater determination.

I can't fail.

There is still time.

As his anger for Pan shifted to the love for his men he slipped through the water like a blade and behind him a wave began to rise. It started as a simple wake behind his body, but soon the wake bent together into a single hump on the water. Constantly it grew taller and instead of running toward the shore with the rest of the waves it followed James, pushing him.

...

"Michael! Where are you?" Wendy called. She was frantically searching the ship for her baby brother. The deck was a loud raging fight with silver clanging, muzzles flashing, and men and boys crying out. Wendy could feel her heart pounding in her throat. She shook with every frantic step she took and every door she opened. Panicked tears had already begun to well in her eyes when she saw a boy wearing fuzzy bunny slippers running down into the gunner's deck.

"MICHAEL!" she shouted and sprinted down the stairs after him. The boy stopped and turned around. He was dirty and had blood on him. He saw Wendy and smiled at her with a delighted little boy smile.

"Wendy!" Michael called to his sister, "I killed a pirate!" he said, excitement rising in his voice, making him jump up and down and clap his hands together.

The ship leaned drastically toward the Island as it sank into a large trough between waves. Michael and Wendy both grabbed a hold of the doorway in which they were standing.

"Michael, you're bleeding!" Wendy said to him, patting him all over with her one free hand, trying to find where he was cut.

"No, Wendy," Michael laughed, "It's not my blood. I'm fine. C'mon, I'll show you how I did it." He started to turn as the ship began righting itself.

"Michael, no! We're getting off the ship. It's time to leave. We have to find Peter!"

There was a loud crash and a huge spray of water on the Island's side of the ship, which rocked it hard back the other direction. Wendy and Michael both fell to the floor, along with the few men in the gunner's deck. Men and boys were heard yelling as they fell over the sidewall from the deck above as the ship nearly tipped over onto its side.

...

James noticed the swim was getting easier. He was swimming down hill, it seemed, if such a thing were possible. He looked behind him and could only see water and sky; the gigantic wave blocked any view he might have had of the Island. The ship in front of him began to lean in the trough created by Hook's giant wave. Then, with great speed and force, almost suddenly, the wave propelled him toward his ship, which began gently rocking back the other way as it tried to right itself.

Just as he flung his arms in front of his face to protect himself from being slammed into the wall of the ship he lurched to a stop and heard the wave crash into the ship instead. The wave had snuck under him and he was left treading water on the standing crest, looking at the side of The Jolly Roger as it leaned away from him. The resulting tipped ship looked like a ramp. Wasting no time the captain ran up the sidewall ladder as fast as he could, getting as high as possible before the ship could right itself again.

"Thus sharply did the terrified three learn the difference between an island of make-believe and that same island come true."
-J. M. Barrie, *Peter and Wendy*

Worlds Collide

Pan picked himself up from the deck. He was weaker today than he would have liked after spending so much energy last night reforming Wendy's memories *twice*, and that left him less prepared than normal. The shock of the wave had caught him off guard and knocked him over, a small mistake. He tumbled, bounced, and eventually smashed his right shoulder into the main mast. The collision knocked the wind out of him, and he had a few large bits of wood in his arm and his golden short sword was caught in the grating over the loading port that separated the deck and the supply hold beneath.

He pulled a battered Tinkerbell out of his pouch and told her to gather up the Darlings and bring them back home.

"Wendy needs to be kept safe no matter what. Got it? She has taken in as much of Neverland as she can. Now all we have to do is wait."

Tinkerbell, roughed up by the recent tumble, struggled to her feet and flew away to explore the ship as best she could before Pan could change his mind. He was up to something, of that she was certain. But she wanted the kids back home safe no matter what else happened and she didn't have time to find out what was going on. She would never die and neither would Pan, and the guilt of bringing the children into this situation was weighing her down.

Peter had just retrieved his sword and chosen his next victim. Smee was crouched, hugging himself and rocking between the staircase to the second deck and the railing of the ship. He was not as confident as he had been when they first met on the Island and this was the perfect time to remove a potential threat while simultaneously dealing a devastating blow to his nemesis. Pan was crossing to the whimpering weakling when he saw something impossible. Captain Hook was hoisting himself up and over the side and onto the deck. He and Peter were the only two standing.

Hook's blood boiled instantly upon laying his eyes on Peter, and for the second time since the Pirates arrived, Peter was afraid for his life and he realized that Tinkerbell was right. She had brought him exactly what he wanted. He wanted to feel challenged; to feel pushed to the ends of his boundaries, and at this moment he was staring at the edge.

Peter's arm ached and there was no time to remove the splinters, so he went at Hook left-handed. Hook had some time to get used to using his off hand, and so seeing his foe come at him southpaw made him smile.

The water had strengthened the Captain. He had returned to his element and gained a foothold. Within his own mind, shackled and in the dark, Cooper shouted out instructions to Hook. They may be fighting one another constantly, but they shared the same body. Hook needed all the help he could get.

Hook's smile grew larger when a familiar thought crept into his mind.

Control the hurricane!

Break him slowly!

...

Jonathan had escaped into the Captain's Quarters after the ship was rocked. There were portraits in frames, books, and maps on the walls. Chills swept up his spine, though, when he saw crude messages carved into the walls, repeated over and over, whittled with a knife and traced with charcoal.

Go backwards through the fog all night.

Sum day yule read this.

Row back in the fog.

You can do it Jimmy.

It repeated on every wall, overlapped and even crept up on the ceiling and down onto the floor in some places. He rummaged through books and letters and realized Captain Hook was not the man who Pan described, and neither were the Pirates. Something terrible had happened to them, forcing them to become the brutes they were now. That was when he discovered Captain Cooper's log on the desk.

He flipped through the pages, hoping to find out how this all began. He read backward through the stinging, agonizing heat, and a hand full of Lost Boy attacks against the ship, and a few pages with the same message hastily written in ink just like it had been carved on the walls. He eventually passed into cleaner handwriting and a more levelheaded train of thought. Jonathan read about the first encounter between the sailors and Peter Pan on the shores of Pan's Island.

The next thing he read made the room darker and his constitution harden. The hair on the back of his neck stood up and his jaw clenched. His fingernails dug into the leather book cover and his arms trembled as he read about a green glowing light that led them through the fog into Neverland.

When he read about Captain Cooper's encounter with Tina Bell he slammed the book shut and yelled an Earth-quaking roar and charged out of the room to find his brother and sister, come demon or pirate, John was going to get to his siblings and leave with them no matter who he had to cut down. John quit. There would be no more politics, no more coercion. No more secrets. It was all out war and no one, not even Wendy would be able to change his mind.

...

Tinkerbell flitted around Wendy and Michael. She was in the process of waking up Wendy. Both children had been knocked around hard when the wave collided with The Jolly Roger and both had been unconscious when she found them. They appeared to have collided with a cannon. Michael awoke quickly when Tinkerbell merely shouted in his ear. Wendy, on the other hand, knocked her head pretty badly and so Tinkerbell was working on reviving her when Jonathan discovered them.

"Get away from her!" he shouted, somewhat surprised by his own strong voice. Shocked by the sudden crash and thunder that was John, Tinkerbell jerked back from Wendy. She had healed only a tiny bit of the girl before she was interrupted and Wendy began to revive only a little. She was hurt and the room spun around her, but she could at least sit herself up. Jonathan picked up a dropped sword from the floor and snatched Tink out of the air.

"You don't understand, Jonathan. I'm trying to – "

"Shut up, liar!" he said, putting the sword to what torso of hers was poking out of his clenched fist, "Don't talk to us. Michael, help me pick up Wendy. We're going home, and you, Tink, are going to take us there or I swear to God I'll take your head off! We're not getting Peter's permission and we're not saying goodbye."

Tinkerbell did her best to look ashamed and afraid. It was best to let John think he was making this happen, lest he think it some kind of trick.

"Okay, Jonathan. I'll take you home. What do you want to do next?"

"We're going to the deck and then flying home, the same way we got here. And no funny business."

Michael retreated the best he could without actually leaving the room. He looked toward the floor and made no sound. It was clear that Jonathan was in control and mad and it was best not to be any trouble. He couldn't help carry Wendy, but after Jonathan tucked the sword into his belt, Michael helped steady her hips as she stood.

As they made their way toward the upper deck, a pair of Pirates tried to face off with the Darlings. Jonathan was steadfast in his determination to leave and didn't check his pace one bit. He pulled Wendy tight to his side, steadying her against his body.

Picking up the clue, Michael let go of his sister and drew his sword, except unlike Jonathan, Michael smiled. He ran ahead of his brother and sister. On any other day Jonathan would have stopped him, but today he found himself watching his brother enjoy himself and never thought of the danger. Michael was protected by the Fairie magic, after all, and on top of that they all were invincible under Jonathan's rage. Nothing would harm them now. Michael was quick and flexible and he rolled, jumped, spun and confounded the slow, malnourished Pirates until they finally yelped and fell motionless to the floor.

He fights like Pan, Tinkerbell thought.

Even though Pan is far away.

Something has changed.

...

Another Pirate was sent tumbling over the side into the waiting crocodiles that were swarming throughout the tumultuous waves. Storm clouds had rolled in to fight the Sun and rain was beginning to drizzle down, making the deck slick. Sunlight burned hard onto the deck in places as it rained cool buckets in others. Peter Pan and Captain Hook fought fiercely in the storm. The Lost Boys kept their distance, keeping themselves preoccupied with the Pirates that were regaining their footing. The Goblins and Pirates alike could feel the heat the ferocious Peter Pan was expending, and as much as the Lost Boys wanted to help him take down his foe, they feared tripping him up and causing his downfall even more.

Captain Hook was blinking fast to keep his eyes from drying out in the intense heat. He had been disarmed but gotten a hold on the boy's left wrist, which he pinned across Pan's body, keeping the dangerous sword locked down. Hook had slammed Pan's back against the mast and would not let him up, no matter how intensely he burned. It had been made obvious again at some point or another during the fight that this was no normal boy. A boy could not have disarmed the mighty Captain Hook. Boys don't have hard, pointy jaws. Boys don't have thick claws. And boys certainly do not breathe visible heat that billows out of their mouths. So what was this thing he was fighting?

Pan's right hand was pressing against Hook's body. He exhaled with force and pushed harder into the Captain's abdomen, making steam rise from the stain of blood and rust on the Captain's shirt. Hook winced at the sudden increase of heat and swung his iron claw at the monster, but did nothing more than stab the air around his head and neck. Another swing, and another, each one aiming for skin but catching nothing. Finally the death swing was on the mark and would have dug a fresh hole in the demon's skull but Pan's small, hard hand caught the hook dead, inches before finding its target.

Pan growled as pain from the splinters in his shoulder shot through his arm like lightning. He had gotten a hold of the hook, though, and he was not letting go. He began deliberately exhaling deep, hot breaths. Smoke curled out from under Pan's hand that gripped the hook and his eyes glowed red like coals. The Captain fell to his knee and yelled in pain as the hook seared at the joint. He let go of Peter's sword in exchange for a grip on his own wrist, trying to choke out the pain.

The Darlings emerged onto the deck just in time for Jonathan to see Peter about to deal a deathblow to the captain.

"NO!" he shouted with authority, drawing his sword.

The word carried across the bay. It echoed off of the cove walls and returned in time to form a chorus with the aftershock in the minds of everyone on board. It stopped the battle. Eyes of all sizes looked as one at Jonathan's new posture. He had the look of a man, insofar as he was able. He felt a man's anger, and a man's hatred. Everything that he had been through at the hands of the demon he'd seen reflected in the pages of that book sitting aft in the captain 's quarters.

"Don't do it, Pan. Don't."

Pan stood over his victim with a hungry look on his face. This was the sort of thing for which he was built. It was how he thrived. It was why he'd brought Cooper here in the first place. After all the games; the years of grooming new treemothers for fuel; of shaping new Lost Boys around those treemothers; here he was, perfectly poised to finally dispatch another foe. And this one had proven himself even more of a fighter than the dragon, or the Cowboys or the Indians.

"Too late, boy," Peter said with a smirk and then turned his attention back to his nemesis. Then, still talking to Jonathan he said, "Say goodbye." He raised his sword back up over his head and swung it down fiercely.

An instinct took over Jonathan. Everything seemed to slow down and his sight pulled into sharp focus. For the second time in his life Jonathan's body took over. The first time he had intercepted a football during recess. This time he let go of Wendy's waist and found his sword. In one smooth movement he sent it whipping through the air, end over end across the ship headed straight for both The Captain and Peter Pan. He did not have to watch it because he knew exactly where it would strike. He saw Wendy flinch toward Peter and she began to call out his name. John turned toward his sister, removing his eyes from the target, and he slipped his arm back around her waist.

The sword arched over the head of Tootles, who was hiding behind a plank of wood he had been using for a shield.

John locked eyes with Michael, who read the meaning in that glance even before it had locked in place. By the time their eyes met, Michael was already pushing off the deck into the air.

O'Neil had just been disarmed and was about to be sprung upon by three Lost Boys before Jonathan's yell stopped the fighting. He bent himself backward, out of the way of the sword as it came hurling past his face, splitting drops of rain as it passed.

The Darlings soared into the storm almost silently. Wendy fought against her brother's grip and continuously reached out toward her love, Peter Pan; all the while calling his name. An instant before the dark clouds could embrace them, Wendy watched the sword make contact.

"...[Mr. Darling] said reproving, 'Be a man, Michael.' 'Won't; won't!' Michael cried naughtily."
-J. M. Barrie, *Peter and Wendy*

Back Through the Window

The clouds seemed to roll endlessly around the Darlings. They flew in silence, none of them able or willing to say anything that could make everything alright. Tinkerbell led the way from John's fist by nodding her head. Jonathan wondered if she might be leading them into a trap, or getting them lost forever. He realized, though, that it didn't matter. If they were going to be lost forever at least they would be away from the liar and devil Peter Pan.

Just as he was getting himself used to the idea that they were not going to be able to go home for a very long time, the clouds began to thin, and pretty soon they could catch glimpses of lights in the distance. The tough veneer on John melted away when he heard the familiar sounds of traffic rumbling below them. A shiver started at his spine and passed over his entire body, causing all of his hair to stand on end. He chuckled and tears hung in his eyes.

Wendy had stopped fighting John a while ago and she was now soaring quietly by his side. Michael had been quiet too, but Wendy's silence was clearly a cold shoulder, whereas Michael's silence was that of a child who tries to remain transparent around angry adults.

Jonathan was contemplating the differences between his brother and sister when Michael broke his silence.

"Home!" he squealed, and rocketed off ahead of his siblings. Jonathan grabbed Wendy's hand and chased after him. Their house was the tallest one in the neighborhood and it had just appeared in the distance. Like an excited puppy, Michael fired ahead and then waited, calling to his family.

"Hurry up you guys!"

"Tinkerbell," John asked, "How long have we been gone?"

"Not long, Jonathan. This is the same night that you left. Your parents have not returned home yet. But they will shortly. You don't have much time to clean up."

John relaxed his grip on the Fairie, letting her go.

"Tink!" Michael called, returning to the group. "Are you leaving? You're giving us up?"

"Michael," she said, "if I could keep you I would. But," she looked at John who returned a cold gaze, "I can't. The Island isn't safe for you. Believe me, this is for the best." She tried to flash a comforting smile, but it only broke Michael's heart.

"I'm going to miss you, Tink. Come back any time," he offered. Behind him Jonathan's eyes pierced through her. He slowly shook his head.

"Come on, Michael," John said, "Let's go home. C'mon, Wendy."

Wendy was crying silently and she leaned in toward the Fairie and whispered something into Tink's ear. Then she turned and followed her brothers back to her mundane life.

...

The sword cut through the air in an arc. Sunlight glinted from the tip of the blade along the edge and disappeared at the top of the sword's curve, only to reappear in a race down the trailing edge. It vanished at the hilt just as the sword finished its second complete rotation and reappeared at the tip once again.

Not a moment later it sliced through flesh and bone and stuck, vibrating, into the mast. Silence fell over the deck of a ship like heavy snow. No one could respond to what they just saw, and more importantly, what it meant. None had imagined that it was possible. He had been untouchable.

And yet with all of the disbelief, the truth remained there, lying on the deck beside Captain Hook's knees. A crew witnessed the salvation of their captain. A scare saw the beginning of the end of its dominance and the dawn of an opportunity to usurp. Even Pan was unable to process what had just happened. For an instant his fire went out and he blinked at his injury as if it belonged to someone else. The silence was broken by a tiny bout of giggling. Heads slowly turned toward the source, Smee, as he giggled and jumped up and down.

"I told you," he squealed, "Hehehe, I told you so. This is the beginning of the end for you! She will come and you will fear her! The end is coming and you brought it here!"

Pan snatched up his severed hand and sword and retreated back to the Island without a word. The rest of his Lost Boys followed him in quick silence. That night as Pan shivered in the dark of his hole no one came to his aid. The Fairies refused to heal him, and with Tinkerbell away for the night it seemed that their strike would continue. Several Fairies died that night before Pan lost consciousness.

His sleep was haunted by the cheerful sounds of celebration, for that night The Jolly Roger was true to its name.

...

The Darling children laid awake in their beds, trying to place order to what had happened to them. Jonathan was counting his blessings that the three of them had returned safely. Wendy's heart broke silently time and again in the dark as she replayed her time spent with Peter. She continuously stared out of the closed and locked window, hoping for some glimpse of him coming back to rescue her one more time. Michael simply remembered. He remembered soaring above the water. He remembered playing with the Mermaids. He remembered his daring victory over the Everfruit tree. His smile slowly began to fade, however, when a strange feeling began to wash over him.

It felt like the Sun was beginning to rise. He felt its warmth creep over him starting with the top of his head. Discomfort urged him to move, but he did not know where to or how, so he sat up. He heard a wind begin to whistle in his ears.

"Johnny...?" Michael asked with worry in his voice.

"Yes, Michael," John asked, then he caught the worry in Michael's face, "Are you alright? What's wrong?" he asked more urgently.

"I feel...funny." The discomfort remained so Michael got out of his bed and paced back and forth. He carried his blanket with him. Then he stopped suddenly. He felt his feet sinking into the floor, like it had become loose. He couldn't move his feet, ankles, knees, thighs and then hips and when it hit his belly button he had a sudden feeling of drowning, like a wave had swirled in around him. He could taste salt.

"What's wrong, Mikey. Do you want some water?" John was on his feet now and went to Michael to both console and inspect him.

"Please come back for me," Wendy whispered. "I need you back."

Warmth had reached up Michael's legs to his knees and he could feel the familiar weight of the Island beneath him. He stood unmoving because he didn't know what else to do.

...

The Sun peeked up over the horizon on Neverland, summoning its prisoners to it.

...

Michael's eyes were closing when his skin felt like it had burst on fire and he felt it bubble and crack. Then, as if a chain pulled him, his feet flew out from underneath him and he flopped onto his belly. John tried to reach his brother, but Michael was yanked out of his reach at the last second, leaving Jonathan with a hand full of blankets. He heard Michael yell, followed by a thunk and creak at the window. John sprang up and saw Michael pinned to the window, which groaned with his weight pressing against it.

"I'll love you forever, Peter. Please come back to me. Rescue me," Wendy continued, lying in her bed.

"Johnny?" Michael whimpered, reaching out to him, trying hard not to upset the groaning glass panes behind him.

John dove for the window in an attempt to fly but only fell to the ground a few feet short of the window. He was out of Fairie dust. He got up and reached for the window, for his brother's outstretched hand, for anything. The window shrilled and squeaked and then shattered, leaving John grasping nothing but broken glass and air. He saw only a speck of his brother soaring off backward through the night sky.

Wendy remained in bed and didn't move. Her lips continued her prayer to Peter, begging for him to come and rescue her. John's hand left a bloody imprint on the windowsill while his mind tried to contemplate what just happened.

Michael, if I could keep you I would. Tink said over and over in John's head and his hatred bloomed.

The End of Book 1

Made in the USA
San Bernardino, CA
21 March 2015